Mountain Girl

Mountain Girl

by

Shelby Cain

OOLICHAN BOOKS
FERNIE, BRITISH COLUMBIA, CANADA
2016

Library and Archives Canada Cataloguing in Publication

We gratefully acknowledge the financial support of the Canada Council for the Arts, the British Columbia Arts Council through the BC Ministry of Tourism, Culture, and the Arts, and the Government of Canada through the Canada Book Fund, for our publishing activities.

Published by
Oolichan Books
P.O. Box 2278
Fernie, British Columbia
Canada V0B 1M0

www.oolichan.com

Cover Painting by Vanessa Croome
Cover Design by Vanessa Croome

Printed in Canada

To everyone who feels trapped in their life.
I hope you find freedom.

Our greatest source of survival is to adapt to our environment. So increasing emotional intimacy with a person who is forcing physical intimacy makes sense in our minds. It resolves cognitive dissonance.

—Rosenna Bakari, *Tree Leaves: Breaking The Fall Of The Loud Silence*

I mean, they call it Stockholm syndrome and post traumatic stress disorder. And, you know, I had no free will. I had virtually no free will until I was separated from them for about two weeks.

—Patty Hearst, about her kidnapping by the Symbionese Liberation Army

PART 1

1.

The sun rose at last. I sat on the porch, my son cradled in my arms. The spasms that racked his body had subsided, but his limbs were stiff, his back slightly arched. I used the corner of his blanket and dabbed at the foamy drool that continued to leak from his strained mouth. He's dying. I'd repeated these words over and over in my head during the last few hours. He isn't getting better. He's dying. The decision we had to make was one that would destroy everything I knew. It would spiral us into a hell I could not fully imagine, but it was the only choice we had. Matty's breath was raspy and irregular. Even in the cold morning air, his skin was unbelievably hot, as though he would melt right into me. I tried not to hold him too tightly. I heard the frantic movements of my husband in the cabin, packing a few supplies we would need for the trip.

We reached the unbearable decision in the night, the world beyond the cabin door inky black, never more distant. We would wait until first light. It would be safer, for all of us. The river raged down in the valley below and would be impossible to cross in the dark, so I sat on the porch, trapped once again, and waited for morning to come. Waited for the chance to save my son—and destroy his father.

"Okay, Kris. We're ready. How's Matty?" His voice was loud but unsteady from within the cabin.

"The same."

Jasper emerged with the backpack slung over one shoulder. Lines of worry creased his handsome face and he appeared older. Different. He secured a lock on the front door, his hand lingering on the wooden planks. He knew he would likely never see this place again. The cabin had been his home when he had nowhere else in the world to go. The home where we'd fallen in love, gotten married, had Matty. He let his hand slide from the door and onto my shoulder, peering at his dying son, whom he loved more than any life he'd built or place he'd known.

"We should go. Come on. It's time."

Jasper planted a quick kiss on my forehead, his beard soft and familiar. I leaned up for more, some more contact, reassurance, but it was gone. I got to my feet and secured the blanket around Matty. His eyelids fluttered and he moaned softly. He'd hovered on the edge of consciousness since last night. The agonizing muscle spasms that had come too often finally ceased. In such a short time, my joyful little two-year-old had become frail and listless. I couldn't stand by and watch it a second longer. I stepped off the porch and didn't look back.

Although the sun had risen over the distant peaks, the forest was still dark. We entered the trail off the clearing, Jasper leading the way. His flashlight illuminated the roots and rocks that could send me flying. We were all weak and exhausted. It had been six days since Matty got sick. Six days with little food or rest. It happened so quickly.

The trail descended steeply, and we followed switchbacks Jasper forged years ago and barely maintained. I walked this trail only a handful of times in the last few years, but it was strangely familiar. We stayed close together, Jasper cutting his normal pace in half so I could keep up to him. I peeked at Matty regularly, his face flushed, his body too light. In less than a week, he'd lost a lot of weight, his frail limbs and translucent skin unnerving. We kept moving. As we got lower into the valley, the roar of the river began. It was always unpredictable. Not always crossable. Jasper figured with a lower-than-average snowpack this year the runoff would be less. We should be all right. As we got closer and the roar grew louder, I prepared myself for what we might find. If we couldn't cross, Matty would die. The river had almost taken my life once, and the fear of being swept off my feet while holding Matty was paralyzing. I forced myself to keep going.

Jasper crested the riverbank ahead of me, the sunlight now streaming over the mountain peaks. He hesitated, and horrible thoughts exploded in my mind. It couldn't end at the river. Not the river.

I screamed at him above the sound of rushing water. "Is it okay?"

"We can make it," he shouted back assuredly.

He reached a hand back and helped me up the riverbank. The water looked angry, forbidding.

Even standing right next to each other, Jasper had to yell for me to hear him. "It'll be fine. I've crossed it when it was higher. Give me Matty, and stay right behind me. Hold on to the backpack straps and don't let go. No matter what."

His gaze was fierce as he held my eyes. I trusted him completely. I handed him Matty, who didn't stir, and I braced for the icy water. Jasper whispered something to Matty I couldn't hear and started walking. I grabbed a strap connected to Jasper's backpack, and I put my running shoe into the water. The rocks were slippery and the cold penetrated to my core instantly. My teeth chattered as I navigated each step. Jasper held Matty with one arm, his other outstretched, bracing for a fall. I tried my best not to pull on the backpack and throw him off balance. The water was thigh-high and my feet were numb. Jasper called something back to me, but I missed it, too focused on each of my steps.

Halfway across, the water swallowing my legs, I slipped. Instantly my feet were out from under me. I clung to the backpack and screamed a gurgled choke as the river enveloped my face. I dangled on my back as the river pulled me forcefully downstream, threatening to drag us all to our deaths. Jasper's fingers curled around my wrist with a menacing grip. He kept wading across while I scrambled to get my feet beneath me again. We made it to the other side, Matty tucked snuggly in his shaking arm and me, a sopping heap. Jasper pulled me onto the riverbank and collapsed to his knees, his breath coming fast and hard. I looked up into his eyes. The fear I saw there mirrored my own. We got to our feet and kept moving.

The truck was parked about an hour down the trail at the

end of a long-forgotten hunting road. Jasper always took time to cover it with branches in case someone happened to stumble upon it. The once-red paint was devoured by rust and the side mirrors were missing. He gingerly handed me Matty, who was barely breathing. His lips had taken on a blue tinge, his skin still burning to the touch.

"We have to hurry." I forced the urgent words through my clenched jaw.

"I know, Kris. I know."

He ripped the branches from the truck and stuck his head under the hood. He didn't look up when he spoke to me, but I could hear his frustration when he barked the words.

"Just get in. You're freezing."

I pried open the door and boosted Matty and myself in, my legs straining and shaking. My wet jeans, worn through at the knees, and plaid shirt stuck to my bony body like a second skin, leeching all the warmth I could produce. I clung to Matty, softly rocking and singing to him as his eyelashes fluttered, and his beautiful blue eyes rolled back into his head. My baby was going to die. It would be my fault.

Jasper tinkered with the engine a few minutes longer and then jumped in, turning the key already in the ignition. The engine sputtered. He tried it again, and again.

"Come on! Please!" He was pushing his worn hiking boot insistently on the gas pedal.

I thought he might finally break, his desperation bordering on panic. Jasper, who never panicked. My rock.

A few more tries and it started. We were moving. The branches scraped the sides of the truck as Jasper steered it out of the bush. Away from the mountain. Away from our home. I kept my eyes glued on Matty's sweet face. It was a couple of hours to town. I feared we left it too late. Jasper was silent, glancing over at our son from time to time. Worry etched across his brow. All of the words had been said. We knew we had to do this, that it was the only way to save Matty. Beyond that, I could only hope that somehow I would still have my husband when it was over.

2.

It was late morning by the time we reached town. I hadn't been back since it all started. Everything looked different: big and busy and unnecessary. Buildings and cars passed in a blur as Jasper sped to the hospital. I could barely find a pulse on Matty. His face was now blue, and I was puffing air into his tiny lips, my tears rolling off his cheeks.

"Hang on buddy. We're almost there," Jasper pleaded softly, his eyes splitting the time between Matty and the road.

Jasper's tone with his son brought sweet memories of them up at the cabin. Jasper never wanted to have kids, but after Matty came into our lives we couldn't imagine any other existence. Jasper spent hours talking and laughing with him, taking him fishing and getting wood. I'd never seen Jasper so happy. We couldn't lose Matty now.

The hospital came into view ahead, and panic rose up in me. This was as far as our plan had taken us. We agreed that nothing mattered beyond getting Matty the help he urgently needed. Jasper careened into the emergency bay and jumped from the truck. I opened my door and Jasper helped us to the pavement. I squeezed his arm and looked briefly into his eyes. Together, as a family, we ran into the building. The shiny floors and harsh lights were so foreign it felt like I was dreaming.

"Help!" I gasped in the direction of a cluster of uniforms near a large desk. "Our son is sick. He's not breathing. Please, help us!"

Instantly there was a flurry of activity. The first nurse to reach us took one look at Matty's face and started yelling.

"Code blue! Child in respiratory distress! Clear curtain

two and get an OR ready. Page Dr. Brown. What happened to him?"

She tore Matty from my arms. I let him go, knowing I could do nothing else. We didn't answer her question as we followed her through the lobby and into a small room. People came from every direction: some pushing machines, others running and holding their stethoscopes tightly to their bodies. The chaos was organized. Precise. They laid Matty down and undressed him. I could barely look at his tiny blue body as they stuck it with needles and inserted a tube down his throat. The dirty bandage on his neck, the last one we had, was curled at the edges and stained with fluid. One of the nurses worked it off, revealing the four puncture wounds that looked angry and festering, not like the innocent red dots they once were. An authoritative man walked through the open door in his crisp white coat. An aura of confidence surrounded him. The room pulsed with energy, but with an unspoken understanding everyone parted to let him get to Matty.

"Dr. Brown, this appears to be a bite to the neck." The nurse sounded disgusted. She turned to us. "Are you the parents of this little boy?"

I opened my mouth to answer but it was Jasper's voice I heard.

"Yes. His name's Matty and he's two years old. Is he going to be okay?"

"We don't know that yet," the nurse said. "He's a very sick little boy. He has obviously been *bitten* by something. How long has he been this way?"

Her disapproving tone said everything she couldn't. *You horrible people. Why didn't you bring him in sooner? You may have killed him.* This time it was me who answered.

"He's been sick for six days. He was bitten by a rat that got into our cabin." The words poured from my lips, my voice shrill and unrecognizable to me. Jasper gently squeezed my hand. "He had a fever, but we were keeping the bite really clean, and then he started having these strange muscle spasms, and his fever got really high. We ran out of iodine and bandages. We got him here as fast as we could. I'm so sorry! Is he going to die?"

I broke down. All the fear and guilt came pouring out of me. Jasper's strong arms pulled me in, and I sobbed uncontrollably into his chest. He held me tightly while his hand smoothed my long hair.

"Is he up to date on his vaccinations? Has he even *been* vaccinated?"

She spat the questions at us. I stayed buried in Jasper, his body stiffened as he spoke.

"No. He hasn't."

"Thanks, Sally. I'll take it from here."

It was a man's voice, soft and calm and free of judgment. I peeked up from Jasper's chest to see the man in the white coat looking back at me with compassion. I liked him instantly.

"I'm Dr. Brown. I know this is difficult for you, and we're going to do everything we can to help Matty. It's pretty crowded in here, and we need to work. We'll be moving Matty to the ICU as soon as we get him stable. You two head out to the desk. There's some paperwork you have to fill in. We'll get you as soon as we have any update."

Dr. Brown started giving orders, not waiting for us to answer, and the nurses closed around Matty like a curtain. The air sparked with urgency. Jasper led me out of the room.

We huddled in the hall. I looked up at Jasper, knowing we were sharing the same thoughts. We couldn't do any paperwork.

"Jasper, I think you should go now." I took a deep breath and feigned bravery. "I think Matty is going to be fine. Dr. Brown's really great, and there are so many people helping him. I think he's going to make it. Go back to the cabin. We'll meet you there in a few days. We can just carry on with our lives."

I tried to appear calm but couldn't control the panic in my voice. I knew as every minute ticked away, so did the chance of Jasper escaping. Being free. He always told me the only way he could survive was to be free. In the mountains. I knew he wouldn't make it anywhere else. Especially locked in a cage.

"I can't believe you're even saying this to me right now. You promised you wouldn't." He kept his voice to a whisper, but rage burned in his eyes. "I told you I would never abandon my son or my family. What kind of a man do you think I am? How are you going to get back to the cabin? Walk? And do you really think they're going to just fix Matty and hand him over to you with no ID or proof he's even yours? Come on, Kris. We've been through this. You know what we have to do now. It's the only way you even have a chance of getting Matty back."

I knew he was right. We spent the last few days in the cabin talking about nothing but this decision. This moment. But now it was here, and it was real, and I didn't know how I could survive a day without Jasper. But we both agreed Matty was the most important thing. We would give our lives for him. We were about to.

"I know! I just, how am I going to live without you?" My voice was catching in my throat. I was crushing Jasper's hand in mine. "How will I raise Matty without you? I'm so sorry this has happened. You know I love Matty so much, but sometimes I wish I had listened to you and given Matty to a normal family."

We were both crying. "Krissy! Don't! Not now. Matty is the best thing, the only good thing I've ever done in my entire life. Don't you dare wish that away. He was worth everything!"

My throat burned with tears and desperation. We stood, clinging to each other, as the sounds of people trying to save our son's life echoed in the hall.

3.

Two nurses trickled out of the room, giving us a wide berth. I looked at their faces for some kind of reassurance but found only judgment. As they retreated down the hall, I heard one whisper to the other. "I can't believe they're the parents! They look like they crawled out from under a rock."

"Yeah, what was Mountain Girl thinking when she had a baby? Obviously she has no idea how to take care of one."

Mountain Girl? Is that who I was now? For the first time, I realized what we must look like coming from our mountain home to this sterile environment. Their words were barbs, each one tearing at the shred of pride I still had. Shame covered me like a heavy cloak. My hand went to my blond hair, which was dirty and tangled. Our soiled clothes and smells, so normal to us, were disgusting and unkempt to the rest of the world. Jasper's beard was long and shaggy, a few needles from the branches he'd torn from the truck embedded in it. I hadn't even noticed until this second. Dr. Brown emerged and we wiped our tears, coming to attention.

"Is he okay?" Jasper blurted out, his voice still thick with emotion.

"Let's have a seat for a minute."

He motioned us over to some chairs against the wall. Jasper and I collapsed into ours. Dr. Brown perched on the edge of his.

"We haven't been introduced. I'm Ray Brown."

He reached out to shake my hand first, and then Jasper's. His skin was smooth and I pulled my rough hand away quickly.

"I'm Kris."

"Jasper."

We were giving ourselves up.

"Matty is very sick. When the rat bit him he contracted tetanus. If he had been vaccinated, he would probably be fine. I'm not going to get into any debate about whether or not you should be vaccinating. That is a personal choice and some people are opting out these days. The bottom line is he got the infection and has had it long enough to do some severe damage to his body. We've had to insert a breathing tube, and he's going to need a machine to help him breathe for a while. It may be several days. He will be on a strong dose of different medications to help with the muscle spasms." He shifted slightly in his chair, pausing until my eyes met his again. "Depending on how long his brain was deprived of oxygen, he may have some brain damage. We'll have to monitor him and wait. Time will tell. At this point he's stable, and we'll be moving him to the ICU shortly. Have you been to the desk yet?"

His words were fast and indigestible. I tried to cling to a few—breathing tube, brain damage—as they flew past. Jasper and I remained silent.

"I know this is a lot to take in. I'm going to get someone from the crisis team to come and talk with you and help you get organized. We'll be moving Matty soon. If I know anything else, I'll come and find you."

He touched my knee as he rose. I didn't want him to go. I wanted him to tell us Matty was going to be fine. Give us an encouraging smile. His shoes squeaked on the shiny floor as he strode away.

I looked at Jasper. His eyes were closed and his head rested against the wall. Before I could get a thought out, we heard a gruff voice from a few feet away.

"Is that your red Chevy parked out front?"

My head whipped around. Jasper scrambled to his feet. The officer's blue uniform filled the hallway. Nowhere to run.

"Yes. It's mine. It's my truck."

Jasper sounded young. Like a teenager being scolded.

"Well, I'm going to need you to move it immediately. It's blocking the whole emergency bay."

As the policeman spoke he looked us up and down, taking in our bedraggled appearance, our dirty clothes and unwashed hair. I cringed from the scrutiny.

"And, I'm going to need to see your licence and registration."

It was an afterthought. A judgment. I hated him. I reached out for Jasper's hand, but it wasn't there. He stepped in front of me, trying to shield me from our fate.

"I don't have any ID. And the truck hasn't been registered in years. I don't live in town. My son, our son, is sick. Really sick."

Jasper's voice trailed off, and he glanced back at me. It had started.

The officer held Jasper's gaze for a few seconds. I reached out and clasped onto his arm as a show of solidarity. *Please*, I thought. *Let the officer be a parent too. Let him have pity on us.*

"You'll both need to come with me. Now, please."

No pity. He took a small step backwards, allowing us space to move with him. Jasper stood his ground.

"I'll come with you, sir, but can my wife please stay here? Our son is being treated in the next room. The doctor said he'd come get us if anything changes. One of us needs to stay with Matty."

His voice was urgent, fraying at the edges. Tears pooled in my eyes.

"No. I need you both to come with me. I'm sure your son is getting the best medical care. Miss, do you have any ID?"

"No."

I hung my head and avoided eye contact. I didn't like the way he said, "miss."

The officer raised his hand, pressed a button and spoke briefly into a small handset clipped to his uniform. His voice was muffled, and I couldn't make out the words. Jasper turned to me and looked deep into my eyes. He held my face in his hands and kissed me softly, and then whispered in my ear.

"I love you so much, Krissy. You made my life worth living. Take good care of Matty, and make sure he knows how much his dad loved him."

"All right, let's go." The officer motioned for us.

Through my tears I saw a sea of blue. Three more officers arrived. One pulled Jasper from our embrace. Another held my arm and they walked us down the hall and out the emergency doors. Our truck was still parked where we had skidded to a stop. My door hung open. There was a police car at either end, and they took Jasper to one car and me to another. I started to struggle.

"Can't you take us in the same car? Can't we be together?"

"No. Not right now," the officer said as he opened the back door and helped me get inside.

The car smelled new, with a mix of leather and plastic. I looked ahead to the car Jasper was in, but I could only make out the back of his head. My heart raced, and the tears that had been pooling released. I couldn't stop them.

Two officers got into the front seats, and the one who had been holding my arm grabbed a clipboard and turned to face me.

"Let's start with the basics. What's your name?"

I choked back my sobs and took a breath. It was time.

"My name is Krissy Mathews."

4.

"Krissy Mathews. Like, *the* Krissy Mathews?" His voice was incredulous. He looked from me, to his partner, and back to me. Staring at me, he fumbled for his radio. "Mark, this girl says she's Krissy Mathews. Yes. I know. Take that guy in immediately."

The engine of the other police car roared to life. I looked up to find Jasper, and this time we made eye contact. I reached up and touched the glass, wishing it was his face. He was gone.

The car I was in remained where it was. Both officers were on radios, their voices a jumble of incomprehensible words: *She's back. We have her. Four years.* I held my head in my hands, shielding my face from their scrutiny. One of the men got out of the car and opened the back door.

"Miss Mathews, we're going to take you back inside. We need you to be medically cleared before we can bring you to the station." He held out his hand for me to take, his expression much softer than when he put me in the car. "Don't worry. The detective in charge of your case is calling your mom as we speak. I'm pretty sure he has her on speed dial. Man, I can't believe it's you." A smile broke out on his chubby face. "Where have you been?"

I felt like I might throw up. My mom. She was coming. I had pushed thoughts of my family so far back in my head. I had locked them away where they couldn't hurt me. Now I was numb. And scared. A barrage of questions swirled in my brain.

"Officer, I don't need to be checked out. I'm fine. Can we go check on Matty now? What are you doing with Jasper? When can I see him?"

I could feel the bile rising in my empty stomach. My mom was on her way. What was I going to tell her? How would I ever explain everything? How would I explain Matty? I was going to devastate her all over again.

The officer reached in and pulled me out of the car, a confused look on his face. I went willingly. I had no fight left. Everything was blurry and in slow motion as I grappled with the screaming in my head. He took me back to the desk and whispered something to the nurse behind it. She was the same one who had been so mean to us earlier. She gave me a shocked look and ushered us to a room farther down from where Matty had been taken, then she avoided my eyes as she rushed past. I wasn't going to let her get away that easily.

"Hey! Have you heard anything about Matty? Is there any update?"

"No. Well, I think they moved him to the ICU. I'm sorry. I had no idea…"

She sheepishly bowed her head and left the room.

The officers and I waited awkwardly. We didn't speak. I wondered if they had been given instructions not to ask me anything. After a few minutes, there was a brisk knock and a doctor walked in. He was much older than Dr. Brown, his hair thinning and deep creases surrounding his eyes. He asked the men to wait outside and he gave me a gown to put on. Then he stepped out. I was alone.

As I peeled off my dirty jeans and unbuttoned my shirt, I saw myself in a mirror above the sink. Jasper and I hadn't owned a mirror. We had no use for one up in the mountains. Jasper always told me I was beautiful, and that was all the mirror I needed. I hadn't studied my reflection in four years. The young woman staring back at me took my breath away. My cheekbones jutted from my face and left dark hollows beneath them. My blue eyes were huge. Long, scruffy blond hair was matted in chunky dread-locks and hung down my back. My skin was deeply tanned and dirty. The part of my chest I could see appeared skeletal. There was a small bump on the bridge of my nose. A souvenir from my first night with Jasper. I looked away and quickly put the gown on, wrapping it tightly around me.

The doctor came back in and started asking me questions. Had I suffered any trauma? Was I in any pain? I kept my answers short and went along with the tests. I'd never had a pelvic exam before, and I tensed as he put my feet in the stirrups. I thought of Matty, his sweet face and the way he said "Momma." As the doctor was finishing up, I heard a commotion outside the door. My mom's voice. She was demanding to see me. Even through the thick guilt, I longed for her embrace, to be a kid again.

"Can I see my mom?"

I couldn't hide the crack in my voice. My eyes burned with tears.

"Yes, we're done. You seem to be doing well, considering what you've been through." He was genuinely surprised, his shoulders relaxing for the first time since he'd stepped into the room. "You're very malnourished, so we'll have to make sure you see a dietitian. And I believe someone from psychology is on their way down."

The voices grew louder outside and my mom's became more frantic. The doctor said a brief goodbye and opened the door. Between the uniforms, I saw her face. We locked eyes. She caught me as I collapsed. Four years of life, of pain and terror and love and guilt, came out in anguished sobs. She held me against her chest as we crumpled to the floor. She cried and repeated my name like a prayer.

The officers left us, and after a while we gathered ourselves off the floor and into the two chairs placed against the wall.

"Oh, Kris, I can't believe it's really you. You look beautiful. Older."

She touched my hair, my face. She couldn't stop touching me.

"I always knew you would come home. I knew you were alive. They had some stupid memorial for you at your school, but I refused to go. This is the best day of my life."

She started to cry again. She had also aged. Her blond hair was greying, shorter than I'd ever seen it. Her face was etched with deep lines and make-up free. She smelled the same, a lotion I couldn't remember the name of. In the darker days, I desperately tried to conjure that smell in my mind.

"Mom, I'm so glad to see you. I didn't know how much I missed you until…I'm so sorry. I'm so sorry you had to go through this." I shook as I spoke, my hands sweating beneath her tight grasp.

"What are you talking about? You're the one who's been through hell. Detective Umbry said they have the guy who took you. That he was the one who brought you here. I can't even begin to imagine what you've suffered through." Her voice became lower and her teeth clenched. "I don't know what finally caused this piece of scum to come to his senses, but I'm just so glad they got the bastard."

How was I ever going to explain?

5.

After her angry words, my mom began taking deep breaths, trying to calm herself. She had four years of hatred built up, and she was ready to unleash it. When she had gathered herself, she spoke.

"Honey, I know you feel overwhelmed right now, but you can tell me everything you want to in your own time. She struggled to get her words out without breaking into tears again. "I'm just so glad to have you back."

Her pained face broke my heart. Even through her words, I could see the questions in her eyes, searching my face for any answers she could find. The one question she so urgently wanted to ask—What happened to you?—was perched on her lips.

"Mom, I need to tell you what happened and where I've been. I have a lot to say."

My husband. My son. Where would I start? And would she be able to love me after she knew the truth? A knock, and the door opened again. It was the nurse.

"Sorry to interrupt. I just wanted you to know Matty has been stabilized. He's in the ICU."

She lowered her eyes and retreated. She was still feeling bad about her earlier treatment of me.

"Who's Matty?"

I took a deep breath.

"He's my son. He's two. His name is Mathew."

The blood appeared to drain from her face and she clutched at her neck as if someone was choking her. My breath came out in rapid bursts. I was desperate for her to understand, afraid somehow that Matty might disappear if everyone didn't know how much he meant to me.

"You have a son? Oh, my God, Krissy! I'm so sorry. I'm so sorry I couldn't protect you from this." She held out her hands to me and they stayed hovering in the air between us.

"No, don't be sorry. You don't understand. Matty is the love of my life! I can't imagine not having him. He's wonderful!"

Her arms shot up in the air and her last question came out as a shriek.

"But, where did you have him? Where have you been?"

I reached up and grasped her hands, trying to reassure her, but at the same time feeling dizzy. It was too much to say. How could I make her understand, and what could I say about Jasper? I had to give her something.

"You're right. I'm feeling really overwhelmed. I will tell you everything. I just need some time."

"Yes. I promised myself I wouldn't do this to you," she sighed. "Do you mind if we bring in your sister? I'm sure she's out in the hall by now and she's been, well, I know I don't have to tell you how hard this has been for her. For all of us."

My sister. I had thought of Jill so many times since I'd been gone, her image frozen like a time capsule in my mind. My younger sister by two years, she always looked up to me. Jill tried to do everything I did. She was my little buddy, my confidante. I'd missed her desperately. If she'd decided to come with me that afternoon, things would have been very different. But I'd learned years ago to stop second-guessing those last hours. Everything happened the way it was meant to, and now I had Matty. And Jasper.

"I'd love to see her, Mom."

My palms instantly went damp with anticipation as I recalled my sister's cheerful face. She would understand.

My mom opened the door and stepped out into the hall. She spoke a few words to the officers and then came back into the room. A large woman was with her. Her eyes were red and bloodshot, and they searched mine with a familiarity that shocked me.

"Krissy!" She was breathless as she said my name, her feet frozen in place, her mouth gaping open and her eyes huge with disbelief. Then, like a veil dropping in front of her face, her emotion disappeared. She spoke again but was now much more reserved. "Krissy, it's me. Jill."

Confusion paralyzed my thoughts. It took a few seconds for me to comprehend that this large woman could be my little sister. She must have weighed three hundred pounds. Her face was swallowed in rolls of fat, her body masked in a giant black cloak of a coat. Her hair was short and raggedly cut, with ugly purple streaks permeating the pretty blond.

"Jilly, oh, my God." I stumbled it out and immediately regretted it.

There was a flash of embarrassment in her eyes as she stepped forward to awkwardly hug me. She began to sob and pulled herself away, retreating behind my mother. My hands dropped to my sides as I stood alone in the center of the room. Even though she looked different, having my sister back was like reassembling pieces of me that had been lost so long ago. This was not the reunion I had imagined.

"Jilly, it's so good to see you. I've missed you." My voice wavered. The tension in the room was thick.

"It's good to see you too. You look…skinny." Her voice was breaking as she spoke. "I'm not supposed to ask, but, what happened to you?"

My mom shot her a look, and she dropped her head.

"Krissy will tell us everything when she's ready. We don't want to pressure her. She's been through an unimaginable ordeal and we're just so happy she's back."

I could tell by the tone and way she was speaking that these were not my mother's words. She must have sought out some kind of counselling to deal with losing me. I was happy she had because she was right. I didn't know where to start. How could I explain what happened and how I got where I was today? Anything important I needed to say was like starting somewhere in the middle. I had no idea how to begin. I kept my mouth closed and let the relief on my face convey my agreement with her. My mom understood, reaching out to squeeze my shoulder, but she couldn't help herself.

"Do you want to tell Jill the wonderful news you just shared with me?"

She stumbled over the word "wonderful." My sister's head snapped up.

"Yeah, okay." I took a deep breath and leaned towards her a little. "I have a son, Jilly. He's two years old, and he's so amazing. His name's Matty. He was bitten by a rat up at our, or, I mean *the* cabin. That's where I was. In a cabin. In the mountains. Now he's really sick. He's in the ICU."

Jill's eyes widened.

"You have a son? Who the hell is the father?"

"Well, I need to tell you about that. Where's Dad?"

I figured if I was going to tell them, I might as well have the whole family together. And I really wanted to see my dad. He was always the calm one in the middle of three crazy, hormonal women.

My mom seemed flustered before she softened her expression.

"Dad is…with the police. You'll see him soon."

"Can't you get him? Is he in the hall?"

"No. He isn't."

The look on Jill's face said something wasn't right. I had a feeling I had caused more pain than I could have imagined.

6.

Seeing my sister and my mom brought everything back to me. Events and feelings I had locked away and tried so hard to forget were surfacing. My last day in town, the day Jasper took me away, was seeming less like a distant dream I couldn't quite grasp. Memories flooded me.

It was one of those perfect early days of spring. The long and relentless winter was finally ending and the sun felt therapeutic and addictive. Everyone I passed had their face turned up to the sky, soaking in the vitamin D with a look of peaceful gratitude. I was in grade twelve and I couldn't wait to graduate. I was planning to go backpacking in Europe that summer with two of my closest girlfriends, Marcy and Sara. The three of us spent hours going over backpacking books, circling hostels and places we wanted to visit. Marcy was obsessed with Italy, so we promised to spend as much time as possible there. I think she was mostly obsessed with the food. After our magical summer, I would be off to university in the fall. There were forty-two students graduating from my high school that year. Most of us had known each other since kindergarten.

Our town was nestled in the mountains and home to about five thousand people. It was the kind of place where most people knew each other, which had its pluses and minuses. As a seventeen-year-old girl, I couldn't get away with anything. If I skipped school to ski at the local hill because there was a huge dump of snow, I would always get busted. Luckily, I usually spotted my dad up there doing the same thing, so we would cover for each other. I was always a pretty good kid, and my parents gave me a lot of leeway.

As I walked home from school that fateful afternoon, I was planning to grab my shoes and head to my favourite running trail on the edge of town. It was a short loop that I had been running for years. My parents loved running and they'd gotten my sister and me into the local running club at very early ages. I loved losing myself in my thoughts, letting my body cruise on autopilot, cranking up my music and finishing soaked in sweat and high on endorphins. After a good run, it felt like I could conquer the world. Sometimes Jilly and I would run together, but she had been getting faster and I had no intention of letting her think she could beat me. When I got home to change for running, I was relieved she wasn't there yet and quickly gathered my gear. I wanted to go on my own without the pressure of proving myself.

My dad worked as a lawyer and generally helped people sort out small-business loans, land issues, stuff like that. My mom worked as a receptionist at a local doctor's office. They usually got home around five, so I scribbled a note on the counter that said "running" and took off. As I drove down our street in my beat up little Ford Ranger, I spotted Jilly and a friend ambling up the road. She saw me and raised her hands as if to ask, "Where are you going?" I held up one of my runners I'd tossed on the seat and she stuck her tongue out at me. That was it. That was the last time I saw any member of my family.

I reached the trailhead and, as it often happened, I was the only vehicle there. I laced up my shoes, put on my headphones and stretched for a few minutes before I started with a gentle lope up the trail. I ran through the trees for about fifteen minutes and climbed up to a small lake. The lake is tucked in against the mountain and has a shale slide falling right into it. The trail meanders around the front of the lake and then heads back down and around to the parking lot.

On that day the sun was warm on my face, and when I came over the rise and spotted the lake it was sparkling so bright it looked fake, like liquid turquoise. I slowed my pace to really take it in. I picked up the scent of a campfire, which was strange because I thought I was alone. My truck was the only vehicle in the lot. Other trails existed in this area so I figured someone had hiked in from another direction. I scanned the shore of the lake and spotted smoke but saw no one.

The lake looked so beautiful I decided to walk up to its edge and splash some of the icy water on my face. As I knelt over, I saw my reflection. Directly behind me I saw a red plaid coat. He looked enormous. He was holding a big stick in one hand. I didn't even have a chance to turn around before my world went black, and changed forever.

7.

An officer knocked loudly and burst through the door, bringing me out of my daze. Back to the present.

"Sorry ladies, but I have to interrupt you. The doctor has cleared Ms. Mathews medically, so we're going to get her down to the station to make a statement. We need to press official charges to have the suspect moved from a holding cell. The guy admits taking her, but we still need a statement from the victim for the judge." The officer turned to me. "You're going to have to come with us. Your mom and sister can follow behind and wait at the station if they want."

My mom jumped from her seat.

"Wait, we haven't even had a chance to talk yet! I don't know if Krissy's ready to get into all the details. The guy has confessed. He's the one who took her, right? Isn't that enough for now?"

She was panicking. And so was I. Jasper had confessed. I needed to see him, to talk to him.

"Detective Umbry is insisting we get her there as soon as possible. He wants to get her story before anything gets blurred. You can have her back soon. I promise."

"Don't worry, Mom. I can go. I want to get this over with. I'll see you at the station. Bye, Jilly."

I got up and gave them each a brief hug, feeling Jill recoil slightly as I let her go. I closed the door and put my dirty, torn jeans and plaid shirt back on. I tried not to glance in the mirror. With a deep breath, I opened the door to the waiting officers and followed them down the hall. I thought again of my dad and anticipated seeing him at the station. I walked quietly with my head down, relieved to have a few minutes to collect my thoughts.

At the main door I insisted we ask about Matty one more time. The nurse said he would be unconscious for several days, at least. They put him in a medically induced coma to help him sleep and allow his body to repair itself. She said he had stabilized, but there was no way to determine the extent of damage until he woke up. I needed to hold him. I mumbled a thanks and left.

As we drove to the station, I could hear the officer on his radio announcing our arrival. I wondered what Jasper was going through right now, and when I would get to see him. We parked in front of the station, and I followed the two officers up the steps and through the door. It was crowded. Bodies everywhere, mostly in uniform. All eyes were on me. I looked to the floor and took a few steps until a pair of black boots blocked my way. Hesitating, I lifted my head and looked into the eyes of the man in front of me. He was tall and very handsome. His freshly shaven face and groomed dark hair, expertly combed back with some type of product, appeared unnatural to me. He was wearing black pants and a charcoal button up shirt, tailored perfectly to his fit body. His chiselled jaw was clenched, betraying no emotion, but the way he looked at me, his eyes stormy and locked on mine, made my knees shake a little.

"Krissy. I'm Detective Umbry. You can call me Jake. I've been looking for you. It's good to have you home. Please follow me."

Although his words were kind, the tone of his voice held an edge that made me nervous. Proficient. Powerful. He turned and walked through the throngs of people without waiting for me to speak. I trailed closely behind, feeling small and fragile in his wake. I was keenly aware of my scraggly appearance and camp-fire smell. My gaze dropped to the flesh of my bare feet showing through the holes in my old running shoes. He led me to an office down the hall and pointed to a chair facing an immaculate desk. I sat, anticipation prickling along my spine. He was not going to like what I had to say. I wanted to see Jasper.

Detective Umbry excused a few officers who had followed me to my final destination, perhaps hoping to overhear some juicy details, and closed the door. It was just the two of us. I tried to breathe regularly but was finding it impossible. Rather than sit in his chair, he perched on the edge of the desk, inches away from me. His perfection was unnerving. I began to sweat.

"So Krissy, let me start by saying again how happy I am to have you back. I realize you don't know me, but I'm the detective who was assigned to your case from day one. I think I've spoken to your mom more than I've spoken to my own mother in the last four years. We've worked our asses off trying to get you back here."

As he spoke, he kept the same steely expression, his eyes never leaving mine, as if my truths were all written just below the surface. My eyes darted around the room, instinct driving my search for an escape. He continued on. "The department, and me personally, have poured every possible resource into finding you. The dollars and man-hours we've spent on your case are unprecedented. And suddenly, here you are."

The way he was looking at me was making me squirm in my seat. He knew. He knew what was going on. And he was going to make me tell him.

I avoided his eyes as I spoke. My voice cracked with weakness and intimidation. "Thanks, Detective Umbry. I really appreciate that you were looking for me, and I'm happy to be home."

I was truly thankful for everything he'd done, but the hostility bubbling just below his professional demeanour made me feel like a wounded bird being batted around by a hungry cat. He was poised to strike. He wanted answers, and I knew I didn't have the right ones. I opened my mouth to attempt some sort of apology, but he cut me off.

His coolness finally began to evaporate. He leaned in even closer to me so our faces were inches apart. "It's Jake. I think we have some major holes in this story we have to patch up. I'd like you to start at the beginning and walk me through the events of the last four years that led you to the part where you and your kidnapper, who is apparently your *husband*, walk into the hospital with a child."

I looked up into his eyes, and the betrayal there shocked me.

"I'm sorry. Thank you for looking for me. Things are really confusing, I'm…I don't really know what to say."

My tears flowed and I crumpled myself into a ball on the chair. My life continued to spin uncontrollably away from me. I wanted Jasper to hold me and make it all better. I wanted Matty. I wanted my mom. My thoughts were splintering in a million directions and I could see no way out.

The detective stood and walked over to a small window on the other side of the room. His every step put welcome distance between us and I felt the air coming back into my lungs. When he returned and sat in his chair, his voice was softer.

"Look, I'm sorry. I have no idea what you've been through these last few years. I can tell you that we've been through hell looking for you, and if I could explain to you the dead-end leads, the sleepless nights…"

He broke off, and then composed himself again.

"Please, just tell me what happened. Tell me the truth. Tell me I haven't spent the last four years of my life desperately searching for a girl who was trying not to be found. Start at the beginning."

I owed him an explanation. That was crystal clear to me. I took a deep breath, wiped my tears on the back of my hand and recalled the first day I met Jasper.

8.

I awoke to a thousand shrill voices screaming in my ears. Harsh
and excruciating. I tried to cradle my head in my hands, but they
were tied behind my back. I was lying on my left side and
attempting to move my arms made me realize they were blood-
less. Asleep. I opened my eyes. In the dim light, everything was
blurry and distorted. I struggled to move my legs. They were tied
at the ankles. I could feel hard, rutted metal beneath me. I was
in the bed of a truck. Slowly, my eyes became accustomed to the
light. Surrounding me were camping supplies: cans of soup, rope,
sleeping bag, rubber bins, rolled up tarps, red gas cans. The smell
was putrid dead animal, musty tarp, and gasoline. The truck had
a canopy over it, with one small window that looked into the cab,
but the tiny pane of glass was plastered in duct tape. I tried to
clear my head and think. What happened? How did I get here?

It came back to me in a rush: standing on the shore of the
lake, smoke from the fire, the man in the red plaid coat—with a
stick. As the images played in my throbbing brain, panic ripped
through me. Adrenaline pumped. I tried to scream, but it was
muffled because of the tape on my mouth. Suddenly, I couldn't
get enough oxygen. My nose wasn't efficient enough to meet the
demands of my body. I kicked and thrashed and tried to pull my
hands free. Where was he taking me? What did he want with me?

This went on for several minutes, or hours, I wasn't sure, until
finally the panic subsided and I lay still. The tape bubbled out
with every breath I took. Tears soaked my face and my throat
burned. *Think. Breathe.* My head pounded and my body ached. I
could tell the truck wasn't moving. I strained to hear any familiar

sounds but there was no distant traffic, no dogs barking. Only silence.

Think. What had I ever heard about being kidnapped? The only thing I could recall was someone saying to never let your attacker take you to another location. I guessed it was too late for that. Not only was I likely in another location, I had no idea where I was or how long I'd been gone. I thought it was night, but I wasn't sure if it was just the lack of light entering the truck. I wondered if my parents knew I was missing yet. My tears started again imagining how scared they would be for me. My family had never been religious, but I had always believed in God, so I prayed. I prayed to God with everything I had. *Please help me.*

I was freezing and I shivered uncontrollably. My lightweight running clothes—tights, a T-shirt and a thin log-sleeved top—were offering no protection from the cold. Where had he gone? Was he sitting in the cab, or had he left me here? Maybe he wanted some kind of ransom for me. I hoped that was the case. My parents didn't have a lot of extra money, but I knew they would do anything to get me back.

A thought struck me. If I was alone, this might be my only chance to escape. Get yourself together, Krissy. Time for action. I shimmied myself down as close as I could get to the tailgate. There were several large plastic bins stacked with boxes of food that blocked my way. I rolled over onto my back and kicked the food off with my feet. Boxes of rice and crackers, beef jerky and pasta fell onto me. I kept kicking through the food until my feet hit the hard metal of the tailgate. It made a loud bang, and the whole truck vibrated. I held my breath and waited. Nothing.

I kicked the tailgate again and the sound echoed into the silence. I figured he must not be around. I kicked with every ounce of strength I had. The truck shook. I tried to get my feet above the metal and to the thinner fibreglass canopy section, where I might be able to pop the latch and raise the door. I kept it up until I was covered in sweat and my breath was ragged. Eventually my hips ached, so I repositioned my feet right where I thought the latch would be. In the momentary stillness I heard footsteps. It sounded like someone walking through long grass. Swish, swish, swish. I couldn't tell how far away it was, but as it got closer, there was a low whistle. I waited. My breath caught in my throat.

He paused and then walked around the perimeter of the truck. The whistling continued. I heard him open the driver's side door and move some things around. The door slammed, and he walked slowly to the back of the truck. I coiled my legs up like a cobra about to strike. When he opened the tailgate I would kick him as hard as I could, try to aim for his face. After that I wasn't sure. He was fumbling with keys, and then he turned the canopy latch. It sprung open, letting in a blast of fresh, cold air. I released and kicked at the space with all my strength.

He yelled as he jumped out of the way. "Whoa! Easy!"

I made contact with the top of the tailgate and it shot open. I heard him laughing. An overhead light in the canopy flickered on. For the first time I saw his face. He looked a lot younger than I expected, maybe twenty-three or twenty-four. He had a long scruffy beard and equally long, tangled brown hair tucked under a black knit hat. He was tall, about two or three inches above six feet, and very skinny. His face was gaunt, his cheekbones protruding above the ragged beard. The red plaid coat hung loosely from his shoulders, the collar of a dirty white T-shirt, riddled with holes, stuck out from beneath it. His mouth formed a smirk that flickered in his eyes.

The light was casting strange shadows on his face. Behind him was blackness. Even though I knew it was pointless, I screamed. It came out as a muffled echo under the tape. I thrashed wildly, sending the food and plastic bins flying out of the truck. He stood there with an amused look. Watching. Waiting.

I realized thrashing around was futile and eventually lay still, breathing heavily and wondering what was going to happen next. Was he going to kill me? Would he rape me first?

"If you calm down, I'll take the tape off your mouth."

His voice was very deep and gravelly, but he still had a little smile on his face, and it gave me hope that maybe he wouldn't hurt me. I attempted to take a few deep breaths. I stayed curled on my side in the fetal position, protecting my body the best I could. After a few minutes, he reached into the truck and pulled me by my feet so I was lying on the open tailgate.

"This might smart a little."

He worked up a corner and then tore the tape off my mouth.

My lips burned and I wondered if they were ripped off with the tape. I gasped for breath, taking in large gulps of the cool air. He took a step back and observed me like I was part of an experiment he was presenting in science class.

"Let me go. Please, please let me go. I won't tell anyone what happened."

It burst out of my mouth before I could even think about what to say.

"Don't worry. I'm not going to hurt you."

"You're already hurting me! What do you want? Do you want money? My parents could get money for you. Please let me call them and you can talk to them and tell them how much you want. They'll get it. I promise."

He chuckled and watched me a little longer, then he walked back around to the front of the truck. I heard him rummaging through the cab. He came back with two large packs and a knife. Its blade glinted in the light from the canopy. My stomach turned and the hairs on my neck rose. I looked at his face and something about his expression reassured me he wasn't going to hurt me with it. I wasn't sure yet of his intention, but it didn't seem to be killing me.

"I'm going to sit you up and cut the tape off your feet. If you try to kick me I might cut you." As he spoke, he leaned in a little closer with the knife and lowered his voice. "If you try to run, I *will* cut you. Got it?"

"Yes. I got it. Please don't hurt me. Where are you taking me? Where are we?" My voice was shrill and I raised my head from the cold truck bed and tried to look past him. In the darkness, the silhouette of a forest loomed over his shoulders. I had no idea how long I had been unconscious, so I didn't know how far we were from home.

"Too many questions," he mumbled. "We have a lot of stuff to get packed and not much time before the sun comes up."

He grabbed my arm and hauled me into a sitting position on the back of the tailgate. With his big knife, he cut the duct tape that was around my ankles. I didn't try to kick him, the knife too close for comfort.

It felt good to have my legs free. I swung them a little to get the circulation back into my feet. I was cold. He grabbed the packs and started loading some of the food and supplies into them. I sat and watched him and wondered if I could make a run for it. It was so dark I didn't even know what direction I would go in, and my bound hands would make it impossible to get away.

He was totally focused on his task, jumping in and out of the canopy with supplies. He kept a close watch on me and the knife lay on the tailgate a few feet away, reminding me what would happen if I tried to run. When he was finished and had secured a tarp around each pack with a bungee cord, he addressed me again.

"All right, we're ready to go. We have a pretty good hike ahead of us, and these packs are heavy. I'm going to cut the tape off your wrists, put your pack on, and then tape your hands back up again."

He was all business. I felt like I was on an Outward Bound trip.

"Could you please leave my hands free? It's so dark out here and that pack looks huge. What if I fall?"

I was thinking if I could get my hands on a sharp stick, I might be able to stab him in the face with it.

"No. Turn around."

He was flustered as he grabbed me and roughly turned my back to him. I could feel the cold blade of the knife against my skin as he cut the tape. My hands sprung loose with the last slice, and I carefully massaged each wrist for as long as I could.

With one hand on my arm, he reached down and grabbed a pack. He swung it easily up onto the tailgate and told me to put it on. I reluctantly threaded my hands through the straps. He stood in front of me and adjusted the strap length one at a time. Each pull made a rough jerking motion that sent pain shooting through my shoulders and back. We were inches apart, and the scent of sweat and campfire wafted into my nose. His breath was warm on my face. He stopped and looked me right in the eyes.

"What's your name?"

"Krissy," I answered quietly.

"Oh. I'm Jasper."

He paused a minute, as if he was going to say more but decided against it, and then he grabbed the roll of duct tape from inside the canopy. He taped my hands tightly together in front of my body and ripped the tape with his teeth. I racked my brain for the right words to persuade him to let me go.

"Jasper, I don't know why you brought me here, or where you're taking me, but I promise if you let me go I'll never tell anyone about you. Ever. Please. Please let me go. Please." I trailed off into desperate sobs.

I was freezing, exhausted, terrified. Judging by the amount of supplies on our backs, I knew he was planning to take me somewhere for a long time. I didn't know if I would ever get back. The now-familiar feeling of panic raced through me again.

"Come on. Get up. We gotta go."

He stuffed the roll of tape into the side of my pack and pulled me off the tailgate. I slid off the cold metal and my feet hit the dirt. My tears had no effect on him. The full weight of the pack cut into my shoulders and nearly buckled my knees. It must've weighed fifty pounds.

"This is too heavy. There's no way I can walk anywhere with this pack. I can barely stand up."

I swayed beneath the impossible weight, my hands unable to help me balance because they were bound in front of me. He either wasn't listening to me, or he didn't care.

Jasper slammed the tailgate closed and pulled the canopy door down. Now we stood in darkness. We were at the end of an old dirt road. Grass grew knee-high between the tire marks, indicating it was rarely used. I was helpless. The pack was a giant ball and chain holding me down. Jasper grabbed a stack of branches from the nearby trees and laid them over the truck. He'd been here before.

My eyes were adjusting to the light. There was no moon, but

the stars were so brilliant and numerous they looked like a giant single cluster. A little clearing stood at the end of the road. Tall grass and several stumps were its only inhabitants. All around us were giant evergreens reaching into the sky. Other than the sound of Jasper tossing the branches onto the truck, it was silent. When he was finished he threw his pack on and walked towards me, fixing a headlamp over his hat.

"We have to move. There's a trail on the other side of the clearing that leads up to my cabin. We have to cross the river. You walk ahead of me. If you try to escape, I'll have to hurt you. I don't want to, so please don't make me. Come on. Get going."

He nudged me forward, giving my pack a shove that almost toppled me headfirst. I took a giant step to recover my balance.

"I can't see, and I don't think I can walk with this pack. Please, don't make me do this," I begged. He didn't care.

"Walk. Now."

He shoved me again, harder this time. I trudged through the clearing towards an opening in the trees. The beam of light from his head cast my long shadow into the forest. Tears filled my eyes and poured down my cheeks. It was like a death march. I wondered how anyone would ever find me up here. I prayed again. It was the only thing I had left to do.

We walked into the morning light. The sun had come up over the jagged mountain peaks, making the journey slightly easier. I heard the river long before we reached its banks. The sound of rushing water grew louder with every step. I tried not to look at Jasper, but when I snuck a glance he was very focused on what lay ahead. We crested the bank and the river raged before me. It could not be crossed. I stopped in my tracks, but once again Jasper shoved me forward.

He shouted above the rush of the water, sensing my hesitation. "Keep moving! There's a spot where it's not too bad."

With the weight of the pack and my shivering body, I knew I wouldn't make it.

"I can't do it. I won't. I'll die!" I yelled, without looking at him.

I wouldn't give him the satisfaction. He shoved me hard and I fell to my knees on the rocky bank. Another layer of pain was coursing through me.

Jasper moved around in front of me and leaned down into my face, speaking forcefully and looking directly into my eyes.

"Get up and follow me!"

He pulled me to my feet by my taped hands and walked into the freezing water, dragging me in with him until the water was knee-high. My feet immediately felt a million icy needles puncturing every cell. I screamed and wobbled to maintain my balance against the river's strength. The thought of submerging my body in its treacherous water kept me walking, but I still lost my footing twice and fell to my knees, the sharp rocks beneath piercing my skin. We made it across, wet and breathless. Jasper released my hands and looked like he might say something, then he turned abruptly and got behind me again. We kept marching.

My lower body was soaked, and I had lost feeling in my feet. My bloody knees poked through my tights from my many falls. The heavy pack dug into the soft flesh of my shoulders, which screamed in pain. My body was hunched over from the weight, but I put my face towards the occasional ray of morning sun that flickered through the trees to soak in every ounce of heat I could get.

Since the river crossing, we had been going straight up a heavily wooded trail for what seemed like forever. I scanned my surroundings constantly, trying to find a mountain or other landmark that looked familiar. Nothing did. I attempted to memorize every tree, every rock in the trail, hoping I would be on my way back out soon.

Jasper was behind me and quiet for most of the trip. When I stopped to rest, he would grumble to keep going, hurry up. He would help me up whenever I fell and lay helpless, face first in the cold dirt, but he refused to remove the tape from my wrists. Each time we stopped, his eyes would dart up and down the trail, and he was anxious to get where we were going.

I wondered what my family was doing. I'd been missing overnight. They would have checked the trail around dinnertime when I didn't come home. My truck would have still been parked at the trailhead, so they would know that was the last place I was. They would be frantic with worry. I wished there was some way to let them know I was alive. So far.

"Jasper." I spit out his name. It tasted like acid on my tongue. "I'm exhausted. I can't go much farther. Please, can we rest for a while?"

I'd decided trying to be nice might be my best chance to survive. Jasper rubbed his face and stared at me with some confusion. I didn't know yet what he wanted with me, but maybe if I could befriend him he might let me go, or at least he might let his guard down a little so I could escape.

He didn't respond. I stopped walking and turned to face him. "Please. Please, can we stop?"

Our eyes met. His were a grey-blue.

"We're almost there. Ten more minutes. Just keep going."

Again he shoved my pack, and I plodded on.

A glimmer of hope stirred inside me. I didn't feel like I was looking into the eyes of a heartless monster. When we got to where we were going, I would try talking some sense into him.

The trail was an endless set of dark switchbacks, except for the odd ray of sunlight breaking through the evergreen canopy. About an hour after we had last spoken, I broke out into a small clearing. A few trees had been cut down and their stumps remained. There was a giant white boulder near one edge of the clearing. A tiny log cabin was nestled in the trees on the other side, almost completely hidden from view. It had a small porch built off the front. Firewood was stored under the porch and stacked chest-high along the side of the cabin. It had a single small window. I could hear the quiet rush of a creek through the trees opposite the cabin. Patches of melting snow littered the ground. It would have been cute, even romantic, given different circumstances.

"This is it. This is where I live," he declared proudly.

His mood shifted. He seemed relieved and calm, as though we were old friends and I had come to visit.

I collapsed on the ground and rolled to my side. My raw shoulders couldn't take another second. He stood watching me for a minute, and then he pulled his buck knife from the sheath on his belt and came towards me. I cringed and shut my eyes. With one quick motion he sliced the tape between my wrists.

"Thank you," I mumbled, as I worked my arms through the pack straps and freed myself.

I kneaded my tender shoulders with my hands as I tried to stand. With the weight of the pack gone I was almost floating, my feet barely touching the ground.

"I have to tie you back up again, but I'll give you a minute if you need to…go to the bathroom or anything."

He seemed embarrassed, averting his eyes.

"Yes. I do. It's been a long time. Where do I go?"

I scanned the area for some sort of facility. He let out a little chuckle.

"Right here. Where do you think?"

I was hoping there was a hidden outhouse or something.

"Well, can I go over in the trees? Can I have some privacy?"

I knew I was in no condition to try and run right now, but maybe if I could get him to trust me I could try later, after I had some rest.

"No. You can't." I was testing his patience. "You can go here now or else I'm going to take you inside and tie you up. Hurry up and decide. I have to get a fire going."

I didn't want to make him mad. When he mentioned it, I realized I hadn't peed since yesterday afternoon, and my bladder ached at the thought of it. I really didn't want to pull my pants down in front of him, but I didn't have any other options.

"Will you look the other way please?"

He considered this for a few seconds.

"But if you try to run, I'll catch you before you get to the trees, and you'll be really sorry when I do. Hurry up."

He turned his back to me. I crouched down and my knees seared with pain. I barely slid my pants down far enough. Silence. My bladder burned, but I couldn't do it.

"It's too quiet, I can't go."

"Hurry up, or I'll make you go in your pants."

He grunted back at me, his back still turned. I willed myself to go. When I was finally finished, I slid my pants up and stood.

"Thank you. I'm done. Could you please not tie me up again? I won't run. I promise. I know you'll catch me, and I don't even know where we are. Where would I go? Please."

He didn't answer. He grabbed me by the aching wrist and tugged me through the clearing and up onto the porch. It creaked under our weight. He jiggled with the old, rusty door latch and then shoved the worn wood door open.

Inside, the little one-room cabin was sparsely furnished. There was a small wooden table with one chair in the middle of the room. Both appeared homemade. A metal cot with a dirty mattress sticking out from beneath a green sleeping bag was pushed against the far wall, and a wood-burning stove was to our right. There were ropes and shovels and a hunting rifle hanging from nails dug into the logs lining all four walls. A small window, the only window, looked out the front into the clearing. It smelled musty, like smoke and dust. Jasper led me towards the stove. Next to it was a grey wool blanket folded on the ground. My eyes fixed on a chain that had been fastened to the leg of the stove at one end and was attached to handcuffs on the other. He had been expecting me.

"Oh, my God. No, please don't chain me up. No!"

I struggled backwards and banged into the table, knocking the chair over with a loud crash. Seeing that chain terrified me. Now it was all real.

Jasper gripped my wrist so tightly I thought it would snap in two. We wrestled for a few seconds, me thrashing and kicking at him like a wild animal. He yanked me over to the stove and reached for the chain with his other hand. It sounded like a metal snake uncoiling as he picked it up off the ground. I lunged for his head with my free hand. He stepped aside and there was an audible *crack* as my face hit the edge of the stove. I landed in a heap beside it, blood pouring from my nose and soaking my shirt. Jasper was breathing heavily as he grabbed my hands, pulled them toward him so I was helpless on my back, and snapped the handcuffs on my wrists. The chain clinked loudly as it dropped to the ground. My fate was sealed.

9.

I needed a break. As I spoke of the horrific way Jasper had come into my life, the fear of thinking I would die at any moment and never see my family again was coming back to me. I hadn't thought of those days in a very long time. After things changed, I locked them away, choosing to be happy and focus on the good. As I recalled the terror, it was like a different man had done these things to me. Not Jasper, my husband and the father of my son. I had no idea reliving everything would drag me back through a nightmare I'd chosen to forget long ago. I didn't want to talk about it anymore.

Detective Umbry was seated, and had been quietly taking notes as I spoke, even though a recorder sat just between us on the desk. I saw flashes of anger cross his face while he was writing. It was fascinating that this man I had never met was so emotionally involved in what had happened to me. I was frustrated at myself for providing so much detail, afraid he may use it against Jasper later. It flowed uncontrollably from me. He opened his mouth to speak, and I suddenly needed space. I stood and walked towards the window. He swivelled to face me and relentlessly continued for answers.

"Okay, Krissy. So he marches you to the cabin and chains you up. At this point you were probably aware people were looking for you. We definitely had choppers in the air searching for you during this time. Did you hear the sound of helicopters?"

"No. I didn't hear anything."

"You're sure?"

"Yeah. I'm sure."

His tone and the way he waited for my answer, eyebrows raised in anticipation, were infuriating. He thought I was lying. I forced myself to hold his gaze in defiance, despite my sweating palms. A few awkward seconds of silence ensued, and then he continued.

"Fine. Let's keep going from there. What happened next?"

He spoke with an efficiency I found incredibly annoying. He was trying to connect the dots and my story wasn't lining up the way he wanted it to. I knew he was trying to bridge some gaps, but suddenly so was I. I was feeling confused. I wanted to see Jasper. I took a deep breath and came back to my chair.

"I think I need to take a rest. I'm not feeling very well. Could I see Jasper? Just for a few minutes to see if he's all right?"

The shock on his face answered the question before he did.

"Are you joking? No, you can't see *your kidnapper*. We need to get your statement so we can lock him away. You are obviously very confused right now." His anger was mounting again, and he stood and walked to the window and back, his eyes barely leaving mine. "Apparently this guy brainwashed you or something, but the next time you see him you'll be testifying against him in court."

He would never understand.

"I realize this is a very complicated situation and impossible for you to understand, but I love Jasper. Very much. He saved my life on more than one occasion. I'm very sorry I ended up hurting my family and wasting your time and everything, but if you just knew him, and what he's been through."

I was trying hard to make him understand. I realized if there was any hope of seeing Jasper I had to make an attempt. I wondered if the detective had ever been in love before, if he knew what it was like to care about anyone else more than himself.

"His mom basically abandoned him when he was little. She'd leave him alone for days in a shitty apartment with a box of cereal. I'm not saying that taking me wasn't wrong, but he was so tired of being alone. No one should have to suffer through that."

He had come back and was now sitting on the edge of his desk, and he leaned in until he was inches from me, his face scarlet with anger.

"What he's been through? What the kidnapper has been through? This is unbelievable! Listen to me, little girl, your family was torn apart by losing you! Your mother had to be hospitalized several times. Your sister dropped out of school and completely shut herself off from society. And your dad is in jail!" He reached out and held on to both arms of my chair, trapping me in my seat as the rage seethed from his lips. My body shook with fear and shame. "You want me to think of what the kidnapper's been through? How about the people who love you and have lost everything trying to find you?"

I covered my head in my hands, trying to simultaneously block him out and process what he said. My dad was in jail. Why? I really didn't know who I was anymore: the mountain girl who was a wife and a mother, or the daughter and sister taken violently from her life?

He pushed off my chair and walked over to the window again, breathing deeply and trying to compose himself. I lowered my hands from my face and spoke. The words coming out in squeaky gasps.

"What do you mean my dad's in jail? Why is he in jail?"

The detective exhaled and leaned against the windowsill.

"I promised your mother I would let her tell you about that, so you'll have to wait. Let's keep going with your story. I have a prisoner in a holding cell who I have to deal with, and I can't do that without your story."

"I won't tell you anything else until I talk to my mom. I want to know what's going on with my dad." I took a breath and tried to regain some composure. I was getting tired of being bullied by Detective Umbry and his agenda. "Until I do, *you'll* have to wait. Otherwise, I will not say another word until I get a lawyer in here."

He cringed when I mentioned a lawyer. I knew that was going to be way too time-consuming for his liking.

"Fine. I'll let you have fifteen minutes with your mom, but then we keep going. And you should have no reason to need a lawyer. This is simply a victim statement. You are the victim here, right?"

I looked away. I didn't know what I was at the moment, but it didn't feel like a victim. I was the one hurting people.

❋

The detective left the room to get my mom. I couldn't sit still. I squirmed in my seat and chewed my fingernails, anxiously waiting to hear my mom's footsteps coming down the hall. I stood up and circled the room like a caged animal, desperate to find out what happened to my dad but nauseated knowing whatever it was, it happened because of me. I paused at the window. The street below was alive and festering with headlights, streetlights and the occasional neon sign. I looked up into the sky but I couldn't see a star. Not one star. I felt like I didn't belong here. Maybe I didn't belong anywhere anymore. I stepped away from the window and scanned the walls. There were a few pictures of Detective Umbry: one in uniform, another standing with a group of men, and one of him with an older lady who was sitting in a red plastic chair on a beach. I wondered if she was his mother. Beside the pictures were several diplomas. I welcomed the distraction and began reading them. The diploma declaring he was a certified detective was dated the month before I went missing. Had I been his first case? As I mulled this thought over, I heard my mom's voice coming down the hall and turned just as she opened the door, Jill right behind her. My mom wore a strained, exhausted expression. I searched Jill's unfamiliar face for my sister. She was in there, but the anger and defiance in her eyes was like a disguise, making the time we'd been apart feel like decades, rather than years.

"Hi, Kris. How are you holding up? Isn't Jake just an amazing guy?"

My mom crossed the room and gave me a long hug. Jill slumped into my vacant chair. "Amazing" wasn't the word I would have used to describe him. "Intense" and "unrelenting" came to mind.

"Mom. I can't talk to him anymore until you tell me what's going on. I need to know about Dad. How can he possibly be in jail?"

I leaned against the windowsill, my knees suddenly feeling

weak. My mom shooed Jill out of the chair and led me to it, keeping hold of my hand, as if afraid to let me go. I sat down gingerly.

"I know, Kris. That's why I wanted Jill to be here. We need to talk about it as a family."

She made eye contact with Jill, and I looked from one to the other, unable to read their expressions.

"Well, we're here," I said, growing more impatient by the second.

My mother settled herself on the edge of the desk and got a tighter grasp on my hand. Hers was sweating.

"The day you went missing was, well, it's every family's worst nightmare. Your dad had gotten home before me, and Jill told him you were out running but should be home any minute. When you didn't show up an hour later, Dad got worried. I was on my way home when he called me on my cell and told me he was going to drive up to the trailhead and see if you were still up there. At that point, the sun hadn't set yet and we thought maybe you decided to go a little farther than usual, or maybe you'd gone to a friend's after your run. When Dad got there he saw your truck and another blue car parked side by side. He thought maybe you met someone to go running. He decided to head back home and finish making supper."

She shifted on the edge of the desk, the deep lines on her face a map of her sorrow. If only my dad had come up the trail looking for me, maybe he would've caught Jasper carrying me away. At least they may have had a better start, had more light to follow the tracks. Maybe he could have stopped this. I wanted to see him and hug him and tell him he couldn't have stopped it. It wasn't his fault.

"So Dad came home and I was there. We got dinner on the table and you *still* weren't home. By now we were getting a bit angry with you. It was getting dark. Dad grabbed a flashlight and his hiking boots and went to find you. Jill and I waited. Dad pulled up and found your truck in the same spot. The blue car was gone. He checked under your gas flap and found your keys, so he knew you hadn't lost them and gotten a ride. He took off up the trail expecting to see you coming around every corner.

When he got all the way to the lake and still hadn't found you, he called home. It was dark now." Jill huffed from her position leaning against the wall. My mom shot her a look that silenced anything she may have been about to say, and then she continued.

"Jill and I both jumped when the phone rang. We were getting nervous because another hour had gone by at this point. Dad was out of breath and sounded scared, on the edge of panic. He got Jill on the phone and asked her who owned the blue car, if it was a friend of yours. He thought maybe you'd gotten a ride somewhere after your run. Jill wasn't sure, so we phoned the police. They alerted search and rescue, and within the hour they met Dad at the trailhead. Dad searched with them for three days straight, and then four more on his own, using every hour of daylight." I squeezed my mom's hand as tears filled her eyes. She was back there, reliving her nightmare, too.

"They found your footprints in some muddy sections, but then they would vanish in others. There was a lot of water on the trail, and it was impossible to tell where you had gone after you reached the lake. They brought in dogs and helicopters; about half the town was up there. Eventually, they called off the official search. Dad never quit on you, Krissy, and neither did Jake. The department was watching Jake pretty closely; he was a brand new detective and so young, but he did everything by the book. Your dad had another idea about what happened to you, and Jake followed up on every lead. He was amazing."

The thought of my dad out there scouring the woods for me brought me back to those early days when I first got to the cabin. I knew my family would be searching relentlessly. Back then, I hoped Jasper had inadvertently left some kind of clue to our whereabouts, maybe someone would find his truck or had seen him carrying me and would somehow find us at the cabin.

"Mom, please. I'm so sorry you guys had to go through that. I'm sure it was agonizing. Just tell me why Dad's in jail."

"I will. But I want you to know the whole story. I don't want you to jump to any conclusions or judgments. Just hear me out."

She looked from me to Jill. Since her small huff, Jill had

remained very quiet. She was fidgeting with a button on the sleeve of her coat and didn't look up during the silence. Mom focused her attention back on me and kept going.

"Eventually, we all realized searching the woods was futile. You weren't there. Your dad just kept going back, persisting, every day walking in your footprints until the rain eroded them. The police were following the lead on the blue car. Dad was obsessed with that angle and was making a list of everyone in town who owned a small blue compact car. After a few weeks of the police and your father tripping over each other to question everyone with a car matching that description, they finally found the owner. It was Blake Thompson."

"Blake was up there? Oh, my God. Did he see anything?"

Blake Thompson was a year older than me. I'd known him since he moved to town in eighth grade. He stuck around after graduation because he had the coveted job of ski patrol at the local hill. Blake was lanky and athletic with bright green eyes and blond hair that hung just above his shoulders and was usually gathered into a messy ponytail. He constantly tucked the stray pieces behind his ears. He was popular. The girls loved him. He was an avid hunter and fisherman, and he was always organizing hiking and camping trips. One night, when I was sixteen, Blake and I happened to be at the same party at a clearing in the forest near town. There was a raging fire and I was sitting near him, trying not to stare, when he pulled a guitar out of his trunk and started singing Sam Roberts songs. I was hooked, but he was interested in girls a little wilder than me. We did have running in common. One time after finishing my lake loop, he was parked in the lot, stretching and readying to run the same route. We started talking and ended up dating for a few months. Blake was my first, and only, sexual experience. Until Jasper.

"The police questioned Blake. Unfortunately, his story was very unclear and details changed from interview to interview. Dad was furious. He thought the police were being way too easy on him. He became convinced Blake had something to do with your disappearance, partially because we had nothing else to go on. Dad followed him and confronted him on the street. Blake became hostile towards your father and eventually took out a restraining order on him. That really put your dad over the edge. It seemed like the police were protecting Blake and doing nothing to find you. One night, when Dad was up walking the trail, he emerged from the forest to find Blake's car parked at the trailhead again. He was sitting in it with a few of his friends. They were drinking and smoking pot. They got out of the car and mocked your dad and pushed him around a bit. Dad went ballistic. I think all the pent up rage he'd been feeling over you going missing manifested itself in a fury he couldn't control."

Her voice cracked and she had to stop, tears filling her eyes again. I was afraid to hear the end. I knew whatever it was, the result was my dad wasn't here, and that was unbearable. He wasn't here because of me. Jill started to cry softly, muffling the noise in her hands. I hesitated, feeling like I might vomit right here on the carpet, but I had to ask the question. I had to know.

"What happened? What did Dad do?"

"Blake had a knife. He pulled it out and tried to use it on your father. Dad grabbed for it and they ended up rolling around on the ground." She squeezed my hand so hard I thought it might break. She couldn't hold the tears back any longer and they slipped down her cheeks. "When the other boys pulled them apart, the knife was sticking out of Blake's belly. They rushed him to the hospital, but he died on the way."

I couldn't breathe. I was trying to digest what my mom said. Blake was dead. My dad killed Blake Thompson. Because of me. She studied the shock on my face, swiping at the tears that had reached her chin with the back of her free hand, and then carried on.

"Kris, Dad was arrested at the hospital. He tried to tell the police exactly what happened, that it was an accident. Blake's friends didn't corroborate his story. With the restraining order and several witnesses testifying they saw Dad harassing Blake, he didn't have a chance in court. He was found guilty of second-degree murder. He's serving fourteen years."

Jill ran from the room, letting the door slam against the wall after she flung it open. I sat motionless. My mom wiped her tears and waited for my reaction. What was I supposed to say? I tried to picture my dad sitting in a jail cell. That's where he'd been for the last four years. While I had been…with Jasper. I opened my mouth to speak, but nothing came out. My throat was dry and raw. Guilt settled on my shoulders, pressing me hard into the chair. When I finally spoke, my mom looked relieved.

"Is Dad okay? Can I talk to him?"

She exhaled and sat up a little straighter, releasing my hand.

"He's hanging in there. The first year was really tough. On everyone. Now he's more or less accepted his fate and is trying to make the best of it. I go up and see him as often as I can. He's allowed a phone call every three days. He knows you're home, and he couldn't be more ecstatic. You can talk to him tomorrow."

She looked towards the door where Jill had escaped. Her face fell.

"It's Jill who's really having a hard time with it. To lose you and then Dad—she really fell apart. I couldn't get her out of bed for months after your dad went to jail. Now she functions but she has to take antidepressants and something for anxiety. She had to drop out of school. She's tried a few jobs, but some days are worse than others, so she usually ends up missing too many shifts and gets fired. I've been really worried about her. But now that you're home with us, maybe she can get her life back."

She trailed off and feigned a little smile. Her grief and loneliness were palpable.

My parents had been married for twenty-four years. I couldn't imagine them being apart. I was realizing I had caused everyone so much suffering while Jasper and I were living out our little fantasy. I wondered what he would think of all this. I wondered if he cared.

10.

Detective Umbry came back into the room. He was annoyed, his furrowed brow and angry eyes betraying his impatience.

"I hate to interrupt, but Krissy and I really have to get this interview completed. I want to get the accused booked and moved to the prison as soon as possible."

My stomach clenched at the thought of Jasper in prison. I was so afraid for him, of what the other prisoners might do to him, and of what he might do to himself. He told me once he would never live in a cage. I needed to see him.

"Sorry, Jake, but I think Krissy has been through enough for one day. I think she needs to be home with her family, take a shower and have some warm food. I can bring her back first thing tomorrow."

"That won't work for us, Cindy. We need her statement tonight. Apparently we sprung her from the hospital a little early. The psychologist didn't get a chance to clear her, so she has to meet with Dr. Bates first thing tomorrow."

I jumped up from my chair, apparently forgotten in all of their planning.

"Excuse me. In case you guys forgot, I'm here. And I have a say in all this. I don't want to meet with some psychologist. I'm fine. Mom, I'll finish this. It won't be much longer. But only if I can see Jasper. I need to see him."

The hurt in my mom's eyes tore at my already guilty conscience. I looked away.

"Why? How can you even look at him after what he did to you and to all of us?"

"I can't explain it to you. Not right now. I just…"

I couldn't finish. The tension in the room was thick and uncomfortable. I walked over to the window and watched the relentless traffic and people below. I missed my son and ached to hold him.

I heard the detective and my mom whispering, very familiar with each other.

"I'll wait in the lobby while you finish up with Jake. He's promised to take it easy on you. After that, he'll escort you to see…the kidnapper. But you have to keep the appointment with Dr. Bates tomorrow. I insist on that. Deal?"

I turned to see them both staring at me. I just wanted to see Jasper. If this was the way that I could do that, then fine.

"I'll see Dr. Bates. Once. That's all I'm agreeing to. And I want to go see Matty after that appointment. I'll be done here soon, Mom."

I gave Detective Umbry a look that said I meant it.

My mom and I hugged, and I sent her off. The detective brought a glass of water over to the edge of the desk and turned the recorder back on.

"For the record, I want you to know I don't approve of you visiting that low life, and I can't imagine why you'd want to. To be honest, I can't figure any of this out. So please, enlighten me. We left off with Jasper beating you and chaining you to a woodstove. What happened next?"

The hint of sarcasm in his voice made me want to stay silent, but I knew telling my story was the only way to see Jasper tonight. And I wanted to make him realize Jasper wasn't a monster. He was a good, kind man. He made a mistake. I wasn't going to argue that. I needed the detective to see it from my perspective. Maybe then he would be able to understand how things got so mixed up. Maybe I would, too.

11.

When I shivered, the chain rattled, so I tried to stay still. I'd passed out at some point and awoke freezing. The clanging of my chain against the stove leg sounded like a locomotive passing inches from my face. The sound crept into my dream, and I half expected to find myself sleeping under a train track somewhere. Instead I awoke into my nightmare, trapped by a crazy man where no one would find me. I had a splitting headache but my mind adjusted to my terror and despair. Slowly. Jasper's fire had long gone out, and he lay sleeping on the cot. In the dim light, I could just make out the shape of him in the sleeping bag. I prayed desperately he would sleep forever, so afraid of what might happen next. I passed out again.

My nose no longer gushed blood, but the grey blanket I was curled up on looked like the scene of a murder. The ache in my head and face were sharp and constant. My clothes were wet, and I could see my breath in the dim light of the cabin. I thought it must be dusk. There was a faint sound of birds and the rush of a creek. My mouth was dry, and tasted metallic, like stale blood. My throat burned with swallowed sobs as tears streamed down my cheeks and soaked into the coarse grey fibres.

After a while he stirred. I closed my eyes and buried my face in the blanket. I heard him turn over and felt his eyes on me. With a lot of rustling from the sleeping bag, he stood and peeled it off. He tied his boots, rubbed his hands together, and walked towards me. I held my breath. There was a loud creak as he opened the stove door. He muttered a bit under his breath and took a large gasp of air, blowing loudly into the fire. I heard a few cracks from the remaining coals. He reached for the stacked wood on the other side of the stove and snapped small pieces of kindling over his bent knee. I kept my eyes closed and my face down. As he placed more wood into the stove the smoke seeped out and stung my nose and my eyes. I tried to stay still, but my lungs burned. Eventually I raised my head and gasped for air. Jasper looked over casually.

"Looks like you broke your nose."

His voice startled me, and I looked up at him before I could decide otherwise. When I met his eyes, anger drove through me.

"I didn't break my nose. You broke my nose."

He was going to say something else, as a flash of defiance passed in his eyes, but he changed his mind and went back to the fire. Slowly as the crackling increased, the heat started to reach my body. I wanted to crawl right through the stove door. I sat up and hugged my knees to my chest, trying to use them as a wall between the two of us. His proximity was unnerving. The little hairs rose on my flesh.

"If you want to warm up, you'll have to take your wet clothes off and dry them on the fire."

He looked into the stove as he spoke, stuffing its round belly with more kindling. He broke and placed each piece as though he was creating some magnificent piece of art.

"No, I'm fine," I muttered through clenched teeth. I would rather die of hypothermia than strip down in front of him.

I couldn't control the shivering any longer and the chain rattled methodically. My empty stomach was clenched into a tight ball, and the anticipation of what he wanted from me was sickening. I tried to keep control, to breathe. I figured if he wanted to kill me he would have done that already, but I hoped what he wanted wasn't worse.

"Do you want to know my parents' phone number so you can make some arrangements to get money? Like I said, we aren't rich or anything, but I'm sure they'll get you what you want. They'll be looking everywhere for me by now. If you could please tell them I'm safe, they'll do whatever you want. Please."

I trailed off. He closed the stove door and stood, brushing off his knees and walking to the other side of the cabin. He didn't look at me; he was looking everywhere else. He sat down on the cot, and it squeaked and sagged under his weight. I tried again.

"Jasper, you could just let me go. I promise I'll never tell anyone your name. You seem like a nice guy. Maybe this was just a mistake. All you have to do is unlock this chain and I'll be gone. Please."

He looked up and into my eyes. His face looked peaceful, with the hint of a smirk playing at the corners of his mouth, almost hidden by the shaggy beard.

"I didn't take you for money. I live off a few hundred dollars a year, and I have enough saved to last me for a long time. People get so obsessed with money. I have a perfect life out here, and I don't need to follow anyone's rules or let anyone tell me what to do." He was very relaxed as he spoke, leaning back on his elbows as if he was basking in his own pride. "There was just one thing missing, and now I have it. I'm never going to let you go, so stop asking me. I know this will be hard for a little while, but soon you'll think of this as your home, and you'll love it just as much as I do. You're going to be my wife."

Wife. I gasped for breath. My brain exploded with screaming voices I couldn't silence.

"What are you talking about? I'm not going to live here with you! I want to go home! Let me go home!" I got to my knees, yelling and yanking the chain, my hair flying wildly around my head. "I'll never *willingly* live here with you. You're crazy! You're completely nuts! I'll run away the second I get a chance, and I'll keep trying until I make it! And if you lay your hands on me, I'll bite and kick and scratch. You'll have to kill me first!"

My chain swung violently and banged against the floor and the stove. He watched with a look of amusement on his face. It was infuriating. When I exhausted myself, I slumped against the wall, stunned and lost for words. My heart ached for my family. They were so far away, and Jasper's words made them seem even farther. Unreachable. Was I really going to spend the rest of my life chained up as some creep's sex slave? My urge to vomit was so strong I heaved and scrambled to all fours, opened my mouth, but only pathetic drops of saliva dribbled to the ground. My empty stomach clenched in a physical revolt from the information I had just received. My tears splashed onto the dirty wooden floor. Jasper just sat on the cot and watched me. He stood and pulled on his red plaid coat. He grabbed a water bottle from the table and walked to the door. As he opened it, he turned.

"Like I said, it's going to take a little while."

When he returned from getting water, I curled into the fetal position so my back was to the room. The heat from the fire finally helped my shivering subside. I'd already run through a gamut of emotions: shock, fear, anger. At least he didn't have plans to torture and kill me. But the fact that he wanted me to live here with him forever, as a happy couple, made it clear he was deranged. I wasn't sure how far I could push him. As hard as it was going to be, I knew my best chance to escape would be to play along until he trusted me enough to unchain me and give me a bit of freedom. The thought of what "playing along" might entail made me nauseated again. As soon as I had an opportunity, I would run.

I heard him fumbling around with the packs, unloading supplies and stacking them around the cabin. There was a clanging noise as he placed something on top of the stove. A few minutes later, I heard hissing and popping. The smell of warm food hit my nostrils and saliva instantly filled my mouth. It was well over twenty-four hours since I had eaten. My stomach, still tender from its relentless heaving, rumbled and churned with the possibility of some nourishment. Jasper stirred the contents of the pot, his spoon scraping the bottom as the bubbling continued.

"You must be starving. If you promise to be good, I'll let one of your hands free so you can eat. Here, turn around."

I felt him standing over me. I wanted to remain stubborn with my face towards the wall, but my survival instincts were stronger than my pride. My body needed food. I slowly turned over and raised my cuffed wrists towards him.

"Are you going to behave?"

He held the key above me and waited for an answer.

"Yes. I will. I promise." I spoke softly and kept my gaze to the floor.

He held my wrist as he undid the cuff. His hands were large, rough and calloused, but he removed the metal from my tender flesh very gently.

When my hand was free, he took a bowl and spoon from the table and filled it with some kind of soup or stew. It could have been dog food for all I cared. It was hot. I was starving. He passed it to me and I gulped it down immediately. It burned the roof of my mouth, but I swallowed it anyway and let it scorch my throat. I could feel the heat all the way down to my stomach.

"Whoa, be careful! It's hot."

I kept gulping until the bowl was empty, and I scraped every last morsel from the sides. When I finished, I placed the bowl and spoon in front of me. He moved back to the little table and sat in the chair to watch.

"Did you get enough? I gave you half but you can have a little extra if you're still hungry."

He sounded a bit surprised at the size of my appetite.

"I'm fine. I'm done."

He picked up the bowl and spoon and scraped the rest of the soup from the pot into the bowl, then sat at the table and ate slowly. I kept as still as possible and enjoyed my full belly and free arm. I stole glances at him now and then.

Jasper ate methodically. Where was his family? Did he have friends? When he finished with the soup, he stood and poured water from the bottle into his bowl and the pot. He swished it around, dumped it into a green basin on the floor, and then went outside and came back with a large load of wood. I jumped when he dropped it to the floor.

"I have to cuff you back up again for the night."

He seemed embarrassed to have to tell me this, and his eyes shifted around the room. I was glad he wasn't going to move me any closer to the bed, which I made an effort not to look at.

"Before I do, do you have to go the bathroom?"

I did. Really bad. The soup had worked its way through me quickly, and I hadn't gone since my arrival. My stomach gurgled and thinking about going now increased the urgency.

"I have to go, but I don't want to go in front of you. I can't. Could you please give me a bit of privacy? I promise I won't try to run away."

He pondered this for a minute. I really didn't think I could try to run yet. I was completely exhausted, and beyond the little window it was cold and black. I knew I wouldn't get far in these clothes before he would either catch me or I would die of hypothermia. And then there was the river. When I did make my escape, it would have to be in the daytime, with enough light to give me a chance at surviving. I did have hope, though, and that made this night a little easier to take.

"I'll stand on the porch, but I'm tying you to a tree. You can call me when you're done."

"That really isn't necessary. I'll just—"

"That's it. That's what we're doing."

He pulled a rope out of his pack. I had nothing left in me to argue. My face throbbed, my shoulders ached and every time I thought of my family frantically searching for me, my stomach tightened into a knot. I pictured their faces: My sister, Jill, wishing she was with me as I drove away. My parents, always telling me to be careful. I never imagined anything bad would happen to me. I just wanted to go home.

I let Jasper free my other hand and tie a rope around my wrist. He led me out of the cabin to the edge of the clearing and into the trees. The moon was the only light. It shone off the patches of snow and illuminated the open space and the cabin. He tied the rope to a tree and made sure it was secure, then handed me a small garden shovel and some toilet paper.

"I have a latrine dug about fifty yards into the woods, but for tonight go here. I'll wait on the porch. Yell for me when you're done."

I watched his back as he retreated. The reality of my situation enveloped me in my solitude. I let the tears fall from my face as

I crumbled to the ground. When I finished, I stood and leaned against the tree, watching his figure pace back and forth across the porch. There was nowhere to go. The cold crept back over my body and I called out. Jasper untied me, leading me back to the cabin like a horse to slaughter, my spirit broken. I stood lifeless as he refastened the cuffs, and then I curled into a ball facing the wall. Sleep came immediately.

✳

I awoke slowly, drowsily, and rolled off my aching hip onto my back. For a few seconds, I was blissfully free, awaiting my first thought. Then the reality of where I was exploded in my brain, making me cringe.

As I moved, I heard a swishing sound. I opened my eyes to find the green sleeping bag draped over my body. I looked over and saw Jasper on the cot, his plaid coat tucked around him, one arm slung over his face. His steady breathing was soft but audible. Glistening rays of bright sunlight shone through the dirty window. I had no idea how long I had slept, but an instant feeling of guilt flooded my body. I'd been missing for two nights now. My family would be past frantic, probably fearing me dead, and here I was sleeping in.

The cabin's air was icy, but under the sleeping bag I was warm. My wrists burned from the weight of the cuffs and the chain. As I rolled, the chain dragged against the floor. I held my breath and watched Jasper for any sign of movement, but he remained still. I wondered what the day had in store for me. How long would it take until he trusted me enough not to handcuff me? I would be patient. I knew I didn't stand a chance without a substantial head start.

Another thought ate away at me. Was he going to force himself on me? He had already said he wanted me here as his wife, not just a friend or someone for company, so I knew he had every intention of becoming sexual. My first sexual encounter had been less than enjoyable. That night with Blake: too much alcohol followed by kissing that led to quick and awkward penetration. I cringed as I remembered grabbing for my pants and underwear after, shocked at my utter disappointment in the whole thing. The two months we dated after that, we had sex a handful of times. It was never much better. I hoped I would be able to escape before this disturbed man became my second.

Jasper awoke and the cot squeaked angrily as he stretched and pulled his boots on. He grabbed his coat and buttoned it over his long underwear, blowing strongly into his cupped hands. I peeked at him while pretending to be asleep, but I really had to pee. My bladder screamed and my mouth was painfully dry. He rose, heading for the door.

"Do you mind if I come too? I really have to go."

He startled, as if he had forgotten I was there.

"Oh, yeah. Hang on a second."

He took the rope that was coiled up on his pack and went outside. The sunlight poured through the door, and I could see a slice of beautiful blue sky. A bluebird day, my dad would say. The thought pulled a heavy blanket of sadness over me. I waited as minutes passed, trying not to pee my pants. Finally, Jasper jumped onto the porch. The cabin floor shook. He came back in through the open door.

"Let's go."

I held out my wrist. He took the key from his jacket pocket and unlocked my cuffs. He didn't have the rope with him, so I stood and walked towards the door, relieved we were making progress towards my independence already. When I walked through the opening and stood on the porch, I had the urge to break into a sprint and head for the trees. As if reading my mind, Jasper's big hand curl around my upper arm.

"Trust me. If you try to run, you will regret it."

He guided me off the porch and into the trees beside the cabin where he'd taken me to pee last night. He held my arm, but didn't squeeze. I wondered if his threat was empty. He didn't give me the impression he wanted to hurt me. He actually acted a bit shy. I was growing more confident by the second that I would escape. I just needed to bide my time until the perfect moment arose. When we came to the trees, I saw the rope had been fastened around one of the larger poplars that bordered the clearing. The other end was in a loop and tied in some fancy knot. The shovel and toilet paper were leaning against the base of the tree.

"I thought this could be where you go to the bathroom."

He stayed a bit behind me as he spoke, maintaining the loose grip on my arm.

"I'll fasten the rope around your wrist and then wait on the porch until you call. If you try to pull, the knot will only get tighter, so don't bother."

He let go of my arm briefly as he picked up the looped end of the rope and positioned it around my wrist. Then he gave it a pull, tightening the rope against my skin. I stood motionless as he walked to the porch. In the daylight, the porch looked closer. Jasper perched on the edge and let his legs swing beneath him.

"Could you please turn the other way?" I hollered.

He let out a bit of a grunt but did as I asked.

I took the opportunity to survey my surroundings. Across the clearing that was in front of the cabin was a break in the trees. This was the trail where we had emerged from the forest after climbing the mountain. It already seemed like a long time ago since I had stepped into the clearing and saw the cabin for the first time. The trail was barely visible in the tangled branches and vegetation. To my right, directly across from the cabin was the head of another trail, which I assumed led down to the creek where he got his drinking water. There was a large white boulder next to this trail, making it more obvious. The jagged peaks of the mountains were barely visible above the dense forest. A small patch of blue sky displayed wispy white clouds. It was beautiful. And isolated. I wondered how long we hiked to get here, the journey already blurring in my memory. I made a mental map of the clearing and where the trail home was, in case my chance to escape came in the dark. Then I called to Jasper that I was ready. He untied me and led me back to my prison. This was now my life. And with the exception of my trips to the bathroom, I sat on the cabin floor, chained to the stove. Three days passed. I cried when Jasper would leave me alone. When he was there, I ignored him. I missed my family desperately. I wanted to go home. Soon I realized ignoring

Jasper was not the way to accomplish that. I had to befriend him.
It was the only way.

※

"Jasper, can we sit outside for a while? It's a beautiful day, and I'd
love some fresh air."

It was day five. When I woke up I was stronger and more
resolved than ever to do anything to get home. It was time to put
my plan into action, and outside I felt closer to home. Closer to
being free. The sun shone brightly in the sky, the temperature
rising quickly. The patches of snow that remained would be in
jeopardy today.

Jasper pondered my request.

"I guess. I have some work to do out there anyway, but I don't
have another rope."

He looked me square in the eye, which he seldom did, as if to
gauge my true intentions. I had no ulterior motives—yet. I held
his stare.

"You can sit on the edge of the porch. I'll be right there
cutting kindling. Don't try anything."

He unlocked the handcuffs and walked me out through the
door and then released my arm. My opposite hand immediately
went to where he'd been holding me, rubbing away his finger-
prints, his control. I sat on the edge of the old wooden porch and
dangled my legs over the side. The sun baked my face and clothing.
It was comfortable and familiar. The stench of sweat wafted from
me. I wondered when I would ever be clean again.

Jasper gathered a stack of wood from under the porch, carried
it to the far side of the cabin and dumped it on the ground. He
grabbed an axe that was stuck in a large stump, placing one piece
on top of the stump. With a large, confident swing, he brought
the axe down from above his head and split the log in two. He
then picked up one half of the same log and did the identical
motion again. Whack. Split. Whack. Split. With a focused precision
he worked his way through the pile. I sat studying him. It was like
he was in a disguise trying to cover up the real him. He tucked

his shaggy hair behind his ears. His scruffy beard hid a good part of his face, making it hard to see his expressions, but his eyes gave everything away. They were deep and stormy and full of emotion. I never saw rage, never evil. I guess that's why I was beginning to lose my fear of him and starting to feel like he was just a lost guy who had made a mistake.

"Jasper, can I ask you a question?"

He stopped chopping and looked up at me briefly, then lifted his arm to sop up the sweat pouring into his eyes with the sleeve of his jacket.

"No, I won't let you go."

He gathered up another stack of wood and was lining up a fresh piece.

"That's not it. I'm just wondering how long you've lived up here?"

"Four years."

Whack. Split.

"Wow. You've lived up here by yourself that whole time?"

"Yup."

"Why?"

He hesitated for a second, but kept working.

"Because I love it. Because it's the only place where I can be left alone to live how I want to live. People don't bug me or make me follow their rules."

Whack. Split.

"So, why did you bring me up here?"

My voice raised an octave as I spoke, part of me bracing for the word "wife" again. While annoying him was not my goal, I couldn't help asking. He said he liked being alone. Maybe he would see I was just going to be in his way and crowd him or something.

"I already told you."

He wiped at his sweat again, and then undid his coat and tossed it onto the porch. He was wearing a thin, grey T-shirt underneath. Sweat-soaked, it clung to his lean body. I couldn't help but notice his muscles protruding from under the wet cotton. I looked away.

"No offence, but if you want someone to be your partner, why not live in town for a while and try dating some girls? You shouldn't have to kidnap someone and chain her up to make her be with you."

He froze. His head shot up. Again our eyes met. I expected anger but saw hurt, like I had stung his pride. He opened his mouth to speak and then closed it again. He did that often, always weighing his words. I did not. We shared an uncomfortable silence. He went back to chopping wood. I regretted what I'd said. So quickly I'd forgotten that just steps away was my chain, my prison. I didn't want to make him mad. Afraid that I may have put in jeopardy my small bit of progress, I retracted.

"I'm sorry. I shouldn't have said that. You seem like a nice guy, other than the fact that you kidnapped me, and my family will be sick with worry, which makes me sick with worry. Maybe if you gave it a try, you could meet someone the old-fashioned way. This is a beautiful place. I'm sure lots of girls would like to live here."

I left out the "with you." I was aware, and I figured he was too, that any guy who would hit someone over the head, kidnap her and chain her up is pretty messed up. I didn't want to be patronizing. I was already trying to dig myself out of a hole.

He began stacking his uniformly sized kindling on the porch, not acknowledging anything I'd said. I decided to shut up for a while. I closed my eyes and tilted my head towards the sun. I tried to send thoughts to my family that I was fine, that I would be home soon. I was now more hopeful than ever I could gain Jasper's trust. I also didn't feel like he had any plans to hurt me, which brought a calm over me, something I hadn't experienced since the second I'd awoken in his truck.

When he finished chopping wood, he made trips in and out of the cabin, stacking the kindling next to the stove. On his last trip out, he brought his water bottle, silently offering it to me. I took it eagerly and chugged some down. The liquid was warm but quenching, sloshing into my empty stomach. Instantly, I was starving. Jasper must have felt the same way because he went back into the cabin and I could hear him rustling in his pack. He came back out with some crackers and beef jerky.

"Here. You must be hungry."

Jasper had been sliding me bowls of food over the last few days, but they were really just a few mouthfuls. He handed me the crackers and laid the jerky on the porch.

"I usually eat twice a day. Jerky in the morning, and rice or noodles with meat, if I have any, at night. I haven't been hunting in a while, so food will be a little slim until I get you settled and can go get an animal. I make great deer jerky, though, way better than this store-bought stuff."

His chest puffed up a little with pride as he spoke, something I hadn't seen much in him. He sat down several feet away from me, and we ate in silence. I wondered if he was happy, if this is what he had envisioned when he took me, the two of us sharing lunch on the porch. We sat that way for a long time. The salty food made me incredibly thirsty, but I saw him drain the water bottle and didn't want to ask for more in case he would chain me up to go get it. Eventually he stood and stretched.

"I have to go get water. Do you want to come?"

"Yeah, I'd love to. Thanks."

I hopped off the porch and followed him across the clearing to the path on the other side. It wound its way through the trees for about a hundred yards. The faint rushing of water I could hear earlier became louder as we walked. We reached the top of an embankment, and the path led steeply down to a small creek that was running strongly from the melting snow. A plastic tube was secured with some rocks and water was flowing out of it like a fountain.

"You can wait here. The bank is slippery. I'll be right back."

Without waiting for a response, he slid down the bank and started filling the bottle. I looked around me and realized if I were to try to escape this way I would be trapped. The bush was thick and the trail ended at the creek's edge. Beyond was a wall of trees. From what I knew at this point, there was only one way out: the way we came in. With my route of escape premeditated, my spirits lifted again. As I stood at the top of the bank, I knew it would only be a matter of time before I would have a long enough window to go for it.

12.

Jake handed me a tissue, which brought me out of my trance. I found myself crying. Remembering those early days at the cabin, my fear and my desperation to go home, my extreme desire to get away from Jasper, was so difficult.

"Krissy, you're doing a great job. I know this is hard. You're a smart girl, and you've got grit. That's what it takes to survive something like this. I just don't understand how things went so wrong. How he managed to brainwash you like he did. It doesn't seem like something you'd fall for."

"Why do you talk like you know me? We've never met before."

He took a moment before he answered, but by the way his eyes widened he was shocked by what I said. When he spoke his words were clipped with sarcasm.

"Yes, I realize that. But I have spent the last four years studying you. I know your family; I know your friends; I know what you eat for breakfast for God's sake!" He leaned into me even farther, then broke eye contact and looked down into his lap, drawing a deep breath to control his emotions. "There was a lot of pressure from my senior officers to write you off as a runaway. After combing through your life, and with what your parents and Jill said, I knew you wouldn't deliberately hurt anyone. I just don't understand how you went from planning escape routes to husband."

How was I ever going to explain this to him? Suddenly I was so angry. I leapt to my feet.

"You don't get it! He didn't brainwash me. He saved me! I would've died without him. And he was so kind to me. He took care of me."

"Krissy! Do you hear yourself? He kidnapped you!" He stood and leaned over his desk, no longer able to control himself. "He beat you and held you captive. You would never have been up there and never needed saving if he didn't steal you from your family! Don't you understand that?"

We were both on our feet, inches from each other. Our frustrations were boiling over. He reached out and grabbed my arm. I thought to pull it away, but didn't.

"You are a sweet, beautiful woman. You have so many people who love you and were frantic to get you back. If Jasper Ryan loved you, why would he keep you from that? Why would he hurt you and isolate you? I don't know what happened up there, or how he got inside your head like this, but please listen to me. You need to let this guy go. Let him rot in jail where he belongs. You need to start a new life."

He squeezed my arm slightly as he said the last part. I was confused and I collapsed back into my chair, breaking his grasp. He let his hand fall to his side and took a few steps back, breathing deeply.

"Look, I'm sorry you don't understand this," I said. "And like I told you earlier, I'm so grateful for everything you've done to look for me and help my family. You've been incredible. But you don't know Jasper or the reasons that led him to take me. He is my husband, and the father of my child, and I want to see him. Now."

He stood and contemplated this for a minute. He raised his hands in concession.

"Fine. We'll go visit your kidnapper. But just so you know, as soon as we get him arraigned, he's heading to prison. The same prison your father is at, coincidentally. Your dad is a pretty popular guy, from what I've heard, and kidnappers don't do so well in prison."

"What are you trying to say? Are you going to have Jasper hurt? My dad would never—"

"No. I won't have to do anything. And I think it's your father's friends that Jasper better be worried about."

I couldn't believe he was saying these things. I would have to talk to my dad about Jasper. About protecting him. How would I do that?

"You get two minutes and then I need the rest of the story. Let's go."

He opened the door and walked out without waiting for me. I got up and followed him. My anticipation created swirling butterflies in my stomach. We walked down hallways and staircases until we reached a desk with a guard sitting at it. The detective mumbled a few things to him. The guard looked at me, then shrugged slightly and pressed a button. The large metal door in front of us unlocked with a thud, the guard eyeing me strangely as I walked by. Through the door was a long hallway of doors, each with a small window about head height. Another guard sat on a chair in front of one. He looked up when he heard us enter and then jumped to his feet when he saw Detective Umbry stride confidently toward him. The detective nodded to the guard who pulled a set of keys from his pocket, unlocked the door, and motioned for us to enter. The tiny room had a toilet in one corner and a cot in the other. Jasper sat on the cot, head held in his hands. He glanced up and our eyes met. I flew to him and buried myself in his chest. He enveloped me, covering my head with kisses.

"Jasper, I missed you so much! Are you all right?"

"Yes. I'm fine." He leaned his head back slightly to look at me while keeping a tight hold on my body, like it might be the last time. "How's Matty?"

"He's doing better. They gave him drugs that keep him sleeping, like a coma, so his body can heal. We won't know anything more, or how much damage there is, for a few days."

I choked on the word "damage." Jasper held me so tightly I thought I might break.

"Kris, I'm so sorry you're going through all this. I'm just—I wish I could go back in time. I ruined your life."

"Stop talking like that! No, you didn't. I love you, Jasper, and I'll wait for you. Matty and I will wait for you. I promise. You just have to be strong. Time will pass and then we'll be together. Forever."

I pleaded with him to believe me. I didn't know what Jasper might do to himself if he lost hope. Detective Umbry cleared his throat behind me. I'd forgotten he was there.

"That's enough. Time to go."

His voice was gruff and mean. He wasn't happy with our exchange, but I didn't care. Now that I was with Jasper I wasn't confused. I loved him. It didn't matter if the detective understood.

"Just a few more minutes. We just got here."

I didn't bother to turn around as I said it. My eyes stayed locked with Jasper's. He tried to put me at ease.

"Go, Kris. I'm fine. Don't worry about me anymore. I want you to promise. Just enjoy your family and take good care of Matty. Make sure you tell him I love him, and that I'm so sorry."

His voice broke, and he brought me in for one more hug. I clung to him, unsure when I would see him again. So afraid I wouldn't.

"Don't worry, Jasper. I'll bring Matty up to see you as soon as I can. And I'm going to make sure the judge knows how good you were to me and how much I love you."

"No, I don't want Matty to see me in jail. I can't do that. I want you to tell him I love him and then get on with your life. Don't visit me. It'll only break my heart. Please don't."

We sobbed and held each other until Detective Umbry squeezed my arm and pulled me from Jasper.

"I've heard enough. We're done here."

He pulled again as Jasper stood and planted one last kiss on my lips, wiping tears from my face.

"Detective, thank you for bringing Krissy to see me. It means a lot."

Detective Umbry froze in the doorway. I could feel his grip tighten around my arm.

"Go fuck yourself."

13.

When we got back to the detective's office, he brought me to my mom. She was waiting in the lobby with a sandwich for me. He mumbled something about five minutes and took off. They were his first words since his exchange with Jasper, but I saw his fury in his clenched jaw. I was exhausted. I sat and ate, realizing I was starving. My mom didn't ask me anything, and I loved her for it. It was getting late and the thought of going back to my old room, crawling into bed and sleeping consumed my thoughts. I knew Detective Umbry would never understand what happened up at the cabin. I decided there was no point continuing to describe what happened the way I had been. When he came back to get me, I stood slowly, preparing to finish this as quickly as I could. My mom stood too, trying to assert herself.

"Jake, she's had enough. She's exhausted and I want to take her home. We'll be back tomorrow."

"Cindy, you know I can't do that. We have to get this done tonight."

"It's fine, Mom. I can finish. It won't take much longer."

I walked past him and into his office. He said something to my mom and then followed me in. I sat down in my chair, ready to end this. I wasn't going to indulge him with details any longer. He walked over and started the recorder. I got a slight waft of his cologne. I hadn't smelled cologne in such a long time. He went back around the desk to his chair, briefly glancing at his notes.

"So when you left off you had been at the cabin for five days and were preparing to escape. Did you attempt an escape?"

"Yes. But it didn't work. And then I was injured. I had Matty. Matty got sick. Now I'm back."

He looked up and glared at me. He was not happy.

"Nice try. I want the whole story, just the way you've been telling me. Moment to moment. You owe me…us, that much."

"Oh yeah? Why do I owe you anything? I know you've been trying to find me, but that's your job. I'm sorry you didn't solve your case."

"Listen. Stop acting like a selfish little brat. You have no idea what we've been through while you were playing house with Bush Boy. I won't get into it anymore. But if you think it was about solving a case, then fine, think that. I need the facts. I need to know why you were living with this guy for four years and didn't try to escape!" He was infuriated.

"But I did try!" I was arguing defensively. "Things went horribly wrong, and if Jasper hadn't saved me, I would be dead, and you would've never found me. After that I can't explain it, and you're not even trying to understand, so what's the point?"

He stood and walked to the window again, his cooling off spot. After a few seconds he turned.

"Krissy, we have to work together on this. Believe it or not we're on the same team. And I know you don't care about me, but your family has been through hell. So can we please do this for them? Tell me about trying to escape, and we'll leave it there for tonight. Is that agreeable?"

I knew he was right. I did owe them my entire story. But I was having a very hard time explaining my feelings for Jasper and how they were possible. I was flustered, and the detective's strong disapproval was making it worse.

"I'm sorry. I know this is important, and you're right. I do owe everyone an explanation. I never meant to hurt anyone."

He came back and sat down.

14.

Two more days passed. This would be day seven: one week missing. I wondered how my family was doing. My vivid memories of their faces were already blurred. My mom standing at the kitchen sink, plucking my coat from the back of a chair and asking me to hang it up *before* I sat down; my dad rolling his eyes from behind the paper. I had taken it all for granted. I would never let that happen again if—when—I get home.

Jasper and I were in a routine. He still chained me up every night, but in the morning he removed the chains and I would be free to follow him around for the day. I was never out of his sight, but I knew the time would come. He gave up the cumbersome bathroom rope, which made things a little easier for me. He waited on the porch and would huff occasionally if I took too long. I looked longingly at the opening across the clearing, but I knew if I went too soon and he caught me, my freedoms would be revoked, and then I would really be stuck.

Jasper spent much of the day working. He was always patching up the cabin, reinforcing the floor or filling holes on the roof. He said I would be grateful when winter came. In my mind I always answered, *I'll be long gone by then, buddy*, but of course I just kept my mouth shut. The sun was warm and comforting on my skin. He would take breaks for water or food, and I would ask him questions. He wasn't much of a talker. I think I annoyed him with my chatter, so I kept it up hoping he would get frustrated and just tell me to go. I asked about his family and his childhood to no avail. He liked to talk about the cabin, the forest, trees and creeks, and hunting, anything that pertained to life in the mountains.

Day eight started in much the same way as every other day. Jasper always let me have the sleeping bag, which I thanked him for in the morning. He would look away and mumble something, never really acknowledging what I said. He still hadn't tried to touch me. We went outside and went to the bathroom. Our food was getting scarce, even with only two meals a day. My clothes were loose. We ran out of jerky a few days earlier. Our diet consisted of nuts and crackers, and noodles at night.

When I came back to the porch, Jasper held a rifle and was looking through the scope. My breath caught in my throat at the sight of the gun.

"I need to go hunting."

He was still looking through the scope when a smile spread across my lips. Excitement was building inside of me. This could be my chance. I tried to play it cool.

"Do you want me to stay here?"

"Yeah. Come inside. I'm going to have to chain you up."

He put the gun down and started to walk through the cabin door. I knew I'd never get away if he put those cuffs on.

"Oh, Jasper. It's such a nice day. Can I stay on the porch? I mean, come on, where am I going to go? I don't even know the way down."

He stopped walking and looked over at me. I tried to keep my expression neutral, but inside my heart was fluttering like a hummingbird. He was considering it.

"Okay, I'll leave you on the porch, but I have to tie you up. I'll leave you some food and water. If you need to go to the bathroom, go off the edge."

I thought of arguing, but he was already heading for the rope hanging in the cabin. He returned with it coiled around his arm and looked for a place to secure it. After a few minutes of finagling, he managed to wrap it around one of the porch planks from underneath. He then looped the other end around my wrist and pulled it tight. I stared at that strange knot, trying to decipher it without looking obvious.

"I'll leave you a free hand in case you need to go to the bathroom, but don't get any ideas. You can't get that undone with one hand."

"I wasn't going to try. I've just never seen a knot like this before."

I didn't think I was that convincing, but he must've been pretty confident in my confinement because he ignored me again and went into the cabin.

When Jasper came out, he was carrying some bullets, the water bottle, a bag of crackers and the duct tape. He stepped towards me, ripped off a long strip of tape with his teeth, and wrapped it tightly around the knot, twisting and flattening it as he went. Then another. Then another. As he fastened each piece, he rubbed the sticky edges into my skin. It took him a while. Finally, he drank from the bottle and shoved a few crackers in his pocket, and then he put the remaining crackers and water down beside me and loaded his gun. I turned away, my mind racing with how to get that rope off. The tape was as thick as a cast. With a final click, he slung the gun strap over his shoulder and hopped off the porch. I sat on the porch's edge and tried to look innocent.

"I have to hike up through the gulley to get to my usual spot, so I'll probably be gone half the day, unless I get lucky right away."

I sensed a new energy in Jasper, like he was going out to play a game or something. He was excited.

"I'll be hanging around here, bored out of my mind."

He pondered that for a second and then bounded back onto the porch and into the cabin. I could hear him rustling around in his pack. He came back out with a well-worn pocket book.

"This is probably not what you normally read, but it might give you something to do."

It was a book by Louis L'Amour. The cover depicted an old, dirty cowboy with a rifle, a story from the Wild West. It looked like it had been read a million times. The pages were dog-eared, and it was twice as thick as it must have been originally.

Still, something inside me softened. It was a sweet gesture.

"Thanks, Jasper. I definitely haven't read this one. I'll give it a shot. Pardon the pun."

A large grin broke out on his face. It was rare, and it made a light twinkle in his eyes. He hopped off the porch and started for the trees just behind the cabin.

"Wish me luck!" he called back over his shoulder.

Wish me luck, I thought to myself as I was already scanning the porch for a way to get free of this rope.

The rope was about five feet long and tied around one of the porch floorboards. I would have to break the board or sever the rope to get free. I wasn't sure how I was going to do either, but I was determined to find a way. I decided to stay where I was for a little while, just in case Jasper was hiding in the trees watching what I was going to do. If he decided to come back and chain me up, there was no way I would escape.

While I was waiting, I indulged in eating every cracker and drinking all the water. I would need the strength, and once I was free I would definitely not waste any time eating. It was a beautiful, sunny spring day. I thought of my family. I pictured their faces and fantasized about how they would react when they saw me. My mom holding me in one of her too-tight bear hugs, Jill jumping up and down like she did when she was really excited. I instantly got a lump in my throat and tears burned my eyes. Then I realized I was getting way ahead of myself. As I looked around the wooden structure I was attached to, I saw nothing that would help me break through the board. It was two inches thick and relatively new. It would have to be the rope.

Enough time had gone by for me to work on my escape. Time was precious. Once I freed myself, I would need every minute to put enough distance between Jasper and me. He could move through these woods a hell of a lot faster than I could. I pulled at the tape with my free hand and teeth. It was almost impossible to tear, but when it did it came off in ragged little pieces. After fifteen minutes, I had removed only three tiny sections. This wouldn't work. My wrist was bright red and my hand was tingling from lack of blood flow. I needed another plan.

I stood and walked back and forth the length of my lead, like a tethered dog. I scanned the inside of the cabin. I could reach just inside the door, but there was nothing there to help me. I stepped back outside and a wave of discouragement flowed over me. Panic rose with each passing second. The perfect opportunity had presented itself: how could I fail? I returned to my relentless pacing. And then I spotted it.

The end of the axe was just visible sticking out of the stump under the porch. How had I missed it? I got on my knees, pulled my rope so tight I thought my shoulder would rip out of the socket, and leaned over the edge of the porch. I reached under the ledge and gripped its smooth handle. It was one of the best sensations of my life. I wiggled it free of the stump, which was quite awkward given my strange angle, and heaved it onto the porch with a loud thump. I almost started to cry but reminded myself I was a long way from home yet.

I moved back over to where Jasper had originally tied me so I had as much slack in the rope as possible. I laid it out straight in front of me and lined the axe up. It only took a few whacks with the sharp blade to completely sever the rope. I was free.

I think I grew wings and flew off that porch. I don't even remember my feet hitting the ground. I was sprinting for the trail, as I wrapped the dangling piece of rope around my wrist. I couldn't control my breathing. When I reached the trees, the narrow trail was impossible to navigate so I slowed down and focused on my footing so I wouldn't trip. I headed down the switchbacks at a fast pace and grabbed at the smaller alders when I needed support. I couldn't believe I had escaped. I didn't know how long it would take me to get off this mountain and out to where Jasper left the truck, but I hoped I had enough of a lead to make it. For a spilt second, I pictured Jasper appearing around the side of the cabin, excited to show me the animal he'd gotten, and his shock at my absence. A flicker of guilt ran through me, followed immediately by shock. How could I possibly feel anything negative about escaping from my kidnapper? I gave my head a shake and kept going.

The trees were dense and the trail wasn't as easy to follow as I had anticipated. In spots it forked off in many directions. I always took the fork that led down. I didn't remember much from the first night we hiked in, but I did remember that after we crossed the river it was up all the way.

Time passed in a vacuum. I had no idea how long I'd been running. The sun was still in the sky, but the forest was so thick it was impossible to tell where it was. Once in a while I would stop and listen for the river, for Jasper, but then panic would rise again and I would bolt. My legs started to ache and my lungs burned. I wished I had brought some water with me. I kept running.

Eventually I heard a constant white noise. The trees and underbrush were incredibly thick. I'd lost the trail a while ago and had to constantly step over and crouch under things, which was exhausting. My throat was tight and constricted, and the only thought in my head was of the river. As I plodded on the noise became louder, the rushing of water unmistakable, and soon, with every tree I pushed past, I expected to emerge on the bank.

When I placed one foot on the rocky shore, I gasped in horror. The river was huge, much bigger than what we had crossed on the way in. I realized my carelessness in not staying on the trail was about to cost me dearly. At the spot where I had emerged, the river was about fifty metres across and gushing so loudly I wanted to cover my ears. To my right was a large rock bluff that hung over the river. I couldn't get around it. To my left, about twenty metres down, was a giant pile of logs and debris about as big as Jasper's cabin. I had three choices: I could try to cross the river here, go back the way I came and look for the right trail, or attempt to climb over the pile of logs and find a better place to cross downstream. None of these options appealed to me. My fortitude wavered. I was terrified Jasper was going to come through the trees at any moment, rifle over his shoulder, betrayal flaring in his eyes.

Feeling cornered, I concluded I would rather die trying to flee than run smack into Jasper in the trees. I grabbed a long stick from the shore and decided to test the river's depth a few feet out. I stepped into the frigid water. It took my breath away. I held my stick in front of me and tested each step before I took it. I reached down and brought a few handfuls to my lips, trying to quench my parched throat. The current was strong, but the water stayed about knee high. My hope surged again. I picked up my legs and hastened my steps. The current ripped the stick from my hands, but I forged on.

When I reached the middle, my legs were numb and the water was thigh deep. I couldn't feel where my feet were stepping, but the other bank looked so close. Once I reached it I could find the road. I would make it. I stepped towards home.

My foot never hit the ground. When I raised it up, the current was too much. I screamed as it ripped me from the earth and carried me away. I tried to put my feet back down, but they banged against the rocky bottom. Pain shot through me. The river was carrying me straight for the giant log pile. I tried to swim for the bank but was completely helpless. As I neared the logs, I reached out my hands to grab them. My fingers were numb and useless on the slick surface, and with a final gasp, I was dragged under the pile.

My body was submerged. I tried to push off the logs from the bottom, hoping to pop up on the other side. A jolt in my arm wrenched my shoulder from the socket. I stopped moving. The violent current pressed my face against the logs but the rope attached to my wrist was caught on the logs and pulling my arm above my head, threatening to separate it from the rest of my body. I knew I would die.

I heard the slap of his hand hitting my face before I felt it. It was like being slapped in a dream, and with the sting of my flesh realizing that it was real. I opened my eyes to see Jasper's face inches from me, and then the space between us evaporated as he pressed his lips to mine. I involuntarily coughed and gagged into his mouth. He turned me to my side as I sputtered and spewed water. I gasped for breath as water crackled in my lungs. Jasper sat back and gave me space. Oxygen started to flow through my body again. I looked up into Jasper's eyes. He looked terrified. He was soaking wet, and blood ran down his face.

I was foggy and confused. Was I looking into the eyes of the monster I had been running from, or the man who just saved my life?

My wet clothes clung to my body, and I shivered uncontrollably. Jasper scooped me up like I was a doll and ran into the trees. I was going in and out of consciousness and struggling for every breath. He was talking as he ran, but I wasn't sure who his monologue was for. I couldn't decipher the words.

A loud squeak from the cot jolted me back to awareness. Jasper had run all the way back to the cabin carrying me. He knelt above me panting furiously and looked down into my eyes, his face white and his voice wavering.

"Krissy, Krissy, you have to hang on, okay?"

He had never said my name before, and it sounded strangely comforting coming from his lips.

"I have to start a fire, and then I have to get you warmed up. You were under for a long time. Stay with me. Try to stay conscious."

His fear was obvious, and as he stood and reached for the wood, I saw his hands were stained in blood. I wondered whose it was. I wondered if I was going to die.

Jasper moved around the cabin, a constant dialogue running from his mouth. I'd never heard him talk so much. I wasn't sure what he was saying, but he kept looking over at me to see if I was listening. I shivered uncontrollably but was blistering hot. I think I was moaning but couldn't be sure. After a while, I caught the first whiff of acrid smoke and heard the crackling of wood in the fire. Jasper came over with the water bottle and brought it to my lips.

"Shhh, Shhh. Drink. You have to drink."

I took some water in my mouth but was shaking so badly most of it ran onto my face. Jasper tried a few more times and then sat back and put the bottle down. He had already taken off his jacket and now he removed his wet shirt. His white flesh glistened in the light of the fire.

"Krissy, I'm sorry, but I have to take your clothes off. They're soaking wet and I think you have hypothermia. Your skin is blue and if you keep passing out, you might not wake up."

He gave me a cautious look, as if waiting for me to protest. I understood what he was saying, and I trusted him. I wasn't sure why, but in that moment I did. I didn't want to die, and I knew Jasper didn't want me to die either.

He sat on the edge of the cot and pulled my upper body to him until I was leaning on his shoulder. My own dislocated shoulder was in agony. I was completely limp and my fingers were numb. I let out an ear-piercing scream as he lifted my arms above my head to pull my shirt off. Before I could stop him, I felt the ball of my shoulder slip back into its socket. The pain was like nothing I had ever experienced—it was red and angry and tasted of metal. The blackness that followed it was so welcome I hoped never to emerge.

I awoke to Jasper's voice again calling my name. I wasn't sure how long I had been out, but the urgency of it scared me.

"Krissy, can you hear me? Krissy, you're not getting warmer. Now you've stopped shivering, which I think is a bad sign, and your hands and feet are white. You feel like ice. The fire isn't enough. I have to use body heat to warm you up. I'm so sorry this is happening to you. You're going to get better. I promise I won't hurt you. Please trust me."

I could barely stay conscious long enough to comprehend what he was saying, but he stood in front of me and unbuttoned his wet pants. He had nothing underneath. His pants fell to the floor and he unzipped the sleeping bag I was in and got inside. I was aware only of the immediate warmth and how good his flesh felt next to mine. He lifted me so I was partially on top of him, my head on his shoulder, as our bodies melded into one. And then we slept.

I remember being conscious on and off throughout the night, Jasper trying to give me water, my shoulder continuing to scream, but it was foggy and diluted. When I opened my eyes the next morning, I had my first clear thought since realizing the rope was stuck. I was lying naked next to Jasper. His head was turned and his breath was soft and even. My breasts were pressed against his body, my head curled into his neck. My thought was that he saved my life. I knew for a fact I would be dead if Jasper hadn't jumped into the river and gotten me out. He risked his life to save me, and in this tiny little world in the middle of nowhere, something shifted.

I lay very still and listened to him breathing. My feet were burning and throbbing, and my shoulder was aching. I had to move but was trying to delay the inevitable. Waking up together naked would be incredibly awkward, and the feelings rushing through me right now were strange and confused. I knew he was my captor, and that more than anything in the world I wanted to go home to my family, but the fear and compassion in his eyes last night were imprinted on me. Primal instincts I couldn't control were bubbling inside of me. I didn't trust myself.

I slept on and off, ignoring the pain and remaining still. Jasper didn't move for what seemed like hours. A few times he would flinch or moan in his sleep, as if reliving part of our horrible ordeal together. He must have been exhausted. Finally, he stirred. I closed my eyes and pretended I was asleep, trying to keep my breathing regular. My stomach fluttered with nerves. Part of me hoped he would sneak out of the sleeping bag and we could pretend this never happened. Part of me didn't want him to move.

He turned his head and looked down at me. I was trying desperately not to hold my breath. His grip adjusted slightly on my body, but he didn't let go. His breathing got quicker and his body started to shake, almost imperceptibly. Then he pressed his lips against my forehead, so gently I could barely feel it. I opened my eyes and looked up at him. Our eyes met. He searched my face for a reaction. I had so many thoughts running through my head, but I was too exhausted to react to any of them, so I just held his gaze and waited for him to speak.

"I'm sorry I woke you up. How are you feeling? Do you need more water?"

"Yes. Please." I continued on. "Jasper, I really need to thank you for saving my life. I don't understand how you…how did you come along at exactly the right time? Why didn't you just let me die?"

Tears formed in my eyes. I tried to prop myself up on my elbow so I could look him square in the face, but my shoulder wouldn't allow it. He tightened his grip on me slightly with one arm and reached for the water with the other.

"Shhh. Don't get worked up. Here, have some water."

He put the bottle to my lips. I drank. It was almost empty, and when I was finished Jasper took the last swig.

We lay there quietly for a while. The pain in my feet was excruciating. Somewhere inside me I knew it was wrong, lying with the man who had kidnapped me, but I was safe and protected in his arms. My skin sparked with electricity at even the tiniest movement he made. I tried to stay quiet as long as I could, but too many questions were running around in my head. I needed to know what happened.

"Jasper, I have to say some things."

I looked up to catch his eyes for an acknowledgement to proceed, but he kept his eyes towards the wall. I went on anyway.

"First of all, I'm sorry I ran away. You've tried to be so nice to me, and I don't know why I did that to you. You must've been really furious when you got back and discovered I was gone. I feel terrible for putting you through that when you were just out trying to get us food."

He was looking up at the ceiling, but he started to gently rub my arm with his fingers. I kept going.

"I just don't understand how you found me. A few more seconds and I would have been dead, and no one would have ever found me under those logs."

I broke off into sobs I couldn't control. Remembering the feeling of the wet wood pressed against my face and the icy water rushing into my lungs was still too fresh to handle. Jasper held me tighter and moved his hand to stroke my hair. He pressed his lips into the top of my head.

"Please tell me how you saved me. Did you see me walking in the river?"

I looked up at him again as tears ran down my cheeks. This time he was looking at me. He had tears in his eyes too.

"I shot an elk about a kilometre out of camp. I was so excited to show you. I thought you'd be really happy if you knew I could provide for you up here. It would show you we really didn't need anybody else. I got it prepared and grabbed a piece to bring back with me. When I got to the porch and found the frayed rope and the axe, I was pretty angry. It seemed like you were getting used to living here. Maybe even liking it. I couldn't believe you were gone. I started to chase you. You were easy to track and I was confident I could catch you. I just didn't know what to do with you when I did. I still felt bad about hitting you in the head the first time."

His eyes darted around the room, looking everywhere but at me, but he kept going.

"When you went off the trail and started to bushwhack I got worried. There are a few really sharp cliffs around here that you don't even know you're on top of until you fall. I quickened my pace and soon I could hear you ahead of me. I had to make a decision then. It was really tough."

He was looking at the ceiling. I had to remember to breathe.

"Why didn't you just grab me?"

"I figured if you wanted to go that badly, well…"

He paused. I froze, strangely frightened of what he would say next.

"I just decided to watch you for a while."

He didn't finish his thought, and I willed him not to. I don't know why, but I didn't want him to put those words out there, and I was flooded with relief when he stopped. He took a deep breath and continued.

"You navigated well to avoid the cliff. When you got to the shore of the river, I figured you'd turn around, since it was impossible to cross."

He looked down at me and emphasized the last part.

"But you just kept going. I couldn't believe how brave you were. I hid behind the log pile and watched you go. I thought if you could actually make it to the other side, well, anyways, you didn't."

I couldn't believe he was behind me the whole time. If he wasn't, I would be dead now.

"So how did you get me out from under the log jam? The last thing I remember was looking up at those logs and knowing my life was over."

He was still stroking my hair. I never wanted him to stop.

"When you fell I knew where the river would take you. By the time I got there you had already been swept under the logs. I waited for you to come out the other side, but you never did. I held onto a log and went under a few times, and I could see where the rope was caught. I think it took me about a minute to get it free, and then I hauled you out. You were so blue, and I wasn't sure I would be able to bring you back. I never would have forgiven myself if…"

I placed my fingers on his lips to silence him. He looked relieved. We lay there together, lost in our own thoughts.

As if snapped to attention, Jasper suddenly disentangled himself from me and sat up. I was vulnerable, afraid of what would happen next. Afraid we would never have this moment back again. He unzipped the sleeping bag and swung his legs over the side of the cot then grabbed his pants off the cabin floor and pulled them on, waiting for the last second to stand up. He zipped the fly and was looking for his shirt. There were crimson scratches all over his body, probably from the logs. I noticed he had cuts on his forehead too. His ribs protruded from his lean torso.

"Jasper, what happened? You're really scratched up. Here, let me take a look at those."

I gingerly sat up and pulled the sleeping bag around my naked body then moved over and made room for him to sit next to me on the cot. He mumbled and pulled his shirt on.

"I have a lot of things to do. The fire is out and we're out of water. I left three quarters of my animal in the bush. A bear has probably eaten it by now. I have to hang the other quarter before it rots. We need to eat."

He'd switched back into captor mode. I was a bit stunned by the change in attitude and not sure what provoked it.

"Can I help with something? What can I do?"

Ignoring my questions, he moved around the cabin gathering the water bottle and twine from his pack. He put his coat on and opened the door. As an afterthought, he turned to look at me.

"Stay here."

And then he was gone.

15.

Jake Umbry sat back in his chair and rubbed his face roughly. The movement broke me out of my vivid recollection.

"Sorry, that may have gotten a bit too personal. That was when things really changed."

"Yeah. Well your attempt at crossing the river is commendable." He exhaled loudly, as if he'd been holding his breath, and stood up. "Like I promised, we'll break there. I expect to see you as soon as you're finished with the psychologist tomorrow. Go get some rest."

He looked wounded. I didn't know why he was so invested in all of this. In me. His eyes held mine too long, his confusion evident in his furrowed brow. I began to speak, addressing him as "detective," but I paused and finally relented. We were past formal titles at this point.

"Thanks, Jake. I'm exhausted. I'll see you tomorrow."

Something fluttered through him, and I saw his throat rise and fall as he swallowed. His first name came out with a softness I didn't anticipate. I stood and walked out of his office. I could feel his eyes on me as I pulled the door closed. It was time to go home.

My mom and Jill were in the lobby, and the three of us walked out of the building and into the dark night. I thought of Jasper sitting in that tiny room all alone, and of Matty, but I was so overwhelmed by everything I just needed sleep.

The car was out front. It was so strange to be back in civilization: the streetlights and traffic were all overstimulating me. There were two men standing in front of our car, watching us as we approached. One had a giant camera. My mom spoke to them before they could get out a word.

"I've told you guys already. She doesn't want to talk to you. If she ever does, I have your numbers. Please leave us alone. This has been tough enough. Please respect that."

As she spoke, the man with the camera started snapping pictures of us. The brilliant flash temporarily blinded me. I instinctually put my hand to my face and jumped into the backseat.

"No offence, Mrs. Mathews, but Krissy is an adult. We have the right to ask her personally."

He turned his attention to me and talked through the glass as if it wasn't there.

"Krissy, how are you feeling? Can you tell us what happened up there?"

The question that was going to haunt me. I knew that even if I were ready to answer it, nobody would understand what I had to say. I shuddered and turned my head. My mom and Jill jumped in and we sped away.

The town was exactly the same, but I saw it through new eyes. It was dirty and crammed together. Even in the darkness, the store-fronts looked faded and forgotten. I was unexpectedly hit with a sense of longing for the pristine forest. I swallowed it instantly, shaking my head to scatter my thoughts.

We drove down the main street. The town was small, less than five thousand people, but the main street was always bustling. At this time of night it was deserted, which suited me perfectly. At the end of the street we made a left. My house was to the right and up the hill, nestled amongst the trees and overlooking the valley below, with the mountains looming above.

"Mom, can we just go straight home? I'm so tired. I don't think I can keep my eyes open much longer."

I couldn't believe she was taking me somewhere else first.

"Kris, we are going home. We haven't had a chance to tell you yet, but we moved while you were…away."

"You moved? What? Where?"

My heart thumped in my chest. My world continued to crumble around me.

"That's kind of something big to leave out, don't you think?"

"Under the circumstances, not really."

She sounded a little taken aback by my reaction.

I knew it was impossible, but I was frustrated I wasn't consulted on such a major change. I'd lived in that house all my life.

"Why did we move?"

I tried to make it sound a little more controlled.

"Well, after Dad's sentencing it was just the two of us, and we weren't sure when you were coming back, and without Dad's salary, and the legal bills, I just couldn't afford to pay the mortgage. I missed some work, but even when I did go back it just wasn't enough. I'm sorry, honey."

I could tell she was trying to keep it upbeat, but her voice was quivering.

"Sorry, Mom. I didn't really think about it like that. I'm sure the new place is great."

I lay my guilty head back against the seat. I wanted my dad back so bad.

We pulled into the parking lot of a condominium complex a few blocks off the main street. We lived in a condo now? I controlled my shock and tried to sound as positive as possible.

"Oh, these look nice."

Jill got out of the front seat and headed inside without us. She was not fooled by my reaction. My mom led me into the building's front entrance and up a flight of stairs. It was nice enough, plain but clean. It had a funny smell I couldn't place. I wanted my old house. This was not the homecoming I had imagined.

My mom droned on about how nice the neighbours were and what a treat it was to have less housework to do. I listened with one ear. I wondered what my dad thought of this.

When we went inside, it felt homier. Our old furniture was stuffed into the living room, looking like it didn't know what it was doing here either. There was a nice, big window overlooking town, and the kitchen was quaint and spotless, just as my mom always insisted on leaving it. Not everything had changed.

"Here you are, Krissy. Home sweet home! I thought this day would never come. I can't believe we actually have you back."

She burst into tears and pulled me to her. I instantly realized how petty I was being. I was back with my family, two-thirds of them anyway, and where we lived shouldn't matter one bit. I hugged her back hard.

"I'm really glad to be back too, Mom."

We clung to each other for a minute before letting go. Jill appeared from down the hallway with a smile that looked like it took effort to maintain.

"Welcome home, Kris. I hope you can stand it here. It wasn't exactly our first choice either."

The sarcasm was thick and it caught me off guard. I wasn't sure how to respond. Jill had some pent-up hostility. I had a feeling I would be seeing more of it, sooner rather than later.

"Thanks, Jilly. I think it's great. I'm just glad to be with you guys. That's all that matters."

"Yeah. Great." She turned and headed back down the hall.

"Let's get you settled, honey. Come with me. The bathroom is to your right. This is Jilly's room, and here's your room!" She opened the door to the master bedroom and there was all my stuff, just like I had left it four years earlier.

"Mom, why is it like this? Shouldn't this be your room?"

From what I could see this was the last room in the hall.

"Where are you sleeping?" I asked her.

"I was sleeping in here, but now that you're back it will be your room. We had most of your stuff in the closet. Jilly set it up for you this afternoon. I'm sleeping on the pullout. It's actually very comfortable."

She was straightening things as she spoke, folding the perfectly folded throw at the end of my bed.

"That's crazy, Mom. I can sleep on the pullout. I'm not stealing your room from you. It's not fair."

"It's already done. I could sleep in a corner on a bed of nails for all I care. I've got my two girls back together. What more could a mother need? I'm going to go get dinner started. Why don't you settle in. Have a bath. I'll be right in the kitchen if you need me."

With that, she gave me one more quick squeeze, possibly to make sure I was really standing there, and left the room.

I could hear Jill's menacing music through the wall. It was a screeching punk band. Jill was angry. I would have to try and explain to her what happened up there on the mountain and hope she could find a way to forgive me.

I walked into the bathroom and closed the door. I wanted to be clean. In the mirror, a stranger stared back at me: she was a woman, not the girl who disappeared four years earlier. My eyes were again drawn to that small bump on the bridge of my nose. It would be a lifelong reminder of the early days with Jasper, and a reminder I didn't want. But since returning home, it was some-thing I couldn't escape. I had repressed our violent beginning— quickly—and now that I was back, I wondered how that was possible. How can you forgive someone who terrified you and took everything from you? I started to shake.

I pushed my tangled hair back from my face. Everything about me was slightly different: my dark skin, my gaunt face, but my eyes were the same. I missed looking into them, which seemed odd, to miss my own reflection. Miss myself. As I held my own stare, the confusion over my identity rained down on me. I gripped the counter as my knees buckled, and a question pounded in my brain, syncing itself with my heartbeat. "What is real?" I didn't know anymore. I was waking from a nightmare— and slipping into another. I had an intense urge to feel something concrete. I searched through the drawers and found a pair of scis-sors. Grabbing a handful of my dirty blond hair just below the shoulder, I cut. And cut. The sound of slicing scissors was melodic and satisfying. I gritted my teeth as the blades chewed through years of neglect. Long tangled pieces fell to the floor, covering my feet. The hair that remained was still matted and would need more work, but it was a start. I took a long, ragged breath and enjoyed the small sliver of relief.

I got into the hot shower and let the dirt and grime swirl down the drain. The sobs surprised me and brought me to my knees. I missed Jasper and Matty desperately. I was lost without them. I didn't know how I was supposed to become a girl I had buried years ago. Up until today, I had let myself believe the old Krissy died in that river, submerged in the chilling water beneath her coffin of logs. Now I was expected to resurrect her, live her fractured life and shoulder all the guilt and shame. How could I do that?

When the water turned cold, I stood and got out. Wrapping a towel around me, I snuck across the hall and crawled into bed. Sleep came before any more pain could.

16.

Dr. Bates's office was a mess. The large mahogany desk was strewn with papers, and plants were decomposing in the corners. Plastic water bottles with varying remnants overflowed from the recycling bin. His worn leather briefcase lay partially open on the floor, with its contents spilling everywhere.

I sat in the chair opposite the desk, scanning my surroundings and questioning who could exist in such a habitat. The sheer volume of overflowing books, furniture and random belongings was making me feel claustrophobic. Why would anyone hoard so many unnecessary things? I longed for the simplicity of the cabin.

His secretary had let me in to wait and mumbled an apology about the mess, rolling her eyes and kicking a gym bag out of my path. She had said he was finishing up with a phone call and would be only a minute. I felt relief. I had an excuse not to visit Dr. Bates again: surely my mom wouldn't send me back once I described this chaotic situation to her.

All morning I'd tried to come up with excuses not to come here, but my mom didn't buy any of them. She said because of my specific situation I had to be cleared by psychology for my statement to be official. I didn't want any questions about my sanity being raised when I pleaded with the judge to be lenient with Jasper, so I went.

I wanted to see Matty, and I knew I had to get back over to the police station and finish my statement. I was sure Jake was wearing out the floor pacing in his office. I hoped to convince him to let me see Jasper again today, before they moved him to the prison. It made me sick to think about it.

I wasn't in the mood to be analyzed by someone who thought he knew what I was feeling. I was already having my own struggles with reality, and after my breakdown in the bathroom last night, I didn't need Dr. Bates telling me my feelings for Jasper weren't real. Now that I saw what I was dealing with, I figured this wouldn't take very long. What could he do: check me back into the hospital? I just had to put up with this one appointment. I tapped my foot and waited.

He came from behind me through a door littered with many coats and sweaters and scarves on hooks that I hadn't noticed earlier. I jolted out of my chair and turned around to see Dr. Bates stepping towards me, a big grin on his face. He had something that appeared to be his breakfast in one hand and his other hand was extended towards me.

"Krissy Mathews! Welcome home. I'm so sorry to keep you waiting. It's been kind of a crazy morning."

He was young, maybe twenty-nine or thirty. His dark hair was messy and still wet from a shower he had come out of very recently. His eyes twinkled.

"Hi. Nice to meet you," I replied apathetically, as I stood up.

We shook hands. His grip was firm, but his hands were soft, not rough like Jasper's.

"Sorry about the office. I keep meaning to clean it up, but you know how it goes. Believe it or not I know where everything is. Please, sit back down. I just have to find your chart. I had it here somewhere."

I watched as he fished around on his desk, placing his bagel between his teeth. This guy was a real piece of work.

"Okay, okay. Here it is. Krissy Mathews. You have quite a story: missing for four years, held captive up in the mountains. I see you have a two-year-old son. You're one tough girl. I know it's only been twenty-four hours since you've been back. I wanted to see you yesterday before you went home, but the police were incredibly anxious to speak with you. How have you been holding up?"

As he spoke, he took a giant bite of the bagel and then plopped it down on one of the piles on his desk. Crumbs scattered across the papers. He looked up at me, anticipating my reply, and followed my eyes to his discarded breakfast. I fought the urge to run to a window and gasp for breath.

"Oh. Sorry again. I know I shouldn't eat in front of my patients, but to be totally honest I had hockey this morning, and Linda schedules my appointments right after to fluster me. I swear she hates me. If I don't eat, I get low blood sugar. It isn't pretty. Trust me. I'm good now. I promise. You have my undivided attention."

I let him blather on. The longer I could keep the focus off me, the better.

"So let me ask you again, how has it been going since you've been home?"

"Good."

"Well good's good. But that's not going to do it for me, Krissy. Please expand."

What was he looking for me to say? That I was racked with guilt, my son was sick, I ached for my husband, my family was torn apart, my dad was in jail, we had moved to a tiny condo and I was pretty sure my sister hated me for life? He was a stranger, and in forty-two more minutes, a quickly forgotten one.

"You know. It's a bit weird, but good."

"Explain 'weird' to me."

He was not going to let me off easy. I squirmed in my chair a little.

"Just, different. Things are a little different since I've been gone. That's all."

"Yeah. I read about your dad. I'm sorry for what happened with him. It must have been quite a shock for you when you got home. Did you know the boy involved?"

"He used to be in my school. I knew him."

"Have you spoken to your dad yet?"

"Not yet. We're going to talk tonight."

"How do you feel about that?"

"Good."

"Good. Okay."

He leaned forward and looked me square in the eyes.

"Krissy, do you think you need to be here? To be seeing me?"

Finally, we were getting somewhere.

"Honestly, no."

"Can I ask why not? I mean, from what I've read in your chart, you've been through an absolutely horrible ordeal that very few people in the world would be able to relate to. Do you really expect to handle all of these emotions by yourself?"

"Well, yeah, I guess. It's not really like that. Jasper and I, we're, well, it's hard to explain. You wouldn't understand. Nobody would."

"You might be surprised. Have you ever heard of Stockholm syndrome?"

"No. What is it?"

"It's a form of what is called 'traumatic bonding.' I know it sounds strange, but our brain can play some funny tricks when our lives are threatened by people, when we feel like we have no way out of a situation. Our survival instincts kick in and can manifest themselves in amplified attachments and connections that, once we return home, seem unnatural."

"Please stop right there, Dr. Bates. I know what you're going to say: that I don't really love Jasper and my feelings aren't real. I can promise you they are. We have a son together. We're a family. You don't know me, and you don't know Jasper. You can't put these fancy labels on me and pretend you know how I'm feeling."

He sat back in his chair, calmly watching me. I wanted to get away from him as quickly as possible.

"Those are very valid points. You're completely correct. I don't know you, yet. But I do know a lot about the brain and how it works to protect us. Can I ask you a question?"

"I don't know. I don't want to try to explain this to you. I don't have to."

"No, you don't. Please believe I am only trying to help you. For you to recover from this experience and go on to live a happy life, you have to talk about your feelings and experiences and fears. Otherwise, this will haunt you, Krissy. You can't keep it all locked away. If you work through it and still find that your kidnapper is the man you want to be with, well, that will be completely your decision to make. Here's my question: did you feel free to leave the cabin at any time?"

"Yes. Well, not the first week. But after that, yes. I fell in the river trying to escape and Jasper saved my life. He could've just let me drown, but he didn't. I would have died without him. After that I was never chained. I could have left. I guess I was injured for a while. I couldn't walk, and then it was winter, and I got pregnant. But Jasper didn't make me stay. Of course I missed my family, but Jasper needed me and..."

I trailed off. He was confusing me. It didn't sound right as I said the words out loud. I felt like a horrible person who had purposely made her family suffer. But Jasper needed me. And I wanted to stay.

"You don't have to figure it all out now. I have studied this topic extensively. I want you to know the confusion you're feeling is completely normal."

Anger welled up inside me. His questions and casualness and shit lying everywhere were driving me crazy.

"Don't tell me what's normal. You don't know me." I leaned into his messy desk and yelled right into his face. "Stop acting like you know what I'm thinking!"

Again he sat calmly, watching me. I was starting to miss Jake. The way he fired back and got mad was easier to deal with.

"Have you talked to anyone about what happened up there? Your mom or your sister, maybe?"

"Not really. I'm working through it with the police. The detective thinks I'm a crazy, horrible person too."

"That's not fair. I don't think you're crazy or horrible. I think you are the victim of a very traumatic crime that has altered your life significantly in ways you don't fully understand yet. I think you have to stop acting like you chose for these things to happen to you and let the blame fall on those who deserve it. You were an abducted child. You did what you had to do to survive."

His words stung. I wanted to argue with him, but somehow

I couldn't. I wiped at a tear, regretful that I'd shown him he was getting to me.

"Can I ask you another question, Krissy?"

"I…I guess."

My heart was pounding in my chest and my shirt was wet with sweat. I wanted out of there.

"Why do you think Jasper kidnapped you?"

I hesitated. I didn't like hearing "Jasper" and "kidnap" in the same sentence. Jasper was my husband. I loved him.

"Well, he was lonely. You don't understand. Like I said, you don't know him. None of you do. He's not some evil monster. He was abused by his mother. He never really had a father, just a bunch of creeps his mom brought home. He spent most of his life alone. Wouldn't you be lonely?"

"Yes. I would. Jasper's childhood sounds terrible. But being lonely doesn't give you the right to take someone from their family to be with you. If it wasn't you, would he have kidnapped someone else?"

"I don't know. Yeah."

"Well, do you think she would be Jasper's wife now? The mother of his child?"

What the hell was he trying to say? That I was completely replaceable to Jasper?

"No! What Jasper and I have is special. No one else could have what I have with him. No one else could love him or take care of him the way I do. He tells me that all the time."

"Are you sure about that? If your sister had been the one up running on the trail that day, would Jasper have taken her instead?"

"What are you trying to say?"

Dr. Bates sat quietly. His expression wasn't smug but rather more patient, with a hint of sympathy. I was shaking. The thought of Jill going through what I went through made my stomach tighten in a knot. Outwardly, I was claiming I wanted to be with Jasper, so why wouldn't I want it for my sister? And if Jasper would have settled in with any girl he happened to grab, then how could I be special?

"Stop! Stop this! You're tricking me! I don't want to do this anymore. Can I go?"

Dr. Bates took a breath and looked deep into my eyes. We both knew he had hit on something I wasn't ready to think about yet; it was a chip in my windshield that could fracture the whole thing. He couldn't resist one more little tap.

"Why do you think your relationship with Jasper is so hard to talk about? Why does it make you so uncomfortable?"

"That's a pretty obvious question. You're not supposed to fall in love with someone who kidnaps you. You're not supposed to be having sex with him while your family falls apart and everyone is looking for you! You're supposed to fight and keep fighting until you're free!"

"Not necessarily, Krissy. Sometimes when you fight, you die."

Like a kick to the chest, his words took my breath away. I opened my mouth to speak, but nothing came out. Dr. Bates leaned towards me.

"I know you're overwhelmed. I can't imagine how scary this is. We're not going to figure this out in a day. I just want to make the point that we do have a lot to talk about. We need to work through this, piece by piece, and get you back to a place where you can enjoy your life, and your son, and a healthy, loving relationship with someone."

"I don't want to."

I sounded like a stubborn child, but I didn't care.

"Why?"

"I don't want to sit here and pour my guts out to you, when I know you're thinking everything I tell you is just some syndrome or something. Besides, you're a stranger. If I talk to anyone, it would be my mom, but—"

"But what, Krissy?"

"I just don't know what good it will do for anyone to hear what happened up there. All it will bring is hurt."

"Maybe. But if you leave it inside it will continue to hurt you for the rest of your life."

We were at a standoff. I sat stiffly in my chair. Each of us waited for the other to speak. He broke the silence.

"I have an idea."

He hopped up and walked behind his chair to a bank of file cabinets and started opening and closing drawers. Every drawer looked completely jammed. Eventually, he came back around the desk holding a skinny, black leather-bound book.

"For the record, I knew exactly where this was."

He smirked and handed me the book. I reached for it cautiously, as though it might burst into flames if I touched it.

"I would like to meet with you again on Monday. Take the week and write everything you can remember about the last four years in that book. Every thought, every feeling. Everything. Start at the beginning and work your way to the end. When you come back next week, you can tell me what the process was like for you, if it brought up anything you want to talk about. If it doesn't, we'll light the book on fire and watch it burn. What do you think?"

I turned the smooth book over in my hands. It was an easy way to get out of talking with him. I wasn't sure if I was missing a catch, walking into some kind of trap.

"So, you're not going to try and read it? If I say, 'Burn it,' that's it. We burn it and we're done. Right?"

"Yes. Although I'm not going to leave you with the delusion that I don't hope we can talk about some things. I do really think it'll help. And remember, everything you say here is strictly between us, no matter what it is. Okay?"

"Sure. Deal."

He stood up and we shook hands. I held the book tightly and walked out of his office.

17.

The ICU was two floors below Dr. Bates's office. As I walked down the stairs, his words filled my thoughts. "Traumatic bonding." It sounded horrible and had nothing to do with Jasper and me. We were in love. I could have left the cabin any time. If I wanted to.

When I reached the ICU, my mom was waiting for me, sitting on a chair in the hallway just before the big double doors. I couldn't wait to see Matty. She wanted to see him too, if I was ready. Jill was still in bed when we left.

"How did it go with Dr. Bates?"

"Hey, Mom. It was all right, I guess. He's a bit presumptuous."

"Are you going back to see him? I think it would be really good for you to have some help dealing—"

"I know. We've been over this a hundred times. I want to see my son."

I walked through the doors and up to the little desk. The nurse on duty looked up as I approached.

"Hi, I'm Krissy Mathews. I'm Matty's mom. How's he doing?"

"Hi Krissy. We've been expecting you. Come on. I'll take you to him. Matty Mathews. He's a little fighter, just like his mom. We're all so happy you made it."

"Um, thanks, but his last name is Ryan, not Mathews."

I tried to keep my voice low, so my mom wouldn't hear me. I didn't look her way.

"Oh! Sorry about that."

She dropped her head so I couldn't read her expression, and she led me across the room and over to a little bed. There he was. He had tubes and machines everywhere, but his colour was better.

I went to him and buried my face in his neck, taking in his smell that I'd missed so much. I couldn't wait to hear his sweet little voice again, to see him running around and getting into trouble.

"When will he wake up?"

"Dr. Brown was in this morning. He said his vitals are looking stronger and he may be able to come off the breathing tube tomorrow. If that's the case, then we'll be able to reduce the medication and wake him up. Would you like me to page Dr. Brown for you now?"

"No. I have to go anyways. I'll come back later, as soon as I can. Please tell Dr. Brown I was here and thank him. Please take good care of Matty for me."

"Don't worry. We're watching him constantly. If anything changes, we have your mother's cell number. I'll see you later."

As the nurse walked away, I saw my mom lingering over by the desk, looking anxious. I stood up and motioned for her to come over.

"Mom, this is your grandson. This is Matty."

She welled up as she reached out and touched his hand.

"Hi Matty. Oh, Kris, he's beautiful. He looks just like you when you were a baby!"

I had always thought he was the spitting image of Jasper, with his piercing eyes and strong features. But he did have my blond hair.

"I can't wait for you to see him when he wakes up. The nurse said they might wake him up tomorrow if Dr. Brown thinks he's ready. He already looks so much better."

"I know you're hopeful, and that's good, but remember what Dr. Brown told you. He may not be the same when he wakes up."

"Stop. He has to be healthy. He's everything to me. He's going to be fine."

I nestled into him again and whispered in his ear. I told him his Mommy loved him and that I'd be back soon to see him. I gave him a kiss and stood up.

"We better go to the police station. I want to get this over with so I can get back here."

*

The drive to the station was quiet. My mom quickly realized I wasn't in the mood to talk about Dr. Bates or Matty or anything at all. I knew she still had so many questions, and I owed her the answers, but I wasn't ready.

When we arrived, several reporters and cameramen stood in front of the main doors. They saw our car and ran towards us, bumping into each other to get to the windows first. I looked at my mom for some sort of guidance.

"I've had it with these idiots. They've been calling my phone all morning. Wait here for a second."

She hopped out of the car before I had a chance to respond and she called them all over to her in a sweet, condescending way.

"Hi everyone! Please stand here. Krissy will address you all when she gets out of the car, but your aggression is scaring her. If you all stand on this side of the car and let her out, she'll tell you what happened."

I will? What was she talking about? The drooling reporters obeyed, and once my mom had them all at her side of the car, she walked around and opened my door. The snapping cameras and incessant flashes started the instant I moved. My mom reached out her hand and I took it hesitantly.

"Mom, what are you doing? I don't want to talk to these people."

With a plastic smile, she pulled me to her and said very clearly, with her real voice, "Run!" I smirked and ran the twenty feet into the station while the reporters yelled and swore and clicked endless photos of my back.

When I got inside, an officer at the desk sent me to Jake's office. As I walked down the hall, my footsteps were heavy with dread over what was about to happen. He wasn't going to like the next part of the story. I hated his disapproval, and the way he was taking all of this so personally, like I was his girlfriend or something, was pissing me off.

I knocked on the slightly open door before stepping through

it. He was sitting at his desk. His tailored shirt clung to his body. I wondered if he ever wore anything loose-fitting.

"Hey. The officer out front told me to come in."

He looked up. The way his eyes swept over me made me want to hide. I hurried to the chair and sat down.

"Krissy. Hi. Wow, you look great, or, good. You cut your hair."

"Yeah. It was a rat's nest. I forgot how good hot showers feel."

I was blushing. I looked down and played with the buckle on the belt I was wearing. That morning I had gone through my old clothes, all meticulously folded and in my dresser, and found a sweater-dress with a belt that would work. All of my pants were too big and they looked ridiculous hanging from my protruding hipbones.

"Before we get going again, there's something I need to tell you. About Jasper."

I froze mid-breath.

"What? Is he okay?"

"Yes, I'm sure he's fine." His eyes darkened for a moment, as if annoyed I would even wonder, and then he continued. "I pulled up a case we'd been wondering about. The incident occurred shortly after you went missing. It was another abduction case. Luckily, the guy who was taken got away. When I looked at the description of the suspect and the vehicle, they match. Krissy, it was Jasper. He tried to kidnap someone just a week after he kidnapped you. He held him up at gunpoint and blindfolded him, then took him out to an old abandoned road. We believe he was planning to kill him and then changed his mind. Jasper is a bad guy."

I stared at him incredulously. Why would Jasper kidnap a man? And then it came back to me in a rush.

"No. You have it all wrong. He had to take that man. He was a pharmacist. It was the only way he could get my medicine. He did it for me."

"Come on! This guy has you so brainwashed you'll believe anything!" He stood up. "Nice guys don't kidnap people at gunpoint!"

"Would you please calm down and listen to me? Let me tell you what happened."

He sat back in his chair and took a breath.

"Fine, tell me your story. But we're having the victim come in later today to identify Jasper in a line. He's going down for this, too."

I collected my thoughts and put myself back at the cabin. Jasper had saved my life by pulling me out of that river, and then he saved it again. I hoped once everyone knew how he helped me, they would understand. Be merciful. But with Jake on the case, my hope was dwindling that Jasper was going to get off easily.

18.

Jasper was able to salvage some of the elk meat. He made several trips in and out of the cabin carrying armloads of wood, and then he got water and filled a large pot. Once he had everything organized, he boiled water and made tea and noodles, frying a few chunks of the elk.

During his activity, I stayed on the cot. When Jasper first left I recovered my clothes, which he'd hung by the fire to dry, and dressed. My feet were in bad shape. They were cut and bruised. When I tried to put weight on them, I screamed in agony. My shoulder was still incredibly tender, but it was bearable now that it was back in its socket. With all his scurrying about and organizing, I sensed Jasper needed to regain order. I wasn't sure what had jolted him out of our blissful state earlier, but I could tell his avoidance of me meant he didn't want to talk about it now.

The elk smelled delicious frying in the pan and my stomach growled in eager anticipation. When it was done, Jasper fixed me a plate with the noodles and meat and brought me a cup of tea. I was sitting on the cot, still wrapped in the sleeping bag. When he passed it to me I thanked him, but he looked away and went about fixing his own plate. Then he sat at the table and ate.

"Jasper, this is amazing. Thank you. I was really starving."

He shrugged and carried on eating. I kept quiet.

After we ate, he cleaned the dishes and asked me if I had to use the bathroom. I did, but I wasn't sure what to do. I couldn't walk, and I didn't know how I would manage to keep any decency if Jasper had to hold me.

"Umm, I do have to go the bathroom, but my feet are really sore. I tried earlier, and I can't walk."

A look of concern passed over his face. He came over to the cot. "Can I see them?"

"Yes. They're just bruised right now. I'm sure they'll be better in a day or so."

I unzipped the sleeping bag and lifted each leg out by the knee, placing them gingerly back down.

"Oh, my God!" Jasper gasped.

They were getting worse.

They were both swollen far greater than their regular size. Bright purple and red bruising patterned their entire surfaces. Both feet had several cuts, most of which had stopped bleeding, but now they oozed a pinkish puss. The redness and swelling was no longer localized to my feet but had spread up my lower legs. They throbbed with their own independent heartbeats. It was excruciating.

"Why have you not told me about this until now? This is really serious! I think they might be infected. I noticed the cuts when I was taking care of you last night, but they didn't look this bad."

The tone in Jasper's voice scared me.

"I didn't know they were getting like this. They were numb, and then I thought they were just sore from when I hit them on the rocks. You've already done so much to help me that I didn't want to bother you."

The look on his face told me this was more serious than I thought. He laid his hands on my feet, pulling them back in shock.

"Your feet feel really hot. That's not a good sign. Were your lower legs red before, when you got dressed?'

I was in such a hurry to get my clothes on before Jasper came back I hadn't really studied them.

"I'm not sure. They do look worse now."

He started to chew his lip. I'd never seen him do that before. He slowly lowered himself to his knees and put his head in his hands. I wasn't sure what to do, but suddenly I was very afraid.

I raised my hand and gently stroked his head. He looked up and there were tears in his eyes.

"Krissy, you need help. You need antibiotics. Your feet are infected, and if you don't get medicine right away the infection will spread throughout your body and kill you. I'm sure I can carry you down the mountain, but I don't think I'll be able to get across the river holding you. With the melt right now it's just too high. I can go and try to get some medicine, or I can get you help. They'll arrest me when they find out what I did, but I'll send someone straight up here to get you. I can't believe this is happening. I guess I didn't think this through enough. I'm so sorry."

He broke off and put his head back down. I put my hand back on his head. He reached up and grabbed it. And I knew what I wanted him to do.

"Jasper, I'm going to be fine. I'm sorry I didn't tell you my feet were hurting sooner. It's not your fault they've gotten this bad. I'm the one who ran away in the first place. I don't want you to go to jail. I just want my feet to be better. And then we can talk about me leaving. Can you please go and get me the antibiotics? I'll wait here. I'll be good. It's the only way you won't get into trouble, and you saved my life, so I owe you."

My eyes pleaded with his to listen to me. He brought my hand to his mouth and held it there, his scruffy beard a sharp contrast to his soft lips. I knew he didn't want anything bad to happen to me, and I knew what he was offering: my life, my freedom, at his expense. He stood, bent and kissed my forehead and then he carried me outside to pee. I was helpless in his arms, and he sat me on a log and took a few steps away to give me as much privacy as he possibly could. When I finished, he carried me back inside and zipped me into the sleeping bag. He brought me the water bottle and enough food for several days, although he promised to be back in twenty-four hours. He had a bottle of Aspirin in his pack, so I took two of those and promised to take a couple later. He put on his coat and stood by the door. I tried to look unconcerned, but I think he saw right through me. He opened the door of the cabin. The sun was setting and the dusky light formed an orange aura around him.

"Trust me, Krissy. I won't let you down. See you soon."

I was alone. And dying.

✳

With the slam of the door, the gravity of my situation overwhelmed me. My brave face dissolved into tears, and the pulsing in my feet intensified exponentially. It felt as if they were being punctured with a thousand sharp knives. I took two more Aspirin and gulped down more water. I was hot and sweaty one second, freezing the next. I took deep breaths and thought of Jasper's face, his eyes, the feeling of his lips on my hand and my head. Could I actually be falling in love with him? What kind of deranged person was I?

I forbade myself from thinking of my family. If they ever knew I had a chance to be rescued, and I turned it down, they would never forgive me. I wasn't sure I could ever forgive myself, but I only turned it down to save Jasper. And I owed that to him, because he saved me. Didn't I? I would go home when I could walk out of here myself, leaving Jasper to live his life on the mountain. Not in a prison cell. My head and my heart were in a violent tug of war, leaving me unbelievably disoriented. Had I lost the ability to determine right from wrong? What was happening to me?

I slept in fits and starts, my dreams vivid and unrelenting. I began to believe I would die in this cabin, alone. That Jasper was never coming back. That my family knew where I was but decided to leave me here and betray me, the way I had betrayed them. The night was incredibly long. Every time I woke and opened my eyes, I prayed for daylight.

Eventually, the sun crept in through the window but brought no comfort. I had lost my appetite, but my thirst could not be quenched, and I emptied the water bottle. The agonizing pain in my legs was now up to my knees, but I refused to unzip the sleeping bag and inspect them. My mental self-mutilation continued. I questioned if I had even an ounce of moral fibre and came to the conclusion that I deserved to die. Here. Alone. I thought of getting up and trying to find a pen and paper to record my final thoughts, to apologize to my family, to let Jasper know I'd figured out his evil plot. I realized it was his plan all along to leave me here to die. I tried to move off the cot but found I was much too weak to stand. I comforted myself in the fact that death must not be far now. I lay back down and awaited its arrival.

The door burst open, and for a moment I wondered if it was a hallucination. Jasper's tall frame filled the doorway. His breath was rapid and coming in gasps, his face glistened with sweat. He was soaking wet from the waist down. In his right hand, he held a white paper bag. He crossed the cabin in three steps and knelt next to the cot, bringing his hand up gently to touch my cheek.

"Oh, my God, you're burning up. Krissy, you're safe now. I'm back. You're going to get better."

He opened the white bag and pulled out several boxes of medication. With his brow furrowed, he studied each box and selected a package. He tore it open and produced a large red pill, then reached for the water bottle.

"Shit! How long have you been out of water?"

I had yet to say anything. I was trying to instruct my brain to believe what my eyes were screaming was real. Jasper was back. He had been worried about me. He cared about me, too. He was back. Once again, he'd swooped in just when I thought my life was over and rescued me. I reached out my hand with a renewed strength and placed it on top of his, relief flooding my eyes. He looked up and smiled at me.

"Hold on. I have to run and get you some fresh water. I'll be right back."

And I knew he would be.

The next few days went by in a foggy blur. Jasper woke me to give me my medication, drink, and even forced me to eat a little. Other than that, I slept. My fever broke the first night, and I slept the dreamless sleep of a contented child. Jasper lay on the floor next to me. Once in a while I would dangle my hand down to make sure I could feel him. He'd brought ointment and bandages and dressed my feet and changed them every day. The pain subsided.

After a few days, he carried me outside and placed me on the porch in a chair to get some sunlight. He draped his coat over my shoulders and propped my feet up on a stump. They were still really bruised and swollen, but the redness was no longer in my legs and the throbbing had ceased. My shoulder ached, but it was improving. Jasper used a bandage to make a sling. As long as I didn't try to raise it too far, it was bearable.

I watched him as he chopped wood and stacked it neatly on the porch. The frayed rope was still tied to one of the porch planks. It felt like a lifetime ago that I'd cut it. I had been near death twice since that sunny morning, and everything had changed. I was so afraid of what I was feeling, but as I watched Jasper working, doing everything he could to take care of me and make me comfortable, a little buzz of excitement flowed through me. Did I love this man?

As if sensing my eyes on him, he looked up at me, squinting into the sunlight. A quirky smile played on his lips.

"What are you looking at?"

"Nothing. Just you."

I returned his playful smirk, and he gave his head a slight shake as he went back to chopping wood.

"Hey, Jasper, I forgot to ask, how did you get the medicine for me? You need a prescription for that kind of stuff, don't you?"

He heard what I asked but kept chopping for a few minutes, and I let him. I was learning Jasper liked to answer questions in his own time. He stacked what he'd been cutting, and with a final whack, he stuck the axe back into the block. Then he dried the sweat off his face with the bottom of his shirt and came to sit on the edge of the porch.

"You might not like this, but it was the only way I could get it, and I was desperate." He kept his eyes down and cleared his throat. "I got to town and headed straight for a pharmacy. I knew I needed a prescription, but I also knew a doctor wouldn't write one for a problem I didn't have. I was worried he might get suspicious and call the cops. I thought maybe if I explained to a pharmacist that I had a friend in trouble and offered him money, he might help me. Well, I was wrong. The pharmacist got really in my face about not having a prescription and what was I trying to pull. I could tell he really didn't like the sight of me, which I'm pretty used to."

He rubbed his beard as he said this, and I suddenly regretted judging him for it. He really didn't have a lot of choice in having it. Shaving up here would be impractical.

"Anyways, I begged him, because I really didn't know where else I was going to go, and I knew you were waiting for me, and your life was at stake. He got really huffy and defensive and said he was going to call the police if I didn't get out of there. I stepped back to leave, but then I pictured your face, and I knew I couldn't take no for an answer."

He looked up and I could tell he was afraid to tell me the next part.

"It's all right, Jasper. You saved my life. You did what you had to do."

I hoped this didn't include hurting the man, but I kept that thought to myself.

"Yeah. Well, all I could think of was putting my hand in my pocket and pretending it was a gun. I told him I wouldn't hurt him if he put some antibiotics and some dressings in a bag. He looked terrified. I don't think it surprised him that I may have had a gun. He did what I told him to, and then I made him walk me out the rear entrance of the store and I put him in the back of my truck. I knew if I let him go he would call the police before I could get out of the parking lot."

Images of the back of Jasper's truck and the horrific fear I experienced there flashed through my mind. I forced them out.

"I drove him out of town and then up an old forestry road I know, where there isn't any traffic. It would have been about a two-hour walk to get back to the main highway. He was shaking and begging me not too hurt him, and I think he was just relieved when I let him go. He knows my face and my truck now though, so I'm sure every police officer around will be looking for me. I'm not sure how we're going to get supplies."

He trailed off as if this hadn't occurred to him until that moment. I was glad he hadn't hurt the man. It was my fault he had to do anything illegal in the first place. Now I'd created a situation where he couldn't even go into town.

"I'm sorry, Jasper. I'm sorry you had to do that, and I'm glad the man's okay. You really saved my life, though. Before you came through that door, I thought I was going to die alone, that you were never coming back. I was so afraid."

I couldn't control the tears that fell and soaked into his jacket, which was draped over my body. I hugged it tightly to me and hung my head, embarrassed. He stood up and came towards me. In one easy motion he scooped me up and then sat down on the chair. I nestled my head into his neck as he cradled me. He smelled like wood. His beard was soft against my face. I draped my arms around his neck, my fingers playing with his hair. The sun soaked into our skin, and I was awash in heat, inside and out.

When I was brave enough, I raised my head and looked into his face. His expression was peaceful and content. We were inches apart. I could feel his warm breath on my skin. Slowly, he leaned towards me, and I closed my eyes as our lips met. Feelings erupted from deep inside me. My hair stood on end. His lips were soft and gentle at first, but as we got lost in each other there was a desperate intensity.

My lips parted and his tongue entered my mouth, strong and warm and confident. His hands were on my face and in my hair, and my body pressed against his hard chest. He moved his mouth over my skin, my face, my neck, claiming every part of me. I surrendered. I could feel him hard beneath me, but he stayed in the chair, kissing my lips raw. I waited for him to take me inside and lay me on the cot, my body ached for it, but we stayed on the porch. I knew it would be completely different from my awkward experiences with Blake.

Eventually, his kisses were soft and sweet again. The sun was setting and the air was cooling off. Jasper repositioned the coat around me and held me tightly to keep me warm. As the sun fell nearer to the earth, it became a giant orb casting gold light on the snow-capped mountains and the tips of the evergreens. It was stunning. We watched its last moments as a perfect circle, before it was pierced by the jagged peaks. Jasper brought his hand up and stroked my hair. Finally, he spoke.

"You have no idea how many nights I have sat out here and watched the day end, wishing I could have someone to share it with. I wanted you to see that, to see how beautiful life can be here. Our life."

His voice was hoarse. I could tell he put his whole heart into what he was saying. He cleared his throat and continued.

"The other day when I first got to hold you in the sleeping bag, I didn't know if you felt threatened or afraid I would hurt you if you didn't go along with it. I really did that because it was the only way to warm you up. As horrible as you may think I am for kidnapping you, I'm not the type of guy who would ever rape you. My plan all along was to bring someone here. They would fall in love with this place, and hopefully with me, of their own free will. They would want to stay and be with me."

"I wasn't afraid, I knew you were trying to help me, Jasper. You've been so...I would be dead if it wasn't for you. You make me feel like I never have before. I want you to touch me, to kiss me. I'm so confused by these feelings, but I can't help it, and right now I want to go with it. When I get better, when I can walk, then I want to talk with you about what's ahead of us. But, for now, I want to forget the other world even exists."

"Can you do that, Krissy? Because now that I have you here, now that this scenario I had planned in my head for so long is real, well, now it's *you*. Everything in me wants the best for you, wants you to be happy. I realized it when we were lying in the sleeping bag. This is something I didn't anticipate. To actually love you means to let you go, to let you go back to your life and be happy with your family. And that means we can never be together."

My head was reeling. Did Jasper just say he loved me? My stomach swarmed with butterflies. I wanted him so badly I couldn't stand it. Being together was the only option.

"Why, Jasper? Can't we have both? Come back with me. We'll explain everything. When I tell my parents how you saved my life twice, and how I feel about you, I know they'll be able to forgive you for kidnapping me. I'll make them understand."

"No, that'll never happen. If I ever get caught in town, I'll be arrested for taking you and for holding up the pharmacy and taking a hostage. I couldn't survive in jail. I can't live around other people. I've known it since I was a kid. I'll live in the mountains forever. And if they ever track me down up here, I'll die before I let them take me in."

19.

Jake's chair scraped against the floor as he stood up.

"Thanks. I got it. I need some water. Do you want some water?"

He walked over to the water cooler. I came back from that other world. From falling in love with Jasper. Now here we were, exactly where he promised he'd never be. All for the love of his son.

"Do you understand now? Do you see why he had to take the pharmacist? He didn't hurt him."

"Didn't hurt him? Why don't you ask Mr. Bailor, who's a father of two by the way, if Jasper hurt him. He thought he was being driven out to the forest to be executed! He hasn't slept more than a few hours at a time since. He's constantly medicated, has nightmares, and he can't work."

"I'm sorry. That would be terrifying. Obviously I know that better than anyone. But don't you see that he did it for me? To save me?"

"Krissy. This guy is a master manipulator. He creates these scenarios where he has to save you, and then he becomes a hero to you. Open your eyes! If he had taken you to the hospital after he fished you out of the river, you wouldn't have needed saving again."

"Well, maybe, but he told me he would go get help if I wanted, when my legs were bad. He said he would go get the police!"

"Yes, I'm sure that's what he would have done. Please! Listen to yourself. There's no way that guy was getting any help. He does these things to make you believe it was your idea to stay. It's all part of his plan. He told you he wanted to keep you there as his wife. Do you think it's normal to get kidnapped and then just decide to stay with the kidnapper?"

"No. But this was different. Jasper didn't mean for me to get hurt. If I had made it across the river, he was going to watch me go. It was my fault for falling!"

"You have to stop with this 'my fault' stuff, or I'm really going to lose it. Nothing that happened to you was your fault. You are a victim! You're the toughest, bravest girl I've ever come across. I wish you'd see you don't have to defend him anymore. You're free, and he can't hurt you ever again. I promise."

We stared at each other. Both frustrated. I wanted to scream at him that he had no idea what he was talking about, that he was so wrong. But I didn't.

"Jake, I'm not going to fight with you about this anymore. And I don't need you to protect me from Jasper."

He sat back down.

"I'm sorry I raised my voice at you, Krissy. I know you've been through a lot, and you're trying to get your bearings. I don't want to see you waste another minute of your time on that guy. But I know that's none of my business. Let's finish up with your statement, and then I can get on with my job, and you can get on with your life."

I knew Jake would not handle the rest of the story details very well, so I stuck to the facts. I told him about having Matty. I told him how Matty was bitten by the rat, which started the cascade of events that brought us here. When I was finished, he turned off the recorder and stood by the door.

"Thanks, Krissy. I'll be in touch when we have information about the court date. The district attorney's office will contact you about your testimony."

"And if I don't want to testify?"

"Give it some time. And please, think about what I said."

"I want to thank you again for all you did to help bring me home. If you had found me in those first few days…"

I trailed off, surprised at what I'd said. Jake looked surprised too, his eyebrows raising, as a mixture of emotions crossed his face. He reached out and touched my shoulder.

"Look, I really do think you're incredible. If you ever need anything, even just someone to talk to, call me. And I really hope Matty's going to be okay."

My skin felt hot where his hand lingered too long. I stood for a moment, and then walked out of the room.

On the way home, we stopped to see Matty again. Several reporters lingered at the emergency-room doors, but I pushed past them with my head down. I hoped they'd soon realize I was a dead end and go away. I had no intention of telling them anything, but I knew once we went to court, all the details would be out in the world for everyone to read and judge me by. Something I didn't even want to think about yet.

Matty was the same, so I made arrangements to meet with Dr. Brown first thing the next morning and then my mom and I headed back to the apartment. My dad was calling, and I couldn't wait to talk to him. I was also terrified. I had completely ruined his life, and I didn't know how to explain myself. He would be so disappointed in me. When the phone rang, I jumped on it. My voice squeaked out of my constricted throat.

"Hello?"

"Krissy, is that you?"

"Dad! Oh, my God. I missed you so much!"

I wanted to hug him desperately.

"Krissy! I'm so happy you're home! I've been bouncing off the walls since I heard they found you. I knew you were alive. I just knew it. I never gave up hope, which is kind of tough in here. But I knew if there was any way for you to survive, you would."

His voice raised an octave at the end, and then there was a muffling sound, like he had put his hand over the phone. I cringed at the icy wave of guilt that crashed over me. I'd never heard my dad cry before.

"Dad, I'm so sorry for what happened. I feel terrible for what you went through and where you are. I wish so badly I could do something."

I broke off into wrenching sobs, the kind where you can't breathe. I could hear my dad saying my name. I think he was crying too. It took me a minute before I could calm myself down.

"Listen to me very carefully, Krissy. You have nothing to do with why I'm here. Do you understand me? Nothing. I'm here because of a horrible accident. It was a mistake, but I made it. No one else is responsible. I never had any intention of hurting Blake. I hope you can believe that. I would do anything to change the circumstances of that night, but I can't. I've learned to accept that. I've had to. I don't want to hear another word out of your mouth about you feeling bad. You had no control over what happened to you. Do you hear me?"

"Yeah Dad. I do, I just—"

"You just nothing. I won't hear another word about it. Okay?"

"Okay."

I didn't have much of a choice but to agree.

"I only have a few minutes, but I want to say some things. I want you to know how incredibly brave and strong I think you are. I could never be more proud of you than I am right now. You stayed strong and survived something so horrible, so horrendous I can't even begin to imagine. You are truly my hero."

I swallowed hard, the weight of my deceits bearing down on me.

"Dad, come on. It wasn't so bad all the time. I mean I really missed you guys, but he treated me fairly well. Things happened up there that we should probably talk about, things you need to know. I have a son, Dad. He's two. His name is Matty."

The line was quiet for a moment, just a faint buzz and his breathing.

"A son. Oh God, I—"

"No, Dad. Wait. He's so wonderful. He is the best thing that ever happened to me. I love him so much. It's indescribable."

"Trust me. I know. Wow. I'm a grandfather."

"Yes! I can't wait for you to meet him, Dad."

"Matty Mathews. That's a great name."

"Yeah. Well…"

I couldn't tell him.

"Kris, I know we have a lot of talking to do. It's going to take us a while to catch up. But I'm running out of time and I want to say one more thing."

He cleared his throat, and I could hear someone yelling in the background. I tried not to picture where he was.

"I want to tell you I am so sorry. I failed you. A father is supposed to protect his daughter and keep her safe. I didn't do that. If only I had gone up the trail the first time I went to check on you. Maybe I could've saved you." His voice was breaking, and I could barely hear him, but he continued. "I have lied awake every night since you've been gone imagining the horrible torture you've been enduring. I made myself do it. I thought I deserved it for not being there for you. All that I can say is I will never forgive myself. I know this will haunt you for the rest of your life. I want you to know it will haunt me too."

"Dad! Stop, please. I promise it wasn't that bad."

I was going to throw up any second. He took a deep, slow breath.

"There you are being brave again. I need to borrow some of that. I have to go here, honey, but Mom is going to bring you up on Sunday for a visit. I can't wait to see you. And I promise, no more tears. I will be the happiest man on Earth from now on. Get some rest."

"I can't wait to see you. I love you."

"I love you too, honey. Bye."

He was gone. I placed the phone on the counter. My mom had left the kitchen, but I'm sure anywhere in the condo was within earshot of my conversation. It must've killed Mom to see what a mess my dad had become. My family was shattered with nothing left but debris.

There was a roast sizzling and spitting in the oven, the delicious aroma wafting through every room, but I'd lost my appetite.

That night I sat at the tiny kitchen table, a blank page staring at me. I didn't want to write about being kidnapped. About how Jasper had taken me. The terror of it all. I'd been through all that with Jake, and I knew I'd have to tell the story again to my family and to the lawyers and the court. I'd had more than enough of that story. But Dr. Bates's words that morning stuck with me all day. Was it possible my feelings for Jasper were something I invented? I really didn't believe that, but Jake had gotten to me too. I wanted to go back to the days that Jasper and I fell in love. I wanted to relive our relationship from the beginning. It wasn't manipulation. We truly loved each other.

My mom and I shared a quiet dinner. Jill was working late. My mom still hadn't asked me to tell her anything further about what happened. I think she was waiting for me to offer it up. I told her about Dr. Bates's request. She thought it was a great idea.

The door sprung open and Jill came in. She was surprised, and somewhat disappointed, to see me sitting there.

"Hey, Jill. How was work?"

"Crappy, actually. Sorry I missed dinner."

She mumbled at me as she dug through the fridge. She came out with a plate my mom had meticulously prepared for her and tried to make a dash for her room.

"Jill. Wait. I feel like I haven't had a chance to talk to you since I've been back. Pull up a chair."

I kicked the chair opposite me away from the table and motioned for her to sit in it. She hesitated, and then came back into the kitchen and sat down.

"So, talk to me. Tell me what you've been up to the last four years."

I was walking through a minefield as I formed the sentence.

"Huh. Well, not much, really. What do you want to know? I ended up dropping out of school after you went missing. Between searching for you and then Dad's trial, I was too far behind to catch up. Mom completely fell apart, so I spent a lot of time making sure she'd eaten and could make it to work. After that, I was so exhausted that I watched TV and ate all day, so I became a fat cow. Now I work at the diner out on the highway, which is just a wonderfully fulfilling job. There's nothing else to tell."

Her hostility threatened to boil over. I wasn't sure where to go from here.

"Jill, I'm sorry you had to deal with everything when I was

gone. Obviously this is not how I had pictured our lives would be. I know you're mad at me. What could I have done to stop it?"

She exploded with a ferocity I didn't know she was capable of.

"I don't know! I know it's terrible for me to be mad at *poor Krissy*, but what am I supposed to do? You ruined my life! Mom and Dad both went nuts! They completely forgot I existed! They didn't even know I dropped out of school until one of my teachers told them three weeks later. And then Dad was gone. It was so awful. And now I'm supposed to be so happy you're home, and you have a son, and Mom said you're calling this guy your husband! How could you do this to us? Why didn't you come home?" The accusatory look in her eye cut me to the core. She started sobbing. She was asking me the question everyone wanted to ask. I knew I'd have to answer it one day.

"Jill, I never wanted any of this to happen."

It was all I could manage. She stood up, the chair slamming against the wall, and retreated to her room.

I sat at the table for the next hour, the book open in front of me, the paper looking anxious to soak up the ink. I was terrified of the words that might flow from the pen, like somehow if I wrote everything down, then I would have to be judged by it. But in the end, I had to face what I had done.

I started writing.

20.

As we sat on the porch, I could feel Jasper's heart thumping in his chest. The light had faded almost completely. We sat quietly for another minute, both of us unsure of what to say next. Where would we go from here? Eventually, he stood and carried me into the cabin. He placed me on the cot and mumbled something about water and food. I knew he would busy himself in work for the next while. Feeling completely useless and exhausted, I zipped myself into the sleeping bag and watched him, wondering how my heart could be so full and so empty at the same time.

Jasper came back from getting water and put soup on the stove. The warm smell filled the cabin, and for the first time in several days, my hunger growled its arrival. When the soup was hot, he brought me a steaming bowl, with a few crackers and some water. I thanked him and started gulping. He ate his from the pot, sitting at the table.

After dinner, I tried putting some weight on my feet, but shards of pain shot up my legs and I winced and receded. I hated depending on Jasper to carry me outside to go to the bathroom, but unfortunately I wouldn't be walking anywhere for a while.

"Could you please take me out to go to the bathroom?" I asked quietly.

We were both lost in our thoughts all evening and had barely spoken. He came towards me and helped me unzip the sleeping bag. We had a look at the wounds together and decided the dressings looked fine until tomorrow. He slid his hands carefully underneath me and carried me outside. The clearing was glowing in the moonlight and the blanket of stars above us was thick and vibrant. Jasper left me on the log and went off to do his own business. When he came back I looked into his eyes. The contentment from that afternoon was replaced with a cloud of sadness. My voice broke through the tension.

"Jasper, here's what I know for sure. I can't walk, and it'll take some time before I can walk out of here and cross the river by myself. You can't take me, or you'll be arrested, so I'll have to do some of it without your help. After everything you've done for me, I would never want to get you in any kind of trouble. So I figure we have some time. Here. Together. With no choice in the matter. Why don't we just enjoy it?"

He stood before me, lit by the moonlight, letting my words soak in. I watched his face intently. I knew what I was saying was wrong, that I was betraying everyone who loved me and was looking for me, but I couldn't stop my feelings. I craved comfort and safety so desperately, and they were right in front of me. Jasper considered everything, and then slowly the cloud lifted and a smile settled on his face.

"When you put it that way."

He picked me up, but this time it wasn't like a caretaker. It was very intimate. He held me closely and brought me to the cabin. As we walked through the doorway I giggled.

"What's so funny?"

He sounded surprised.

"Nothing. It kind of feels like you just carried me over the threshold."

I was embarrassed and buried my face in his neck.

"And that's funny?"

"I don't know. Isn't it?"

I peered up at him, trying to gauge his reaction. He sat me gently on the cot and knelt in front of me. He took my hands in his. My whole body vibrated, and I couldn't breathe.

"Krissy, from the first moment I saw you, I knew I wanted you to be my wife. Now I know it more than ever. I also know that I want you to be happy, and I hope I can be a part of making that happen. I love you. More than you can know."

The sight of Jasper on his knees in front of me made my heart race. I didn't know how this happened, and right then I didn't care. All I knew was I wanted him, in every way possible.

"I love you too, Jasper. So much."

I bent down and kissed him, parting his lips with my tongue and exploring his mouth. He wrapped his arms around me and slid his hands up the back of my shirt. Our skin touching was electric. He slipped my shirt over my head and took his off. Every muscle on his torso rippled as he raised his arms above his head. I moved closer to the edge of the cot, resting my feet gingerly on the floor and spreading my legs wide. Jasper pressed himself against me and kissed my breasts, lingering on each nipple until I thought I would explode. I ran my hands through his hair and down his back. He stood up and laid me down, directing me with hungry kisses. I put my hands above my head as he kissed his way down my body, sliding off my pants and then letting his fall to the floor.

The cabin was dark except for the flickering firelight that danced across the table and on the walls, casting shadows on Jasper's naked body. He reached for my underwear, sliding his fingers under the band, and then he paused.

"Are you okay?" he asked, his voice gruff and thick with desire.

"Yes."

I was dizzy and aching with anticipation. He slid the soft cotton slowly down my legs, carefully removing them from my feet. There was no pain. When he came back to my mouth his kisses turned sweet and soft. He was hard against me, and then he was inside me. I gasped as he rocked gently, watching my face and planting kisses on my cheeks. As we moved together, I knew I had never felt more whole. Jasper's touch, his passion, was exquisite.

We made love three more times that night. We filled the spaces in between whispering and kissing and exploring. I had never given myself like this to another person. Flashes of guilt surged through me, but I brushed them aside.

I was Jasper's.

As spring turned into summer, my feet began to heal. It was a slower process than I had anticipated, but I was beginning to walk.

We spent our days lost in each other, him attending to my every desire. I couldn't move very far, but Jasper would get us water and make our meals, always checking in to make sure I had what I needed. In the afternoon, we would make love in the clover and sleep in the sun, my head resting on his chest.

I wanted to keep track of the days I'd been gone, but they blurred, one into the next. I told myself my family was fine, that they missed me, but they would understand when I showed up healthy and explained everything to them. I pictured my sister running, spending time with her friends, getting ready for her final year of high school. I had missed my own graduation. I tried not to picture my parents. I really didn't have a choice. There was no way to get back to them without putting Jasper in jeopardy. I kept these thoughts of going home tucked away and rarely indulged in them. I was a girl in love.

While we were relaxing in the sun one day, lying side by side in the clearing, I couldn't resist the urge to ask Jasper a few questions. We were completely consumed with the present, but my thoughts were beginning to take me beyond that, and I wanted to know more about this man.

"Can I ask you a question?"

He moaned. He hated when I asked him questions, which he said I did far too often.

"Come on. Please? It's just that, I love you, and you are so special to me, but I know nothing about you. It isn't right."

Neither one of us was very fond of discussing our families, but at the beginning I'd mentioned mine constantly. Now it just made things awkward, so I tried to keep the thoughts to myself. He lay quietly for a few minutes, and just when I thought he might completely ignore me, he spoke.

"A few questions. What do you want to know?"

"Well, where were you born?"

"On a farm."

"On a farm around here?"

"No. Down south. I can't even remember the name of the town. We weren't there long. We weren't anywhere long."

"Here's another one: how old are you?"

"Twenty or twenty-one. Honestly, I can't really remember, and I rarely know what the date is anyways."

"Wow, you're only twenty-one? You're so young!"

He was slightly irritated, but I pressed on anyways.

"So where are your parents? Why is nobody looking for you?"

A look of disgust crossed his face, and I knew I was treading on thin ice. I stayed quiet, hoping he would answer.

"My parents. Well, Kris, not everyone has a loving family like you. My dad left as soon as he found out my mom was pregnant. Can't say I blame him. She was a real sweetheart."

Jasper must've been able to taste the bitterness in his voice. He leaned over and spit on the ground.

"Do you know where they are now?"

"I have no idea. I left when I was fourteen. My mom moved us around so much before then I never knew where we were or what loser would be living with us next. Some of my earliest memories are of being alone and scared in a nasty apartment. If it was a good day, I'd find some cereal. On a bad day there was nothing. She'd lock me in and be gone for days. I used to pretend I was in the woods, trying to survive by myself. I always feared she'd never come back, but eventually she did. She'd be so strung out when she returned; it would take at least another day before she talked to me. I'd sit by her bed and try to take care of her, unless she brought company. Then I'd hide. My mom had a wonderful talent for attracting the biggest asshole in every town. Most of them loved beating on me for fun. After one guy put me in the hospital, my mom just didn't pick me up. So I left. I didn't care. I had no money so I broke into some guy's garage and stole a bunch of camping supplies and started living in the bush."

I could tell he was trying to sound tough, but I heard the pain behind his words. I laid my hand gently on his arm.

"I'm so sorry. How did you find the cabin?"

I knew how much he loved talking about the cabin, the only thing he showed real pride in. I hoped this question would bring him out of his dark memories.

"I was moving through a town a few hours from here and I had to get some work to pay for supplies, so I walked onto a site where a guy was building a house. He needed a labourer and agreed to pay me cash. As the weeks passed, we started talking a bit. Nothing personal, just about hunting and fishing. This guy knew the area really well, and when I asked if he knew any remote hunting spots he told me about this place. He said he used to come here with his grandfather before they demolished the old dam upriver. Since then, people avoided this area because the river was too full and dangerous to cross. I knew it would be perfect, and I was confident if I waited until the right time of year, when the water was lower, I could find someplace to make my way across. I stuck around with him for a few months, saving all my money and learning everything I could. He had a broken-down truck he wasn't using, so I fixed it up and he gave it to me for next to nothing. The day I left, he put an old rifle in the cab, said he had others. I was so happy. It took me a while, but I found this place eventually and fixed it up."

Jasper always lit up when he talked about his home. He really loved this place.

"You should have seen the cabin! It was all grown over with grass and bushes. There must've been fifty mice and a few huge packrats living in it. It took me over a year to get it into the shape it's in now, but I loved doing it." He beamed with pride as he reminisced.

"So, I have to ask you one more thing."

"What is it?"

"Why take me? You had everything you wanted. Why did you risk it all to take me?"

He sat up and looked me in the eye, his expression very serious.

"That was the thing, Kris. I didn't have everything I wanted. I lived up here for four years by myself. Four long winters. In some ways, it's like I've lived my whole life alone. I considered ending things so many times. People aren't supposed to live alone for years on end. It makes them go crazy."

At this word he diverted his stare. It sent a jolt through me.

"Why didn't you move back to town or live in town part-time? Get an apartment. A job. If I met you in town I would have—"

He jumped up angrily, cutting me off mid-sentence.

"You would have what? Dated me? A stinky, long-haired guy with no education or social skills? Like hell you would have. You would've looked at the ground as you passed me, like every other girl I've ever seen. The only girls attracted to someone like me are skanky ones who're looking for trouble. I wanted a sweet girl. A quiet, sweet girl who would live up here with me and want to take care of me. And I would take care of her. I will never live in town, around people. People are evil and mean. I want to be here, with my wife."

He sat back down as he said this, taking me back on his lap. I hugged him, but my thoughts were jumbled.

"So how did you come up with the idea to kidnap someone?"

He took a deep breath. I was incredibly confused.

"One day I was picking up supplies and saw the picture of a beautiful young girl that caught my eye. She was on a milk carton and she was missing. From that moment on, I was obsessed with the idea. I bought the stuff I would need: the chain, handcuffs, tape. I started hanging around the high school. I camped close to town. That's when I saw you. Your ponytail swinging behind you as you ran up to the lake was the most beautiful thing I'd ever seen."

I felt sick. Remembering that day and the flash of Jasper's coat before my world went dark. The crippling fear when I woke up in his truck. I wondered if I was on a milk carton. It stuck me that sitting on Jasper's lap as he smoothed my hair was twisted. I stood, pretending to stretch. He sensed my conflict.

"Kris, none of this shit matters. Don't you get that? We were meant to be together. I know it was not a pleasant way to find each other, but we did. I love you so much. No man will ever love you like I do. My life was so empty before you. Any girl I've ever met, or been with, is a shadow compared to you. And I know with all my heart that I don't want to live a day without you. I can't."

He knelt at my feet. I put my hands in his hair, as my brain deciphered what he was saying. Would he kill himself if I left? I was trapped again. I loved him. He saved my life. He also tore me from it.

21.

We needed supplies. It had been months since Jasper went into town, and we'd eaten through most of the packaged food. Meat was abundant, as Jasper had recently killed another deer, but I longed for other things. Specifically, chocolate and pizza.

Jasper would laugh when I went on about all the foods I missed. He said he could live on meat and noodles, no problem, but I think he secretly agreed with me. Fall had arrived, and winter would be here before we knew it. I hobbled around with a walking stick Jasper carved for me. I didn't travel far, though, and we never spoke of me returning, or when that would happen. After our conversation in the clearing, a kernel of doubt surfaced about what I was doing and how I felt about Jasper. Most of the time I managed to push it down with everything else I suppressed.

He decided the only way to get in and out of town without being identified would be to hide his truck just outside of city limits and to cut his hair. I was shocked when he said it, but excited too, picturing what he would look like without all that scruff. He boiled water and sharpened his buck knife until it gleamed. We sat on the porch: I was on the chair and he was on the floor at my feet.

"I'm going to start with your hair, and then I'll do your beard. Are you sure you trust me with this sharp knife?"

He looked up at me with a mock sneer, and I kissed his cheek just to make sure he knew I was only teasing him. Then he turned away from me.

"How short do you want it?"

"I don't know, Kris. Whatever you think. Really short, I guess."

He sounded a bit unsure, but we both knew it was necessary.

I started sawing away, chunk by chunk. The blade was sharp, which made it easy, and I tried to keep it as even as I could. It didn't take long before Jasper and the porch were covered in hair. I cut it all until it was about two inches long, then I went around and took another inch off, at his request.

"So, how do I look?"

He stood to brush all the hair off and ended up removing his shirt and shaking it out. Now he stood before me shirtless, running his hand over his head. The cut was chunky, but in a stylish way. His light blue eyes were even more piercing. He was adorable.

"Pretty cute, if I do say so myself." I looked up at him, my heart full.

"Cute? I was looking for manly, sexy, even handsome. Definitely not cute."

He feigned offended. It made him even cuter.

"Sit back down. Let's get that beard off."

He laughed and plopped down, this time facing me. I bent and kissed him, softly at first, but I couldn't stop the electricity that crackled between us. Our lust for each other had been unrelenting since our lips first met. He pulled away and held my face in his hands.

"I would love to strip you down right here, right now, but the water's getting cold."

"I just wanted one more kiss with that beard. I probably won't see it for a while."

I pretended to pout as I grabbed the bar of soap and dipped it in the lukewarm water. Then I worked it into a thick lather on his face. I had never shaved a man before. I was nervous.

"I really wish you had a mirror up here, so you could do this yourself. What if I cut you?"

"I hate mirrors. Besides, you'll probably do a way better job than I would. Don't worry. I trust you."

He looked into my eyes, and I knew he did.

I started by cutting the bulk of the hair away. Then I rinsed the knife and scraped it gently down Jasper's skin. It sounded rough, like sandpaper. We stopped midway so he could sharpen the blade again, and then I finished. I'd left his neck for last, and as I slid the knife over his throat, sweat beaded on my forehead. He kept his face pointed at the sky, appearing completely at ease. With a final scrape, he lowered his head, revealing the young man he really was.

"Jasper! Oh, my God! You look so young. So different."

My mouth gaped open. It was shocking. His face was several shades lighter in the middle, but he was incredibly handsome. He looked like a movie star. He was slightly bothered by my reaction, his hand exploring his new skin.

"Do you like it?"

"Yeah! I mean it's amazing, incredible. You look so sexy!"

At that, he beamed and reached for me. It occurred to me as nervous as I was about his transformation, Jasper was equally nervous for my reaction to it. In a way, he had been hiding behind all that hair, and this was the first time I truly saw him.

He carried me inside and stood me in front of the cot, removing my clothing one piece at a time as he covered me in kisses. His face was foreign and exciting, but his eyes and hands were Jasper, and I begged for more. We made love and skipped dinner, curled together like every minute might be our last.

The next morning, he got dressed and made me a fire. We were both a bit scared about his trip to town, but with his new makeover I was confident no one would recognize him. When he was ready to go, he came and kissed me. We sat and held each other, neither one of us wanting to break free. I knew he would be back soon, and he knew I would be waiting for him. After he left, we both counted the minutes until we would be together again.

I spent the day hobbling from one spot to another, trying to keep my mind on anything but Jasper. It didn't work. The cabin was desolate without him, and when I sat outside I felt vulnerable and afraid. Not having him around made me realize I never wanted to be without him.

I'd been terrified to be alone with my thoughts, but as the

day passed, I grew more resolute than ever that my place was with Jasper. I was meant to be with him. My love for him consumed me. My family would adjust to life without me. They would be all right. I only wished I could let them know I was happy, so their torment of wondering what happened to me would end. Maybe someday. Jasper needed me. I knew he wouldn't make it if I left. With fierce resolution, I made my decision. I would stay.

I wanted to look special when he returned, to show him I'd been thinking about him and to let him know what I had decided. The wildflowers that bloomed so abundantly in the clearing that summer were mostly gone. I found an errant daisy and tucked it behind my ear. With a small piece of twine, I gathered my knotty hair into a loose braid and tied it behind me. I poured water into the pot, warmed it up, and then washed myself the best that I could with a piece of old cloth Jasper had saved for that purpose. I peered into the murky water when I was finished, looking at the broken reflection of the girl in front of me. I didn't recognize her, and I sunk my hand into the cooling water to erase her heavy stare.

I wished I had a pretty little dress to change into. Instead I put on one of Jasper's black T-shirts and belted it with another piece of the twine. My skinny legs poked out the bottom. I hadn't given much thought to my appearance in months. I knew I'd lost weight; my clothes were baggy all over, but he remarked daily how beautiful I was, and I believed him. He was the only mirror I needed.

As dusk fell, I sat on the porch, the sleeping bag wrapped around me to ward off the chill that was encroaching more by the day. I strained my ears to hear any rustling in the trees. It was silent, except for the odd bird calling from its invisible perch. Time passed. I grew anxious. What if the police had arrested him? He said he would never let anyone take him. What if he'd been shot? My nerves got the best of me, and I stood and paced back and forth on the porch, my mind running worst-case scenarios.

When my aching feet became unbearable, I sat on the edge, dangling my bare legs in the cool night air. The dusk had turned to dark, and I strained my eyes to see across the clearing where Jasper would emerge. I could hear the stove was still crackling. I had stoked it all day to make sure it was cozy in the cabin when he returned, wet from the river.

At last, his large frame broke through the trees. He startled me when I first made out his face. I'd forgotten how dramatically different he looked. He was wet from the waist down. His giant pack was bulging, and he had supplies latched to every available bit of space. It must've weighed eighty pounds. How he kept it dry while he crossed the river was a mystery. He grinned from ear to ear, making him look even younger. My heart skipped a beat.

"Jasper! I've been worried sick about you! I thought you got caught or something bad happened!"

I leapt off the porch, ignoring the searing pain in my feet, and ran to him. He dropped his pack and wrapped me tightly in his embrace.

"There's my girl. I missed you so much, Krissy. Wait 'til you see what I brought you!"

His eyes sparkled with a secret he couldn't wait to tell. I wrapped my legs around his waist and planted kisses all over his face. I was safe. I had never had any problem being alone before, but now I knew I didn't want to spend another minute without him.

"Wow! You really did miss me."

He laughed as I almost toppled him over.

He carried me over so I was sitting on the porch. I kept my body coiled around his, and he took my face in his hands and kissed me deeply.

"You look pretty," he mumbled into my ear.

I ran my hands over his face and hair. I couldn't believe he was mine, and he loved me. I was the luckiest girl in the world.

"Come inside and get dry. You must be freezing."

I released my grip on him reluctantly and pulled him by the hand into the cabin.

"Hold on a second. Let me get my pack. I have some great surprises for you."

He walked over to where he'd dropped it. I couldn't believe he could carry it. Once he had slung the pack on his shoulder, he climbed onto the porch and into our warm home.

"I never want to leave here again," he beamed, looking over at me as he dropped the pack next to the table and stripped off his wet clothes.

I perched on the edge of the cot and admired his chiselled body. With his new haircut, he looked like he could be in an ad for Abercrombie & Fitch. I wanted him immediately.

"Get over here. Let me show you how much I missed you."

"Trust me. You can show me all night long. But first I have a few things for you."

He slid on a dry pair of pants and then opened the pack and rummaged through it. On the outside, he'd loaded our regular supplies: rice, pasta, crackers, soup. Everything looked so delicious I was suddenly hungry. With everything fastened on the outside of the pack, I puzzled over what was bulging from the inside.

"Close your eyes and open your hands."

I started to giggle, but I did as I was told. Jasper placed something sleek and hard and triangular in my hands.

"All right! Open them!"

I did. In my hands I held a giant Toblerone bar. The ones you see in the supermarket and wish you could have, but know you would look ridiculous buying.

"Chocolate! Thank you so much. It's amazing!"

My mouth watered. I couldn't wait to rip into the box. I turned it over in my hand, looking for the tab you tear to open it, but Jasper stopped me.

"Wait. You're not done yet. We're just getting started."

He was loving this just as much as I was.

Next, he pulled out a green plastic bag. He handed it over to me looking very proud of himself.

"I hope you like them. I wasn't sure what size you were. The lady helped me. They're just from the thrift shop."

I was stunned as I looked into the bag. It was full of clothes. I pulled out a pair of jeans and immediately brought them to my nose to smell the clean scent. They felt thick and warm and amazing. I was speechless. Next, I pulled out a beautiful royal-blue sweater. It was soft cotton, a bit worn at the elbows, with three brown wooden buttons at the neck. It was the most beautiful thing I had ever seen. I held it to my chest.

"I thought that one would look pretty with your eyes."

He lowered his gaze and blushed, his cheeks now visible without his beard as a mask. I crossed the few feet between us and buried my face in his neck.

"I love them, Jasper. It's the nicest thing anyone has ever done for me. I don't know how to thank you."

I didn't need to find the words. From the tears shining in his eyes, I knew that giving gifts was something new to him. It was filling him with love and pride to be taking care of someone else.

"Keep looking. There are a few shirts, underwear, socks, even a dress."

I stayed motionless, clutching my sweater, so Jasper took over. He pulled out a plaid button-up and navy and white striped T-shirt.

The underwear was lacy and pretty, and I couldn't wait to put a pair on. I had been washing mine almost every day for four months. The last article he held up was the dress. It was emerald-green jersey, low-cut with little flutter sleeves, and it flared out about mid-thigh. It was gorgeous, and tiny.

"I love it."

The thought of him in the store thinking of me and choosing each item so carefully made my heart swell.

"I really don't know what to say. I hope it fits!"

"I know it's not very practical for up here, but the lady told me every girl loves a new dress. You could wear it in the summer."

"Now it's your turn to close your eyes."

I took the dress from him and made sure he wasn't peeking. Then I undid my twine belt and pulled Jasper's T-shirt over my head. I selected the prettiest pair of underwear, red-and-white cherries with red lace edging, and slipped the green dress over my head. It fit perfectly, even a little loose, which made me realize how skinny I had become. I smoothed the soft fabric over my body, feeling like a supermodel.

"Ready. You can open them."

I put my hands on my hips and struck a little pose.

He opened his eyes. His lips curled into a grin as he took me in from head to toe. He shook his head slightly from side to side.

"Krissy, you're stunning. You're the most beautiful girl I've ever seen."

His face grew more serious. I froze.

"You make me happier than I have ever been in my life, and I never want to spend one day without hearing your laugh or tasting your skin."

He stepped towards me and took my hands from my hips. Our eyes locked, the light from the fire glowing a soft orange in the cabin. The intensity of the moment made my skin tingle. I held my breath, unsure what he would do next, but sensing he had more.

Jasper reached in to his pocket and took out a tiny gold ring. It shone like he had plucked a flame right out of the fire. He lowered himself to one knee, and my breath caught in my throat. He held the ring up to me, his blue eyes swimming in tears.

"Krissy, will you make me the happiest man in the whole world? Will you marry me?"

His tears spilled over and made paths down his newly exposed cheeks. His magical words hung in the air around me. They were the words I dreamt of hearing growing up, but nothing prepared me for how they actually sounded coming from the lips of the man I love. I had no doubts.

"Yes! Yes, Jasper. I'll marry you. I'll be your wife."

My knees buckled. My body ached to be closer to him, and the inches between us were too much to bear. He slid the ring onto my finger and put his hand behind my neck, drawing me on top of him. We consumed each other with a shocking ferocity. Our appetites could not be satiated.

That night we lay together, sweaty and dizzy with pleasure and exhaustion. I twirled the ring on my finger with my thumb. I had never been so happy.

22.

We said our vows in the clearing next to the white boulder. I wore my green dress and left my hair down, knotty as it was. The air was cool, and my teeth chattered as I promised to love Jasper and be by his side forever. I never imagined having a wedding without my family. My mom would have organized everything and cried when she saw me. My dad would have been proud walking me down the aisle. Jill, my maid of honour. But that was all impossible, and I tried not to let it distract me.

I had taken the ring off and given it back to him. He said he never wanted to see my finger without it again, slid it back on, and kissed it into place. He promised to always provide for me, to always keep me safe. We shared a long, lingering kiss and walked hand in hand back to the cabin. We were married. Our lives together lay before us, but I could focus on only one day at a time. The future presented me with too many questions I had no idea how to answer.

We had a quiet contentment about us that day as we got back to our regular chores. I organized all of our supplies and tried to make the cabin as homey as possible. Jasper was stocking up the woodpile for the winter. He figured the snow would come in the next few days, and he said he hoped I wouldn't be too bored during the long winter. I told him that was impossible: I would be with my husband.

It started to snow the very next night. Big, soft, beautiful flakes floated through the air like feathers. They rested on the trees and blades of grass, painting everything with a fluffy white brush. I made Jasper go outside with me and we danced around the clearing, catching flakes on our tongues.

It turned out Jasper was right about the snow and the boredom. It snowed through the night, and the next night, and the next three months. It turned bitterly cold, making trips outside brief and uncomfortable. We attempted them only when absolutely necessary. Some days stretched on endlessly, but we were secure and warm in our little cabin. The daylight hours were fleeting, and we had only a few tasks that needed completing every day: keeping the fire stoked, getting water, cooking our meals, going to the bathroom. Once these things were accomplished, we spent the remainder of the day sleeping, making love, and reading.

Jasper picked up several books on his last trip into town, fearing I would have trouble adjusting to winter in the cabin. We took turns reading to each other. When we had read and re-read every book, we made up stories. His stories always involved some fugitive on the run. Mine were of lovers torn apart by uncontrollable circumstances.

I had asked him to find out what day it was when he'd gone to town, but in all the excitement he'd forgotten. At least that's what he told me. He said it didn't bother him not to know; the seasons were the only calendar we needed. It drove me crazy. I wanted to know.

On a particularly quiet day, when the snow was thigh-deep in the clearing, I decided it should be Christmas. I asked Jasper to cut down a little tree, which he did begrudgingly, mumbling something about me going nuts. He came back with the top of an evergreen that stood to my waist. I held it while I sent him back out to make a stand from some firewood. We didn't have anything to decorate it with, so I collected some witch's hair that I used like tinsel and mossy bark that I carved into circles and hung with twine. I had been saving the Toblerone box. I used some of the witch's hair and cut holes in the box and poked twigs through it. My angel.

Jasper busied himself with the wood and the water, but he couldn't hide his amusement with my little project. When the tree was ready, we sang Christmas carols. Jasper pretended he was in some kind of choir, mocking me and making me laugh. I thought of my family and told Jasper about all of our Christmas traditions. He hadn't celebrated Christmas in years and couldn't remember anything special he used to do. After a few days, the tree started to die and Jasper took it out on the porch and chopped it up for firewood. The holidays were over.

The next months passed much the same as the first ones had. Our big excitement was when we could hear the distant rumble of another avalanche cutting a swath down the mountain. Once in a while, the debris would come close to the cabin. Jasper told me a couple of years ago an avalanche came right through the clearing and stacked snow on the porch and against the door. He had been stuck inside for three days, until he dug himself out. I shuddered.

I hadn't been feeling well. Sometimes I flung open the door and gasped for a breath of fresh air. The cabin was becoming stale and musty. I longed for the sensation of sunshine bathing my face in warmth, for the colours of the green grass and the wildflowers when they bloomed. Jasper told me I had cabin fever and that endlessly talking about summer wasn't going to make it come any faster. I could tell he was a little worried about me though. He was more attentive to me and went out of his way to be silly and make me giggle.

Spring was a welcome relief. Each day the sun stuck around a little longer and soon we could spend more time outside than in. The snow in the clearing started to melt, and Jasper made me a trail around the cabin's circumference, digging all the way down to the grass. It was nice not to sink up to my knees in snow with every step. I paced my trail like an animal in the zoo, but at least I got out walking, which helped clear my head.

We bathed by warming water on the stove and using rags to wash our bodies clean, a messy process, so I was happy when the weather improved enough to do it outside on the porch again. I brought out a hot pot of water and a towel just as Jasper finished chopping the wood.

"It's bath day, and by the look of you my timing is perfect."

He glistened in sweat and had already stripped out of his shirt. His beard had filled in, but we were planning to shave him again when he went for supplies, and I secretly looked forward to it.

"You and your bath day. Wasn't it just bath day a few days ago? I've never been so clean in my life. You're not living in the city anymore, you know."

Jasper and I differed in our opinions on how often people should clean themselves. He was coming around to my way of thinking, but I knew that was just because he liked me bathing him so much.

He hopped onto the porch and stripped the rest of his clothes off. The sun shone high in the sky and defined every muscle. I didn't think I would ever tire of looking at his naked body. It made my pulse race every time.

Steam rose like thick smoke from the pot as I dipped the cloth in it and rubbed his dirty skin.

"Ouch!" Jasper jumped and turned to look at me. "Wow, that's hot. Are you trying to melt my skin off?"

"Oh, stop being such a baby. You're fine."

I pressed the cloth into his face to quiet him down and handed him the soap. We had a system that worked pretty well. The person being washed would soap up their body on one side while the washer wiped down the other. I remember being so embarrassed, aware of my naked flesh the first time Jasper bathed me. Now we were so comfortable with each other I barely noticed my nudity.

When I finished with him, he towelled off and put on a clean shirt and the same pants he had been wearing. He never wore underwear. When I asked him why, he said he hadn't had any for a long time, and then he just got used to it. I found it sexy. While the water was still hot, I stripped down and grabbed the soap. I stood perfectly still with my head tilted to the sky and soaked every ray into my skin.

"I better stop feeding you so much. You're getting a little belly."

I opened my eyes to find him staring at my naked body, a half grin lighting up his face.

"What are you talking about? I'm skin and bones!"

I couldn't believe he had said that, and I glanced down at my taut flesh. My hands went to my mid-section. Sure enough, I found a little lump there.

"What the heck is that? Do you think it's from being malnourished or something?"

I rubbed my hands over my little bump, shocked I hadn't noticed it until he pointed it out.

And then it hit me like a linebacker coming full steam. I grabbed the towel and wrapped it around my naked body just before I crumbled on the porch.

"Jasper! What if I'm pregnant?"

The last word stuck in my throat, and my voice broke as I said it. The grin playing on Jasper's lips immediately vanished. His eyes grew wide.

"Pregnant? How could that be? I thought you weren't…you didn't…you know." His voice broke off, but I knew what he was asking.

Ever since I had come to the cabin, I hadn't gotten my period. I always had a weird cycle, and I would miss a few months now and then if my weight got especially low or if I was running harder to train for a race. I figured the initial stress when I got to the cabin and then the severe weight loss from barely eating had made it stop permanently. I wondered what would happen if I did get it, but I figured I would deal with that when it arose. Jasper never mentioned it, but he knew it wasn't a problem since we made love at least once every day.

"I don't know Jasper. I haven't had a period since I came here. I thought that meant I couldn't get pregnant."

My head spun, and I couldn't keep my train of thought. I kept hearing the words "I'm pregnant" echoing in my ears. I was scared. What if this ruined everything we had? Would he even want me anymore? He sat down on the porch with me, a very noticeable two feet away. He looked stunned. I wanted to devour the space between us and bury my face in his neck, but fear paralyzed me.

"Jasper, I think we're overreacting. We don't even know if that's the problem. It could be anything. Maybe I'm just bloated, maybe its malnutrition. I bet you that's what it is. I don't think it's possible to get pregnant without a period."

He stared straight ahead. I wasn't sure if he was listening to me or not. I started to shiver. The sun went behind a cloud, and the world shifted abruptly. Everything changed in those five minutes. I stood and dressed as quickly as I could, noticing now how my pants stretched over my stomach. He stayed motionless. I knew when he acted like this it was best to let him be. I was dying to know what he was thinking.

I brought our bathing supplies into the cabin and was putting them away when he walked in.

"You're right. We don't even know if that's the problem. I'm going to town tomorrow for supplies, so I'll buy one of those test things. Just keep your fingers crossed it's negative."

He turned around and walked back out. For the first time in a long time, I felt alone. And scared.

That night we didn't make love. Jasper sat at the table and read until late. When he came to bed, I reached out for him, craving even the slightest gesture of affection. He turned his back to me and spent the night tossing and turning. The cot seemed to have shrunk to half its size. I cried softly when I knew he had fallen asleep, and I prayed I didn't have a little person growing inside me.

Jasper was more like himself the next morning. He kissed my head before getting out of bed, and it left a heat that radiated throughout my body. Everything would be fine. While he got the pack ready, I made him breakfast and then boiled the water to shave him. We cut his hair and shaved his face as cleanly as possible. He looked thin and drawn, his worry lines evident without his mask. I told him he looked wonderful. When he was ready, I stood on the porch and kissed him goodbye. He was full of trepidation and I tried to reassure him. I spent the day convincing myself it was completely absurd to think I was pregnant. I couldn't be. I tried to remember everything I could about pregnancy from health class. Jasper returned as the sun was setting. I had missed him and wanted his arms around me. He wore an unfamiliar expression when I saw him in the clearing. I opened my mouth to speak when he approached me, but he silenced me with his hand on my lips. He dropped the pack and took my face in his hands, kissing me fiercely. We walked into the cabin and over to the table, kissing and groping and pulling at clothes. I wore the green dress, hoping it would remind him of our wedding day and of how much he loved me.

At the table he took my wrists and turned me roughly, bending me over and pushing my face down. Jasper had always been so sweet with me. Even when things were incredibly passionate, he never hurt me. This was different. He lifted my dress and pulled my underwear down to my knees. I could hear the buckle of his belt as he undid it. I turned my face to look in his eyes, but he forced my head back down on the table with his hand. With his other hand, he grabbed under my hips and thrust himself inside me. I let out a small scream. He held me now by both hips and the table shook as he drove himself deeper into me, completely lost in his world. I bit my lip and tried to brace myself. When he was finished he lay on top of me, breathing heavily. I stayed silent.

Without a word, he stood and buttoned his pants. He walked out the cabin door and came back with the pack slung over one shoulder. I pulled up my underwear and tried to straighten the dress, tears stinging my eyes.

"How was your day? Did you get the wood chopped?"

He asked his question as if he was seeing me for the first time. I was throbbing and sore.

"Um, yeah. I did as much as I could. I really missed you. How was town?"

He busied himself unloading supplies, avoiding my eyes.

"The same. The river was really high, but I found a better spot to cross farther down. Everything's getting more expensive.

I'm going to run out of money soon. My savings are almost completely used up."

He pulled out pasta and crackers and stacked them on the table that I had just been pressed against a few minutes earlier. I stood motionless, unsure of how to gauge these mood swings.

"Could you get a pot of water boiling? I'm starving. I haven't eaten all day."

He gave a quick glance in my direction, but still we didn't connect. Shaken out of my trance, I grabbed the pot and went to fill it at the creek. When I came back, he was lying on the cot, breathing softly. A rectangular white box lay in the middle of the table. I knew what it was and my cheeks reddened as I pictured poor Jasper having to buy it. I ignored it and got his supper ready instead.

His breathing grew heavier, and I could soon tell he was fast asleep. I put the cooked noodles on the edge of the stove to stay warm. The box was alien to me and out of place, and as I stared at it, I wondered how one little box could have so much power. It would determine the course of our future. Just a few short days ago, I thought nothing could affect the love Jasper and I shared. Now I realized love was incredibly fragile. I would do anything to protect it.

All day, I tried to figure out a solution to my problem that didn't involve the end of our relationship. I couldn't come up with anything. If I was pregnant, I could have an abortion. The problem would be seeing a doctor without identification and not being recognized. I didn't know if that was possible. If I had to have the baby, there was no way I could do that here at the cabin. Giving birth meant going into town and checking into the hospital, where I would be identified immediately. If Jasper came with me, he would be arrested. If he didn't, I would probably never see him again. I would have to give the baby up for adoption and then willingly walk away from Mom, Dad and Jill, breaking their hearts all over again. Could I do that?

I knew Jasper agonized over the same dilemma. He handled things differently than I did, and as I watched him sleeping peacefully, looking so young and innocent, I forgave him for everything. I wasn't sure why he had taken me so roughly, but maybe he needed to regain some control. The throbbing had subsided. I loved him so much, and I needed to find a way to make this nightmare go away.

23.

I stood up and stretched. My mom had gone to bed an hour ago. I hadn't seen Jill since our fight. She had always been my best friend, my confidante, and I didn't know if she would ever forgive me. The way her life had unravelled was horrible, and it was my fault. I felt completely alone.

I walked to the fridge and opened it up, appreciating the variety as I reached for the milk. I wished desperately I had someone to call. Someone who would listen. I didn't want to wake up my mom. I still wasn't ready for that conversation. I wondered about my friends from high school. They would be twenty-one now, too, and probably at university living the life I was supposed to live: worried about tests and roommates and boyfriends. My mom had mentioned a few of them contacted her, wondering when they could see me. I had no interest in reconnecting with them right now. I had enough people to explain things to, without adding anyone else. Maybe someday I would be ready.

As I closed the fridge, I noticed a business card taped to the corner. Jake Umbry. Detective. He had scrawled a cell number under his work number. It had twenty-four hours written beside it. Before I knew what I was doing, I picked up the phone and dialled.

Jake answered on the second ring.

"Hello?"

Panic surged through me. What was I thinking? I held the phone away from my ear, about to hang up.

"Hello? Cindy? Is that you?"

"Hi, Jake. No, it's me. Krissy."

"Krissy? Hey! What's going on?"

"Sorry to bug you. I know it's late. Were you sleeping?"

"No. I never sleep. I'm glad you called. I'm just working too late. What are you doing? Are you okay?"

"Yeah. I guess I'm just, feeling a little lonely. My mom and Jill are sleeping. I had this huge fight with Jill, she totally hates me, and I have no friends and no one knows what I'm going through and—"

"Do you want to go for a walk? It's a nice night. It always helps me calm down, so I can sleep."

What had I gotten myself into? I didn't know why, but I wanted to see him.

"Sure. I don't know my address. Should I meet you somewhere?"

"No. I know where you are. I'll meet you downstairs in ten minutes."

He hung up. I stood staring at the phone, confused by my own actions. I loved Jasper. We were married, in our own way. I looked down at my tiny gold ring and gave it one spin on my finger. What was I doing?

Jake was standing on the sidewalk when I walked out the entrance door. He wore jeans, a black jacket with the collar flipped up and a ball cap. He looked good. I was self-conscious in my loose jeans and an old grey sweater, with my hair piled on my head.

"Hi."

"Hey. Good to see you, Krissy."

He walked over and gave me a slightly awkward hug. I was surprised, and I leaned into him, feeling a small flash of guilt. His smell was intoxicating.

"How did you get here so fast?"

He stepped back, but stayed close enough to make me uncomfortable.

"I live about four blocks west of here. And I brought my bike."

I noticed the shiny black motorcycle parked at the curb. It suited him perfectly.

"Oh. Nice."

I took a step back to distance myself and started walking down the street. Jake chuckled and quickly caught up to me. We walked in silence. I kept waiting for him to question me, but he didn't. Blocks passed with only the sound of our feet on the pavement.

"There's my school, or, my old school, I guess. It looks different. I can't believe I missed graduation."

"Well, if it's any consolation, they did a beautiful tribute to you."

"Really? How do you know?"

"I went."

"You did? Why would you go to high-school graduation?"

"To try to find you, of course. That's pretty much all I've been doing for the last four years. That was before the incident occurred with Blake and your father. I watched Blake like a hawk and had a man on him constantly. Your father was so convinced it was him. It was really tragic what happened. Just so you know, I did everything I could to help him get the lowest sentence, and the guards know if anyone touches him they have to answer to me. He's a pretty likeable guy, though. I don't think he needed any help from me. And really, what father wouldn't do the same for his daughter?"

I stopped walking. I was touched by Jake's concern for my dad. He had become such a presence in my family's life while I was gone.

Standing on the street looking at my old school was surreal. I had a strong desire to go back in time, before any of this ever happened, before my family was destroyed. But then I wouldn't have Matty. Or Jasper. It was all too much to handle.

"How will I ever be normal again? I've caused so much pain, and I'm not the same girl that drove out of this parking lot four years ago. I'm a mother, and a wife, and the man I've loved more than anything is gone. I don't know who I am, or where I'm supposed to go from here."

I wiped the tears from my face. I was exhausted. Jake stood in front of me with sadness in his eyes. I wanted him to hug me again, to feel like someone was supporting me, but he didn't.

"I think you've probably had enough for one day. I can't imagine how overwhelming this would feel. I don't know how you're going to survive this, but I know you will. You already have. I guess you just have to find out who the new Krissy Mathews is. Come on, I'll walk you home."

As we moved, he left more distance between us. Why did I care? He was right. I had to be a new me. When I looked into my future, the idea of raising Matty by myself while I waited years for Jasper to be released seemed lonely.

"I'm so sick of talking about me. Please, tell me about you. How is it that you're a detective already? You're so young."

"I'm not that young. I'm twenty-nine."

"Well, I was reading your diplomas and noticed you became a detective four years ago. So you were twenty-five. Isn't that young to be a detective?"

"Yeah. A bit. But I've always known this is exactly what I wanted to do. My dad was a detective for thirty years. I went into the academy straight out of high school and put everything I had into it. Finished first in my class. I put in some years undercover; that was really tough. When I think back on that time, I can relate to how it feels to be confused about your identity. I started to lose who I was completely. And I was lonely as hell. So when a job came up for detective out here, I jumped on it. The chief was an old buddy of my dad's, so I think that helped."

"Wow, your dad must be so proud of you."

"He's dead. Died in the line of duty six years ago."

"Oh, my God. I'm sorry. You must miss him."

"Yeah. My mom couldn't handle it. She lives with her sister now in Florida. I don't see her much. She doesn't like Colorado. Too cold."

"So you're alone too. I mean, unless you have a girlfriend or something. You probably do. Of course you do. Sorry, none of my business."

I wanted to crawl into a crack in the sidewalk. Why did he make me so uncomfortable? I could feel his eyes on me, but I couldn't look up.

"I've been pretty busy the last few years, but I've made some good buddies here. And no, I don't have a girlfriend right now."

He laughed a bit as he said it. Relief ran through me. Why? I needed to get home.

"Sorry I kept you so busy. And I know I've said this, but I am so grateful for all your work. I didn't make it very easy for you."

We walked quietly for a few minutes. I could see my mom's building just up ahead, the streetlights reflecting off Jake's bike. He broke the silence.

"I always wondered if my father had been working your case instead of me, would he have found you? Was I making some rookie mistake that was costing you your life and your family so much pain? I guess I'll never know. I'm just really glad you're back. I've been thinking about you every day for four years. It's a hard habit to break."

We were standing in front of my new home. Jake looked me straight in the eyes as he spoke.

"I'll see you tomorrow at the arraignment, Krissy. Good night."

He jumped on his bike and took off. I stood still, afraid to move.

I crawled into bed and attempted to sleep, but it wouldn't come. My guilt about calling Jake was haunting me. There was a connection between us. The way he looked at me, the longing in his eyes, was unnerving. Even though somewhere deep down it raised a red flag, part of me wanted to be around him. I felt safe around him. He was the only person who knew what had happened up there, who knew all my dirty secrets now, and he still wanted to listen to me. I wondered if it was his passion for the case and his desperation to find me that made it feel so personal. I found him attractive, but who wouldn't? He probably had women lining up to date him. I rubbed my face in my hands and resolved to stop thinking about him. Why did I care if he had any real feelings for me or not? I had to stay focused on my family. Jasper and Matty were everything to me. Finally, sleep came.

24.

Sunlight shone through the flimsy blinds. I got up and got dressed. It was going to be a big day, and my stomach did flip-flops as I walked into the kitchen. I would be meeting Dr. Brown to discuss taking Matty off the ventilator. I couldn't wait to see him awake and talking. I missed his sweet little voice so much. Then I would see Jasper at his arraignment. It might be the last time I see him until I visited him in prison, unless the judge granted him bail, which was highly unlikely. I wondered how he was feeling. Picturing him in that little cell, worried about me, sent another surge of guilt through me. I stopped and leaned against the wall until the feeling passed, and then I left the bedroom.

"Good morning, honey. How are you?"

My mom was whirring around the kitchen. The smell of bacon hit me with a force I wasn't ready for.

"Good, Mom. Thanks. I might just have some tea. I'm feeling a little sick right now."

I pulled out a chair and sat down quickly.

"Oh, Kris, you have to eat! You're skin and bones, and you have such a big day today. You have to have something in your stomach."

"I know you're trying to help, and I really appreciate it. But I feel sick, and food is not what I want. We never ate, well, I'm not used to eating in the morning anyways. I'll have something later."

She stood before me with a heaping plate of food. A family of four couldn't eat that much. I felt bad that she'd cooked it all for me, but I hadn't asked for it.

"Fine. But take a granola bar in your pocket. I'll get you some tea."

She put the plate on the table, probably hoping I would change my mind. I pushed it away.

"I heard you go out pretty late last night. Where were you going?"

Oh, God. I needed my own place.

"Nowhere. Just needed some fresh air. I walked to school."

"You shouldn't be out walking by yourself at night. I know you're an adult, but that doesn't matter. It isn't safe."

"Thanks, Mom. I was fine. I wasn't—I was fine. Let's go. I need to see Matty."

I didn't want to answer any questions about Jake right now, and I knew she'd have a million if I told her he was with me. I hated lying to her, but I simply couldn't talk about it.

The bright hospital whirred with activity. When we arrived at the ICU, the nurse paged Dr. Brown. I waited with Matty, holding his hand and whispering to him. I couldn't wait to pick him up and hold him.

Dr. Brown swept in, and immediately nurses appeared and buzzed around him, passing files and papers.

"Hi, Krissy. Good to see you. How's Matty this morning?"

"Hi, Dr. Brown. Good I hope. You tell me."

He gave me a brief smile while studying what the nurses were giving him. He spoke quickly to one, and then he turned his full attention to me.

"It looks like Matty is very stable and his vitals are strong. We have reduced his medication, and if he does well when the ventilator is out, we'll continue without it. All the people here have a job to do to remove the tube. If we have to put the tube back in for some reason, I'll ask you to step out and let us work because it may appear a bit chaotic for a few minutes. How does that sound?"

"That sounds great."

The words caught in my throat. I wanted my healthy little boy back.

"Okay, team. Let's turn off the vent and remove the tube please."

The nurses and technicians stepped in and began working. I let Matty's hand go and backed up to give them room. My mom appeared at my side and put her arm around me. We waited. Over the shoulders of the healthcare workers, I could hear Dr. Brown giving calm orders, and I could see the tube being pulled out and hear Matty coughing. I wanted to push through everyone and get to him. Minutes passed as machines were hooked up and numbers were called aloud. Finally, Dr. Brown turned to me.

"Little Matty here is a fighter. His numbers look good. Everything has stabilized. It'll take some time before he is fully conscious and can speak. His throat will be sore. We'll have to take him for further tests over the next few days, but things went very well."

I let out a deep breath that I didn't know I was holding. Matty was going to be okay. I couldn't wait to tell Jasper. Dr. Brown gave me a reassuring look and turned to the nurses at Matty's bedside.

"Let's clear out and let this mother get to her son."

The people parted and I could see Matty's sweet face. He looked much more like himself with the tube gone. His eyelids fluttered and he moaned quietly. I planted kisses on his soft blond hair and tiny face. I was so excited to hear him speak soon, but I was dreading the first time he would ask for Jasper. When Matty was first born, I didn't think Jasper would ever warm up to him. It took a while, but over time they became best buddies. Matty was going to want his dad. I didn't know how I would ever make him understand all of this.

We had to leave Matty for a while. My mom had gone to the hospital administrative office to take care of some paperwork before we could go to the arraignment. I sat in a hall chair, stuck in my memories of when Matty first came into my life. In my bag, I had the black book Dr. Bates had given me. I was too afraid to let it out of my sight, especially with Jill at home and still so mad at me. I wasn't ready for anyone to read about my relationship with Jasper. I pulled the book out and opened it to where I had left off the night before. I had to add the missing piece: Matty. Once Matty came into our lives and began to bond with Jasper, I couldn't bear the thought of tearing them apart. It was another reason that leaving wasn't an option. Until it became the only option we had. I took a deep breath and started to write.

25.

The promise of summer lingered in the smell from the wet grass that showed more of itself daily from beneath its winter blanket. A week had gone by since Jasper had returned from town. I put the small, unopened cardboard box back in the pack that hung on the wall, and neither one of us said a word about it. I think we both longed to go back to our carefree existence.

Things had improved but weren't the same. Although Jasper cuddled and kissed me again, we hadn't made love since that night on the table. In an unspoken exchange, we understood he was waiting to see what the box said. Just as silently, I tried to convince him the test results didn't matter.

One morning he got up early and went hunting. I closed my eyes and opened them again to find the sun high in the sky. Lately, I found sleep was a precious commodity I couldn't get enough of. I got up, stretched, and pulled some clothes on. The jeans Jasper bought me that used to require a belt were so snug around my waist I ended up leaving the button undone. The denial I had been shrouding myself in the past week had to end. With a deep breath, I walked to the pack and slid my hand inside, feeling for the smooth cardboard. I pulled it out and scanned the cover, studying the pink plus sign on the box and praying not to see one on my stick.

The urge to pee came over me and I ran out of the cabin and tore the box open. The stick was wrapped in another plastic sleeve and I ripped at that with my teeth as I worked my pants down. I pulled off the plastic cap and peed on the white end. I wasn't sure how much of a sample was needed, but I was pretty confident

I had given enough. I laid the stick on the grass in front of me, chanting softly, "Please be negative. Please be negative."

The plus sign appeared almost instantly. Everything happened so fast I didn't prepare myself for that result. But there I was, squatting in the grass with my pants around my ankles and a very real pink plus sign staring back at me. I was pregnant.

I pulled my pants up and sat on the edge of the porch, the little white stick looking strange and out of place in my hand. I turned it over and over, hoping to see a different result with every rotation. I put my hand on my belly and for the first time thought about the little person growing in there. I wondered if it was a boy or a girl. Would it have Jasper's beautiful eyes? My blond hair? Something I hadn't anticipated tugged on my heart.

Quickly, I realized it didn't matter. Jasper clearly wanted it to be just us, and that's what I wanted too. I condemned any thoughts of a baby and locked them behind the iron wall I had built in my heart and my head. The one my family also lived behind. It was only Jasper and me now. We needed each other, and his happiness was all that mattered to me. He would be home soon, and I'd have to tell him. I didn't think it would come as any surprise, but knowing the reality of our child felt different. I hoped he would understand and that he would still love me. I wanted so desperately for things to go back to how they were. I couldn't believe I might ruin everything. I had to find a way to make this go away without putting him at risk.

I spent the rest of the afternoon running options through my mind and always finding reasons why none of them would work. Even if I could sneak into another town and get an abortion under a different name, I knew they didn't perform them after a certain time. I wasn't sure how far along I was, but since I already had a belly, I figured it must have been several months. I found myself no closer to an epiphany when Jasper came bounding around the corner of the cabin.

"Hey, Kris! Wait until you see the moose I got! It's a monster! We'll have meat for six months at least! It's going to be a ton of work to get it all dried but totally worth it. It took three shots to bring him down. I thought he was going to get away. It was awesome!"

He vibrated with adrenaline, his hands and shirt stained in blood. He had a giant piece of meat strapped onto his pack, and his joy was infectious. I tucked the stick into the pocket of my jeans, not daring the risk of ruining this moment. The old Jasper had come back. He planted a kiss on my forehead and ran off to get water from the creek. When he returned, I had deposited the box with the stick and the plastic sleeve back in the pack that hung on the wall. Another day.

We worked into the night getting all the meat hung. I fried some up, and we ate out on the porch by the light of the moon, Jasper still excited, regaling his story and admiring his kill. That night we made love.

It took us several days to get all the meat cut and ready to be dried. One of the quarters had been chewed on, and Jasper thought wolves had gotten at it, but there was plenty left. Killing the moose brought Jasper back to his joyous state. We both forgot about the box in the pack. I would tell him when the time was right, and things would just find a way of working out. I was doing much better. I wasn't as tired and Jasper's happiness lifted my spirits. Spring had arrived, and we spent our time outside soaking in the sunshine and enjoying each other.

I was very careful only to eat a few bites of food a day, which helped keep my belly from getting any bigger. Being hungry was an easy price to pay for regaining Jasper's love. I wore my bulkiest clothes and made sure he never saw me totally naked or put his hands on my stomach. We were making love daily again, not with the passion we originally had, but it was sweet and gentle and I could see the love in his eyes. It was impossible for him not to notice my belly, but he never mentioned it. Somehow we'd come to a silent agreement to ignore it. I guess the prospect of dealing with it overwhelmed us so much that denial was the easier path. That was enough for me.

Spring turned to summer. Our supplies were holding up well, and Jasper thought we would be fine until fall. He never mentioned how little I was eating. I kept my belly hidden from him. It had grown slightly and become quite hard, but I could still manage to cover it with a loose shirt tucked in or a sweater. The days were long now and we lived very simply. Jasper loved fishing in the creek and would spend hours with his hook tied to a poplar branch, sitting at its edge. He caught a few small fish, more bones than meat, but I praised him endlessly and fried them up for dinner, making a huge production out of it. Truthfully, the smell made me gag. We spent the evening reading to each other from books we had read dozens of times. Something to fill the silence. Jasper promised to get new ones when he went for supplies.

I ignored the thumping in my belly. It was the only reminder that something wasn't right. I started sleeping in my sweater, telling Jasper I had a chill so he wouldn't see the strange protrusions, which were always more prominent at night. I didn't let myself imagine the tiny little limbs flailing inside me.

The nights cooled and the days grew shorter. Jasper decided the time had come to stock up for winter. He left in the morning after starting me a fire. I welcomed the seclusion and spent the day in bed. I awoke midday to rain pelting the window and my fire diminished. The sky looked grey and gloomy, the sun absent. I had no idea how long I had slept, but I didn't want Jasper to come back and find me in bed: no fire, no wood, no water. I pulled myself up and into some clothes. My back screamed in agony, violent spasms causing me to have to sit several times before I could get myself out the door. I accepted that as my punishment for spending the day horizontally.

Outside, I squinted against the freezing droplets. My sweater flapped in the gusty wind and I bunched it tightly around my protruding belly. I held the water bottle in one hand and made my way off the porch and over to the trail that led down to the creek. Suddenly, I had to pee with such force I barely got my pants down as fluid gushed from my body. It was a strange feeling, but I had been noticing changes in my body lately, and figured this was another. I carried on to the creek.

The rain made the dirt bank slick with mud. I held on to the evergreen branches and lowered myself down until a back spasm drove me to my knees and I slid the rest of the way. Barely stopping myself with my hands, the rain fell harder and I became more vulnerable to it on the exposed edge of the creek. When the spasm released, I filled the bottle quickly and looked up the muddy slope that I had just descended. It appeared ominous.

My breath came hard and fast. I tried to slow it down and get control. I got to my feet. My pants were caked in mud, and rainwater cascaded down my face. I reached up and got a good grip on some of the boughs that intruded on the path. I dug my feet into the muddy slope and pulled myself up the bank, the water bottle in one hand and a branch in the other.

I made it to the top just as another spasm gripped me in searing pain. I let out a primal wail, its enormousness muted by the heavy rain, and then I dropped to all fours, unable to find a position that would allow release from this tightening vice. I had never in my life felt pain like this. I wanted Jasper. I wanted my mom. The cool raindrops mixed with my warm tears and fell from my face in rapid succession. I think I moaned, but I was living so inside myself at that moment I couldn't be sure. Finally, the spasm relaxed and I gulped for breath, unaware until this second that I had been holding it through the pain.

The water abandoned, I stood gingerly, afraid any sudden movement might trigger another spasm. I shuffled my feet towards the cabin. Jasper would be disappointed that the fire had gone out, but I was shivering and drenched and afraid I might be dying. I needed to get inside and lie down.

I had barely reached the porch when the next one hit, harder and more severe than the last. I clutched the wet boards between my fingers and squeezed until not a drop of blood remained in my hands. I grunted and moaned into the pain. The pressure increased between my legs, until I thought I might split in two. I had a sudden, violent urge to go to the bathroom. I tried to squat down but ended up on all fours again. I worked my pants down with one hand as the urge threatened to overwhelm me. My body's loss of control terrified me.

I screamed for help. I knew nobody could hear me, but I couldn't suppress the panic. Without warning, the pressure between my legs became a searing burn. That's when I first realized: I was having my baby.

With understanding, came a slight calm. I started to pant like I had seen women do on television. It helped. I didn't know what I would do when the baby came out, but at least I knew what was happening. I wasn't dying. I was giving birth. The excruciating burning was followed by an overpowering urge to push. I did. I was on all fours with my pants around my ankles. I looked down between my legs. A patch of blood was on the ground and a small black lump protruded from me.

I didn't want the baby to fall onto the wet grass, so I removed my sweater and shirt and laid them down on top of the blood. The cold rain stung my naked body. With a final scream and push, the baby slipped from me. A boy. I caught him with one hand and eased him onto the sweater. He was tiny, hardly bigger than my hands. As fast as it came, all the pain disappeared. Nothing but white noise. His little eyes opened and he squinted into the rain. He had yet to take his first breath.

I pushed back onto my knees, scooped him up and wrapped him in the sweater, using the shirt to wipe the goop from his face and body. He scrunched his mouth, but still no cry. I began to panic.

"Come on, baby. Breathe! Come on, little guy. You can do it."

I kept chanting these words over and over as I rubbed his tiny body. The umbilical cord pulsated between us.

I put my pinky finger into his mouth and scooped. Chunks of blood and black stuff poured out of him. With a few sputtering coughs air entered his lungs. His cry was one of the sweetest things my ears had ever heard. I looked into his eyes, and he looked into mine. It was instant love.

I had never seen a newborn baby before, but I was pretty sure they weren't supposed to be this small. He couldn't have weighed more than three pounds. His skin was thin and translucent, and his little bones threatened to poke right through. His eyes bulged out, giving him an almost alien appearance. His chest rose and fell sharply with each breath. I watched him with my heart in my throat, knowing instinctually if I didn't get him help soon, he would die.

I had to cut the umbilical cord, which had now stopped pulsating. I didn't have any scissors, and Jasper had taken the knife with him. I turned to that axe again to release me. I stood, holding him tightly against my chest as he cried softly. He sounded like a baby lamb. My knees wobbled as I moved towards the cutting block, the pants still around my ankles, to where the axe protruded. I had another strong urge to push that buckled me over. Twins? I was afraid to look down. The pain was much less, and with relief I saw something black and strange slip from my body and fall to the ground. I couldn't believe it had come from inside me, but I had no time to dwell on it. I took a deep breath and with my other hand rocked the axe free from the block.

I laid my little boy on the porch and held the cord tightly as I ran it over the blade of the axe. It took a few tries but I severed it. I tied it in a knot and then scooped him back up again. His lips had turned blue. I needed to get him out of the rain. I needed to get him warm.

I yanked my pants up, brought him into the cabin and placed him gently on the cot. His crying became softer, and his breathing was laboured. Panic rose in me. I quickly pulled some clothes on and then cradled him to my chest. At that moment I wanted him to live more than anything in the world.

I expected Jasper any minute, assuming everything had gone the way it normally does. I knew I couldn't get down the mountain and across the river without his help. Each second was painful as I watched the baby struggle for breath, his tiny body shaking. I talked and sang softly to him and willed him to hang on.

Jasper burst through the door, a look of fear in his eyes, and his pack nowhere to be seen.

"Krissy, what happened out there? There's blood all over, your clothes are—"

He froze in the doorway. His face went from red to white as

he registered the sight of me on the cot, something cradled close to me. He walked toward me slowly. I held the baby out slightly from my chest, so he could see his son.

"Wow. It's—"

"A boy. We have a son, Jasper. But I think he's sick. We have to take him to the hospital. Now."

The edge in my voice told him I meant it. Jasper looked from our son to me, with shock and fear on his face. Then he turned and walked out of the cabin. I heard the click of the lock, sealing us in.

26.

I couldn't write anymore. My tears dotted the page, mixing with the black ink. I'd forgotten about Jasper locking me in the cabin with Matty. I think he felt threatened, or he thought I might leave or something, and he went right back into captor mode. Luckily, Matty recovered. Every day he got stronger and ate more. Jasper kept his distance at first, making sure we had food and water, but he kept us in the cabin most of the time. After Matty got better, I didn't mention leaving again, and eventually he relaxed and returned to normal. Very slowly, he warmed up to Matty. He built a crib, and he would hold Matty if I ran out to the bathroom or went to get water. I remembered feeling more than ever that I couldn't go home anymore. How could I show up with a baby? As Matty learned to crawl and eventually walk, Jasper spent more time by his side teaching him things and laughing at his adorable attempts to be just like his dad. Jasper's eyes lit up in a way I had never seen before. He fell in love, and the three of us were happy.

My mom returned and I slipped the book back into my bag. I wanted desperately to see Jasper and hurried her to the car. We snuck into the back of the courtroom right before the arraignment was about to start. Jake sat in the front row next to two men in suits. As the judge announced Jasper's case, Jake turned around and looked right at us. At me. I couldn't decipher his expression. His steely gaze held a hint of something intimate. My stomach flipped. My mom raised her hand in a small wave. Jake nodded his head and turned to face the door that had just opened. An officer came through holding Jasper's arm. His hands were clasped together and hanging limply in front of him. He wore one of those orange suits and was shackled at the feet and wrists. His hair was short and his face clean-shaven, exactly how I used to cut it so he could go to town undetected. He looked young and handsome and scared. I sat up straighter and tried to catch his eye. He stared at the floor and then sat in the chair pulled out for him by one of the officers. My mom clenched my hand. I watched the back of Jasper's head and willed him to turn around. I wanted to lock eyes with him. To let him know: *I'm here*. The judge spoke for a while, mentioning two counts of kidnapping and a long list of other things. Then he asked Jasper how he was going to plead.

"Guilty, Your Honour."

He spoke loudly and clearly. Tears rolled down my cheeks. The judge said Jasper would be held in the federal prison until his trial and that bail was denied. The trial date was set for six months from now. Everyone stood and Jasper shuffled towards the door. I wanted to run to him or call his name. At the door, he finally turned and scanned the courtroom. Our eyes met, and I mouthed the words *Matty's okay. I love you.* I tried to reassure him through my tears. Offer him some sense of hope. I saw only sadness and defeat. He stared at me until the officer behind him pushed him through the door. As it closed, I lowered my gaze to see Jake staring at me. He looked sad too. And something else: Disappointed? Angry? His shoulders hunched and he looked away. He said a brief word to one of the guys in the suits and left the courtroom.

27.

We went to see my dad at the prison several hours drive from town, hidden in the forest at the side of the highway. I'd never taken the exit that curved around and brought us through the trees and directly into high fences and barbed wire. Although there was a main gate, the prison was divided into several large buildings that housed different types of prisoners. My dad was in the medium-security building, which allowed him freedom to be out of his cell during the day. My mom said he had a job and spent a lot of time in the library. I didn't know where Jasper would end up. After his arraignment, I asked a guard what would happen to Jasper next. The guard said new prisoners had to go through a security classification screening and risk assessment that would determine where they would be placed, and part of this process included a review of his mental-health status. I didn't know how well he would do on this part. He was living his worst nightmare. I was terrified he would try to kill himself. I hoped the love he had for Matty and for me was enough to keep him alive.

A long line-up of cars waited to enter the prison grounds. Two guards with rifles stood by the front gate, talking with the driver in each car. They weren't in much of a hurry. My mom and I sat in the front of the car. Jill lounged in the back, her earphones playing music so loudly I had a headache from trying to talk over it. She hadn't said a word the whole way up and had barely spoken since she'd screamed at me for ruining her life. I hoped one day we would be sisters again, or at least some kind of friends.

"Settle in, Kris. This whole process with the guards can take forever. They never let you forget who's in charge, that's for sure."

"I can't believe you've had to do this regularly for four years," I said quietly. "Poor Dad. It's going to be so strange to see him in there."

There was a loud huff from the backseat. I was shocked Jill could actually hear me over her music.

We made our way through the gates and clerks and security checks. An hour later, we were sitting at a table with our visitor badges on, staring at the metal door my dad would walk through any moment. I was nauseated with anticipation and eyed the closest garbage can, just in case.

The room was filled with people waiting to see their loved ones. I watched a small boy ask his mother incessantly when his daddy was coming, pulling on the bottom of her shirt until she bent down and whispered something harshly into his ear. At last, there was a loud buzzer and the sound of the metal doors releasing. Before I could stop myself, I jumped to my feet. An officer came through the door first, a huge man with a scowl on his face, followed by the line of prisoners. My dad was the third man through. It took me a second to recognize him. He was thin, and his hair was completely grey. The last time I saw him it was salt and pepper. His shoulders curved down more than I remember, his head lower. But it was my dad. I squealed and ran to him, causing the guard to sidestep and warn me about something. I wasn't listening. I grabbed my dad and we embraced, and didn't let go, my tears marking his blue jumpsuit.

"Dad! I missed you so much!"

"Kris! It's so good to see you!"

He held me tightly and we stayed that way until the guard came over and said if we didn't sit down the visit would be over. Dad held me at arm's length and gruffly wiped the tears from his face.

"You look beautiful. Skinny, but beautiful. You're all grown up."

He looked over at my mom and they shared a moment. Something only two people who'd been through hell and come out the other side could decipher. He reached out to hug her, kissing the top of her head and wiping her tears too. Jill stood behind us, the odd man out as we shared this special moment. Dad went over and whispered something in her ear, and she smiled. It was the first authentic look of happiness I'd seen on her face since my return. When the grumpy guard cleared his throat, we all took our seats fearing it may be our last warning.

"Well, aren't I the lucky man? My whole family back together. This is amazing, guys."

He started to well up again. I couldn't help staring at him. How was he living here?

"Kris, tell me what it's been like since you've gotten back. How are you adjusting?"

"Pretty good, I guess. You know, it's a bit weird. Mom's trying to feed me every time I turn around. I like the new condo, and it's nice having a bed. Matty got his ventilator taken out yesterday, and he's doing great. He can't talk yet, but we saw him this morning and he opened his eyes and smiled at me. I can't wait for you to meet him, Dad. He's so special."

He was uncomfortable as he shifted in his chair. Jill appeared completely bored. My mom jumped in to fill the space.

"It's true, Mark. He looks just like Krissy when she was a baby, with that golden blond hair, blue eyes, and his cute little nose. Just like Krissy."

He sighed and seemed to take it in. I knew it would be hard for him to accept Matty as his grandson, but what I had to ask him today was going to be much harder.

"Well, I'm looking forward to meeting him. Can you...have you talked about what happened yet?"

"It's been a little hard, so far. I haven't really talked much to anyone, except Jake I guess. And Dr. Bates, the psychologist, made me write a bunch of stuff down. I have another appointment with him tomorrow. It's kind of hard to explain everything."

"Mom said you've been talking with Jake. That's good. You need to take your time and work through all of this. Like I said to you on the phone, I can't imagine what you've been through. But as long as you know you have a family that loves you unconditionally, then I know we'll figure this out. We're here for you whenever you need us. Isn't Jake an amazing guy? He has been such a gift to this family. When I think of the work, the hours he has put in trying to find you and to helping me with my situation. That boy is a saint."

"Yeah. He's pretty dedicated."

"'Dedicated' is an understatement. He's been working his butt off to get me out of here early. And from what I've heard, he's doing everything he can to see this bastard who took you gets the maximum time. I can tell you one thing: there's quite a welcoming committee waiting to meet Jasper Ryan when he comes here. With me at the front of the line, of course."

"Mark! What did I tell you about that! You are forbidden from being a part of any violence in here. You know that! If you so much as yell at him, it can affect your early parole."

"Cindy. Please. I know that. I just want to say "hello." There are plenty of guys anxious to have more than words with our new guest. No one knows what block he'll be in yet. I don't think they're stupid enough to put him in mine."

I couldn't hold it in any longer. I stood up and got the look from the guard again, but I didn't care. I was desperate.

"Dad! No! You can't! Please don't hurt Jasper, or let anyone else hurt him. Please, promise me. Jasper is, well, he saved me, Dad. He saved my life, and he's the father of my son, and I really care about him. I love him. I know you can't understand that, but I do. He treated me nicely while I was up there and, just please don't let him get hurt."

I scanned my family, begging for sympathy. Jill gave me an icy glare.

"What? What are you talking about? Cindy, have you heard this? Did he brainwash her?"

The table rattled as my dad's fist pounded against it. His confused expression polluted with rage.

My mom sat quietly, not knowing what to say.

"Oh yeah, Dad, haven't you heard? Krissy *loves* her kidnapper. She calls him her husband. Check out her ring! She's going to wait until he gets out and then they'll be together. He's going to be your new son-in-law!"

"Jill, enough!

My mom stood up as well.

"If you're going to talk like that, you can wait outside. Krissy has been through a severe trauma and is working through her feelings."

"Jesus, it's always about her! Doesn't it piss you off that while you were drugging yourself into oblivion and Dad was rotting in jail, Krissy was up in her love nest with her *husband,* not even trying to escape?"

With that, Jill spun on her heels and walked out of the visiting room. My mom and I sat back down, and the three of us were stunned into silence for a minute, left with painful, unanswered questions. No one knew what to say next. I spoke.

"I'm so sorry. Dad, I know you can't understand this, and I guess I can't ask you to. But I have to ask you to protect Jasper, because I don't know what else to do. I know you hate him for taking me. I hate that he took me too. But once we were there, up at the cabin, things happened, my life was in danger, and he saved me. Now I need to try and save him. I don't know what will happen in the future, but I do know that he doesn't deserve to be beat up or killed. He had a terrible life before he met me. No one loved him. Please, Dad, promise me you'll protect him."

I reached out and grasped his hand. Begging him to do something that was almost impossible. Protect the man who hurt his daughter. The man who destroyed his family. Tears welled up in his eyes.

"You know I love you more than I could ever try to explain. But what you're asking me is too much. I told you about the nights I lay awake thinking of this man and what he was doing to you. I don't know what really happened up there, and maybe I shouldn't. But I have lived it over and over for the last four years, and I have gone through hell: I was arrested and sentenced, your mom fell apart, Jill self-destructed, you were ripped from us—all because of him. I have promised your mom I will do everything humanly possible to get out of here early, and I will keep that promise."

He looked deeply at my mom, his anguish tangible.

"But the promise you are asking me to make is impossible. Your abductor must deal with the consequences of his actions, as every man does. There's nothing I can do about that."

I was speechless. I understood completely where my dad was coming from. The thought of Jasper being hurt made me feel so helpless, but maybe it wasn't my battle to fight. I didn't know what else I could do. My family had been stretched to its limits. I could not ask them for anything else. My throat was raw and aching from guilt and despair.

The buzzer sounded to end our visit. We reached across the table and hugged, both still reeling from our passionate exchange. My mom held my hand as we walked across the parking lot and over to the car. Jill leaned against the trunk. The smell of smoke lingered in the air. We all got in and rode home in silence. We'd said enough for one day.

28.

I wasn't surprised Dr. Bates was late. I sat in the chair and marvelled again at the complete disarray in his office. I held the black book on my lap. I hadn't opened it since I quit writing, leaving off with my happy family and the good years the three of us had together until Matty got sick. Thinking it all through the night before, I was still surprised I called Jake. Why did I have to go and stir that pot? The way he looked at me at the arraignment, like I hurt him, was terrible. I didn't want to give him the wrong idea. I was committed to Jasper, and I knew it would be a long time until we could be together, but I would have to wait. I had Matty, and soon I would be able to take him home. We could get a little apartment, and I'd have to get a job, but I'd figure something out. I just wanted to feel normal again. Dr. Bates burst through the door just as I opened my book to read the first few words. I closed it quickly.

"Krissy! Hi! It's really great to see you again. Sorry I'm late. I ran out to my car to get this book I brought for you, and after I grabbed it I ended up locking my keys in. I tried a coat hanger, but you can't do that with new cars. Anyways, a tow truck is coming."

I sat and watched him. He was such a disaster, waving his hands around wildly, his hair a tousled mess, but I couldn't help smiling at the way he was always trying to catch up with himself.

"No problem. Maybe you should have a seat? You look a little frazzled."

"Yes, I will. Thank you. So, how are you?"

"I'm not too bad. I saw my dad yesterday. It was so nice

to be with him, but it was really hard leaving him there and—everything."

"That's great. I'm sure he was overjoyed. What was hard about it?"

"Well, you know. It was pretty emotional. My sister stormed out, which wasn't surprising. My dad definitely doesn't understand how I could possibly have any feelings for Jasper, and I guess I don't blame him. I mean, when you really think about it, Jasper completely ruined his life, in a roundabout way."

"Yes. But I would bet that your dad is mainly angry with him for what he did to you, Krissy. Jasper caused you a great deal of pain. Wouldn't you agree?"

"Yeah. I mean yes, at the beginning. But after that we were really happy. I loved him."

I caught the slight raise in Dr. Bates's eyebrow. I'd used the past tense to describe my feelings for Jasper. Why would I do that? I quickly corrected myself.

"I mean, 'Love him.'"

He waited, his silence saying more than any words could.

"How did you do with your writing assignment? How did it feel to write about everything that happened up at the cabin?"

"It was fine. I didn't write about the beginning. I'd just been over the whole thing with Jake, and he couldn't handle hearing about how things changed when Jasper and I fell in love, so I wrote about that. About our relationship and how great he was to me. About having Matty. All that stuff."

"Who's Jake?"

"Jake? Oh, he's the detective who worked on my case. He's gotten to know my family pretty well and spent a lot of time looking for me. He's been great. To my family. They all love him. He helped my dad with his sentence and stuff too. I think he became a little obsessed with the whole thing, to tell you the truth. He doesn't like to fail, that's for sure."

"Why do you think Jake wouldn't be able to handle hearing about your relationship with Jasper?"

"Trust me. He feels the same way as you: that Jasper manipulated me and my feelings aren't real. He seems to take it personally, like I'm his girlfriend or something. It's crazy."

"How does that make you feel? That Jake might be interested in you that way."

"Well, I don't know if he is for sure. He probably isn't. I'm sure he could get any girl he wanted. He's just very protective. But the other night when we went for a walk he looked hurt when I mentioned my feelings for Jasper. There's this energy between us. I don't know. It's hard to explain."

"You went for a walk together? That sounds nice. Did he ask you to go for a walk?"

"No. I called him. But it wasn't like that. I just finished writing everything, and I felt really alone, and I haven't seen any of my friends for years and my mom still doesn't know anything—I'm not sure she *wants* to know anything—and I just wanted to talk. I don't know. I don't know why I called. I feel really guilty about it."

"Why do you feel guilty, Krissy? If Jake is just a friend, then you shouldn't feel guilty about calling him to talk. Do you think Jasper would be upset if he knew?"

"Yes! Of course he would! Jake's mission in life is to put Jasper behind bars for as long as possible. If Jasper knew I was hanging out with him, letting him put ideas in my head, he would feel so betrayed."

"It looks like Jasper is going to be out of the picture for quite some time. You are going to want friends. You need people in your life you can talk to, and Jake might be someone you really connect with. But can I offer a bit of advice?"

"I guess. That's kind of your job, isn't it?"

He laughed at that and contemplated it for a minute.

"Maybe. Sometimes. Sometimes my job is just to listen. But back to Jake: I want you to be careful with any romantic feelings you may develop at this time. You're very vulnerable to connections after what you've been through. I think it's really important to focus on yourself and feeling confident in *you* right now."

"Romantic feelings? Whoa. I didn't say that. I love Jasper. I would never cheat on him. Ever. But you said yourself I need friends to talk to. Right?"

"Definitely. And you can't worry every time you're with someone that you're betraying Jasper. If your feelings for him are real, you shouldn't have anything to worry about. And neither should Jasper."

"Yeah, I guess. Let's not talk about Jake anymore. And you can't tell anyone about this, right? My mom doesn't know. I didn't want to get into it with her."

I was sweating. The seat felt hot beneath me. I looked around anxiously for a window.

"Nothing you say here will ever leave this office. It's between us. I promise. Now, how do you feel about what you wrote in your book? Is it something you would feel comfortable discussing with me?"

"Is it hot in here?"

"Maybe. Are you feeling hot?"

"Dr. Bates, why do you answer everything I say with a question? Do they teach you that at psychology school or something?"

He tried to hide a smirk but wasn't very successful. After a moment, he collected himself and looked me square in the face.

"Yes. The book. Talk."

Even as I walked to the hospital that morning, I wasn't sure what I would do with the book. The thought of burning it, of not having to explain my actions, was very appealing. But after talking with Dr. Bates more, I thought maybe he had a point. I should talk to him, to someone, about how I was feeling. Jasper wasn't going to be there for a long time. I would have to deal with everything on my own, which was daunting at the moment.

"Yes, I think I'd like to talk about it. But I don't want to defend myself the whole time. Don't keep telling me you know why I feel the way I do. Because you don't."

"Great, Krissy. That makes me very happy. And I will try to keep my opinions in check. But that brings me to the reason I will soon have a tow-truck bill to pay. I have something I think you might find helpful."

He handed me a hard-covered book. Several of the pages were dog-eared and the jacket cover was torn and marked, like it may have spent some time as a coaster. The title was *Stockholm Syndrome: Through the Eyes of Survivors*. A pretty girl's face, her eyes closed and lashes brushing her cheeks, was on the cover. I flipped the book over and read the back cover.

In 1973, two men entered a bank in Stockholm, Sweden. For more than five days they held three women and one man hostage. During this time, the prisoners were terrified and abused. They thought they might die at any moment. When police ended the standoff, the hostages shunned their protection. After they were free, several hostages raised money to help defend the criminals. One female hostage became engaged to one of her captors.

A psychological condition that had been recognized for years— where prisoners bond with their captors—was given a lot of publicity and finally a name: Stockholm syndrome. Since then, Stockholm syndrome has been displayed in countless cases when people are threatened and imprisoned, including domestic abuse. Survivors describe the intensity and authenticity of the feelings they developed for their captors, and how they came to be free. Physically and emotionally.

Before I could stop it, a tear fell, splashing the tattered paper. I took a minute before I looked up at Dr. Bates, who was looking at me kindly.

"I promise I'm not trying to tell you what you're feeling, but this may give you another perspective on why some people have the same experience you did. It isn't as abnormal as you may think, and you have to stop beating yourself up. You don't have to validate what you did up at that cabin these last four years, Krissy. You don't have to prove it was real. You survived. You kept your son alive. It can be as simple as that. If nothing else, maybe this book can show you you're not alone."

I couldn't speak. I wanted to argue with him, but the air had been sucked out of me. I could only look at him helplessly.

"Let's stop here for today. I know this is painful. Take a few days. Try to read some of the book. Maybe after that we can talk about what you wrote. I'll see you again on Thursday. Does that sound good?"

I took a long, ragged breath and stood up, covering the girl's face with my sweaty palm, as I turned towards the door.

"Thanks, Dr. Bates. I'll see you Thursday."

"Great. Oh, and Krissy?"

"Yeah?"

"Be gentle with the book. That baby's in mint condition."

29.

I needed to see Matty. I raced down the stairs, anticipating his warm little body in my arms. He had been sleeping when I checked on him before my appointment, but I was hoping he was awake now. Maybe even talking. I turned the corner and walked past the row of chairs that served as the ICU waiting room. There was a single man sitting in one of them. As I got closer, I realized I knew him. It was Jake.

"Jake? What are you doing here?"

"Sorry to surprise you. I tried calling you at your mom's this morning but you were already gone. You need to get a cell phone. Do you have a minute? I really need to talk to you."

He stood up, and as usual he was too close for comfort. I stepped back and sat on the edge of a chair. He sat back down next to me.

"What is it? Is something wrong with Jasper? Or my dad?"

"No. Nothing like that. Your dad's great. He has a parole hearing coming at the end of the year. Hopefully we can make some headway there. If we could just get the witnesses to explain that the whole thing was a complete accident."

"Yeah. That would be great. Is that why you're here? What's going on?"

My pulse was racing. Something about the look on his face, the way he was talking quickly, told me I wasn't going to like what he was about to say.

Just then, three young nurses came through the ICU doors. They glanced at us, and then took a longer look at Jake, staring until they almost tripped over each other and started giggling. He didn't seem to notice.

"I'm here to talk to you about Jasper. I was in the processing room after the arraignment, when we were getting ready to send him to lockup. He gave me something and asked me to give it to you. It's a note. Honestly, I should be putting it into evidence. I was just going to throw it out. You know how I feel about this guy, and I think he's had more than enough time to communicate with you. But I figured you might care what he wanted to say, even if nobody else did, and I thought it might be something about Matty. So, here."

He reached into his pocket and handed me a folded piece of paper. I held it out in front of me, stunned by its existence, not sure what to do next. I didn't want to read it in front of him.

"Thanks, Jake. I know giving this to me was hard for you, but it really means a lot."

"Yeah. You're welcome. I guess I should go. How's Matty doing?"

"Oh, really good, thanks. He has his ventilator out, and he might even talk today. At least that's my hope. The nurses said this morning if he keeps improving, they might move him out of ICU in a few days."

"That's great. Hey, I saw this yesterday and I thought he might like it. I didn't know if he had any toys or anything. If it's too old for him, just leave it in the waiting room or something. It's really no big deal."

Was Jake actually blushing? He reached over to the chair beside him and grabbed his motorcycle helmet. Inside was a small white plastic bag. He handed it to me, looking sheepish. I took it and peeked inside. It was a small black motorcycle, possibly the same kind Jake rode.

"Wow. Thanks. It's really cute. Or cool. I think he'll love it. It's very thoughtful."

I smiled at him, the blush slowly fading from his face. It was a sweet thing to do, and before I could stop myself, I leaned over and planted a kiss on his cheek. The second I lingered there was too long, his delicious smell overwhelming me. I stood up quickly, my books dropping to the floor.

"Here, let me get those."

He bent down and scooped up the books, scanning them both before handing them back to me.

"Thanks. Sorry. I'm such a klutz these days."

"No problem. That one looks good."

He gestured to the cover with the pretty girl. I looked up at him with a flash of defiance.

"Yeah. We'll see."

We stood for a moment in the hallway, our ever-present awkwardness heavy in the air. He cleared his throat.

"Well, good luck with Matty and everything."

His eyes went to the crumpled paper in my hand.

"Thanks. And thanks again for the motorcycle. It's really great."

I stepped past him and in front of the large automatic doors that swooshed open. He stood where he was, watching me go inside. I clutched the motorcycle in one hand and the note in the other as I made my way to Matty.

30.

I was desperate to rip open that note and read it. Desperate. But when I got to Matty's bed, he was alert. His eyes were open, and he recognized me when I walked over. For the moment, I forgot all about the note. The nurses were busy taking vitals and checking tubes. I sat next to Matty and we looked into each other's eyes. He tried to talk, to say "Mama." It came out in a whisper, but that was enough. He was going to be healthy and relief flooded through me.

I spent the next few hours holding Matty's hand and singing silly songs to him, trying to get him to drink some juice. His blue eyes were bright again, and his blond hair wild. I kissed his little fingers and the palms of his hands. His touch warmed and relaxed me. Something I hadn't felt in a long time.

I pulled the black motorcycle out of the bag and showed it to him. He was fascinated. Jasper had picked up a couple of little toys in town when he'd gone for supplies, but they were really just baby toys. Nothing like the shiny bike. I let him hold it for a while and then put it back in the bag and took it with me. I didn't want him to swallow any of the little pieces. It wasn't designed for a child Matty's age, but the fact that Jake thought about him and went to a store to buy it really touched my heart. When Matty fell asleep, I said goodbye to the nurses, who were becoming quite familiar to me. Rhonda, always efficient, with her thick glasses and prominent scowl, smiled at me today. I watched her go to Matty's bed and coo at him as I stepped through the doors. My son was in good hands.

The note sat folded in my pocket, and I rubbed it gently

between my thumb and forefinger, fearing it might disappear if I let it go. I walked out the main hospital entrance and let the fresh air flood my lungs. Near the front entrance, I found a bench and sat down. The spring was turning to summer, and the warm breeze and smells from the flower garden behind me were wonderful. I put my face to the sky and let the sun soak in for a moment, preparing myself for what I would read. Words to get me through the years until Jasper and I could be together, I hoped. The thought of raising Matty alone in a tiny apartment without anyone to love me was terrifying. Maybe the note would reassure me that what we had was real, not some syndrome or survival strategy my brain created. I sat the book with the girl's face down beside me. Something about the words on the back had struck a chord, and it scared me.

Slowly, I removed the white, lined paper from my pocket and unfolded it. The letters were blocky. All capitals. The writing was unfamiliar, and I realized I'd never seen Jasper's handwriting before. There were only three sentences.

Don't wait for me.
Don't visit me.
Get on with your life.

As if I'd been kicked in the stomach, I leaned over and gasped for air. The paper fluttered to the ground. This couldn't be real. After everything we'd been through together, how could he hurt me like this? I remembered what he'd said to me in the cell the last time I'd actually spoken with him. It was something just like this. But how could he be so cold? No "I love you but…." Nothing. It was brutal. Who was this man I had spent endless hours obsessing about? This man I had forsaken everything for? Rage consumed me.

And then it hit me. Of course he could do this. He'd hurt me before: Taking me and chaining me up and not caring when I pleaded for him to let me go. Locking me in the cabin after I had Matty. Matty almost died up there, and in the very end he did the right thing, but it was his love for Matty, not for me, that led him here. Jasper was not a good man. He was sick. And reading this note, seeing how he could cast me off like this after he took everything from me, made it sink in. I was sick, too. But I could get better. With Matty and my family and Dr. Bates and maybe even Jake. I would get better and put this whole terrible ordeal behind me. I was a fool for believing what Jasper and I had was real love. He'd manipulated me into trusting him, into making me think he loved me more than my family did. That he needed me more. And that I needed him. I would have to live with that shame, and some day I'd have to explain it all to Matty. But I would never regret having him. Matty was my silver lining, the only thing that could bring Jasper to his senses. For a brief moment, anyways. I would make sure Matty knew that.

I picked up the paper, refolded it, and put it back in my pocket. I wanted it to be my reminder that Jasper didn't want me. Maybe he thought he was doing it for my own good, but it didn't matter. How could you feel something so strongly for someone, and then in a flash it could be gone? I was realizing I had a lot to learn about myself, and reading Dr. Bates's tattered book looked like the best place to start. I admired the girl on the cover once more. Her fragile beauty was haunting. I started to read.

31.

That night, I sat down with my mom. It was time. I'd read about half of the Stockholm syndrome book, sitting on that bench in the sunshine. Reading about the other women and what they went through was an awakening for me. I wasn't alone. Other women had been through similar situations, had similar feelings, and once they were safely home, they gained perspective that was impossible to grasp while they were with their kidnappers. They were victims. I was a victim.

I asked Jill to join us, to hear my story, but she mumbled something about friends and took off. I hoped one day we would repair our relationship, but she needed time.

I walked my mom through that first horrible week: the fear that Jasper might kill me at any moment, and then the hope that I might get free. Her tears flowed, but she let me speak. When I told her of my escape attempt, how close I was to death, she was horrified. As I retold the story, I started to see the cracks. If Jasper had been a good man, he would have brought help. I was so close to death when he returned that it could have gone either way. The antibiotics could have been unsuccessful. If I had died, I think he would have buried me and moved on, and maybe tried again with another young girl. The thought made my stomach turn.

When we got to the part where Jasper and I became a couple, I stopped. I told her if she wanted to know, it was all in the journal Dr. Bates gave me. I welcomed her to read it. She declined. That was enough. I didn't tell her about the note. I figured that was between Jasper and me. I wondered if Jake had read it, but I realized it didn't matter. I would do exactly what it said. I would move on.

My mom and I talked long into the night about a plan for my future. I wanted my own place. A place for Matty and me. As much as I loved my mom, I needed to remove myself from her watchful eye and make my own decisions. She said she totally understood, and I was welcome to use my university fund to get myself back on my feet. I couldn't believe she kept it, even when they'd clearly needed the money. We cried and hugged, and I went to bed exhausted.

The next day Matty was moved to a regular unit. He had his own room, and I could stay with him as long as I wanted, not like the strict ICU visiting hours. He grew stronger by the minute, talking and eating Jell-O and popsicles to his heart's content. Everything fascinated him, and it was amazing to see the world through his eyes. The way the hospital bed moved up and down automatically, and the toilet flushed loudly, even the magic of turning the faucet on and off entertained him endlessly. I hadn't exposed him to a television yet but could only imagine his excitement at seeing his first cartoon. We were both adjusting to our new surroundings.

Dr. Brown checked on him and said he had progressed quickly and would likely fully recover from the tetanus. He would be a regular little boy. Because he had been born prematurely and so small, his lungs were showing signs of damage. He would need to be monitored for asthma and potentially have an inhaler. After being so close to losing him, these were things we could deal with. He had said "Dad" several times over the last few days, his little brow furrowing up into a worried question. Each time, I explained Daddy had gone away, and we wouldn't see him for a while. A sad shadow would pass his face, but then I could usually distract him with a toy or a snack. When he was old enough, I would have to explain it all to him. For now, I wondered if time was merciful enough to let him forget and grant him a clean slate. What a gift it would be.

Matty was thrilled with the motorbike from Jake. He rolled it all over his bed and eventually fell asleep with it clutched tightly in his little hand. While he slept, I finished the book from Dr.

Bates. There were four different stories: two were kidnapping victims and two were domestic-abuse victims. I wanted to thank them all. The bravery they showed in sharing their stories changed everything. I tore out a page from my journal and made a list:

1. Write letters to the Stockholm syndrome women.

2. Get an apartment.

3. Call the Single Mothers Society and sign up for a sponsor (pamphlet from Mom).

4. Get a cell phone.

I decided to take Jake's advice, and there was only one number I could think of programming into my new phone: Jake's. I couldn't get him out of my mind in the last twenty-four hours. I was leery of jumping into any kind of relationship right now, and I knew that I wasn't ready for anything sexual. That might take time. But I wanted him around. His presence made my skin tingle and my palms sweat in the best kind of way. And I loved the way he looked at me.

I pried the motorbike from Matty's tiny hand. He didn't budge. I kissed his sweet face and told the nurse at the desk I'd be back later that night. I had things to do.

PART 2

32.

"Dr. Bates, are you ever going to clean up this office? It's a complete disaster. You know you can't find anything in here, and to tell you the truth, it smells."

I stood in the middle of his office, my new place of employment for the past three months. I had been home a total of six. During that time, I'd checked everything off my list, and then some. I had a job, a cute but tiny apartment a couple blocks away from my mom's, a support system including a few friends from high school I'd reconnected with, and most importantly, some clarity. Dr. Bates and I had worked extensively through what had happened at the cabin. I saw my time there, and what I had to do to stay alive, through new eyes. Dr. Bates was brilliant and patient, and he always made me laugh. I didn't know how I could have survived my re-entry into the world without him. As a boss, he was hopelessly disorganized. And wonderful.

"What? It smells? First of all, you know this is my unique organizational system. Do I eventually find everything?"

"Well, yeah, eventually, but—"

"Second of all, if you don't like it, you have my blessing to clean it up. Except the desk. Never the desk. And that grey plant in the corner, that was from my ex-girlfriend. If she ever stops by, I want her to know I still have it. I think I still like her."

"That plant is so dead it's already charcoal! And it's grey because it has an inch of dust on it! I'm not cleaning this place. My job is to answer your calls, make believable excuses when you're late, which is always, and enter your billing. I did not take the job of maid, although I think you really need one."

"Fine, I'll clean it myself. Tonight. Please send in my next patient. And tell her why I'm late."

"I will, but then I have to go. I have a date, and don't say anything! I'm being careful, taking it slowly. Linda's coming in for the afternoon. I'll see you tomorrow. And I look forward to seeing your sparkling clean office."

"No comment on the date. We'll discuss it at our next session. As for the office, you should be excited. Does it really smell in here?"

"Yes."

I walked out of the office and told the patient in the waiting room that the doctor would see her now.

Dr. Bates hired me when his secretary, Linda, was ready to kill him and wanted to downgrade to part-time, which was perfect for me. Now I work the mornings until one, and Linda takes the afternoons. Matty goes to daycare and he loves it. He has so much fun with the toys and the other kids. Sometimes I have to peel his hands from the door to get him out of there. Dr. Bates and I are working with the lawyer to prepare for Jasper's trial, which is coming up in a few weeks. Dr. Bates is going to be an expert witness, testifying about Stockholm syndrome and explaining how it can be possible to be in love with someone who is hurting you so much. He is testifying for the prosecution, Team Krissy. I don't really like the idea of teams, but I just go along with it. I want people to know there's a reason I acted the way I did, why I didn't take every opportunity to escape. I was trying to survive.

Jasper's defense team will try to push the fact that I stayed at the cabin voluntarily for most of the time I was missing. Jake had to hand over my statement to them, which they are using to build their case. Although there was no debate over the kidnapping charge, they will argue Jasper never actually raped me, that our sex was always consensual, and that after the first week I was never confined against my will. That's where Dr. Bates will testify I wasn't in my right mind. Jake said Jasper isn't co-operating and won't talk to his lawyers.

A few weeks after getting the note from Jasper, I became very angry. What gave him the right to decide the last things we said to each other? I talked to Dr. Bates about it and he thought I should see Jasper, if I was angry, to get some closure. When I called the prison to inquire about visiting him, they said if I wasn't on his visitor list then he had a right to refuse, but they would put the request through. Also, he was in solitary confinement and barred from having any visitors for the moment. I asked why, but the guard just mumbled something and hung up. When I went to visit my dad, I always asked if he'd seen or heard anything about Jasper, but he said no, other than the fact that he had been in solitary confinement almost every day since he'd gotten to prison, for one offence or another. That didn't sound like the Jasper I knew. I figured once he got to jail he would keep to himself and put his head down. He was in another cellblock, so my dad didn't have any more detail than that. I wasn't sure if he was telling me everything or not, but I didn't want to push it.

I wrote Jasper a letter. I told him that I missed him, and I hoped he was going to be okay. It was the truth. Even though I had come to realize what an unhealthy, controlled relationship we had, Jasper was my first love. I told Jasper all about Matty, about what he was saying and doing and how much he loved daycare. I included a picture of him. In the picture, Matty's clutching his favourite toy, the motorcycle from Jake, but I figured Jasper would never know where it came from. Nothing could change that Jasper was Matty's dad, and some day I would explain everything to Matty. I didn't know how I would feel about them having some kind of relationship, but I'd have years to sort that out. Lastly, I told him I didn't appreciate his note. He should have given me the opportunity to talk to him in person and at least say good-bye. I sent the letter knowing he wouldn't receive it until he was back in a regular cell. I didn't know when that would be, but sending it gave me some peace of mind. It was time to concentrate on my own life.

As the trial date grew closer, I became anxious about seeing Jasper. I would be testifying against him. I was going to tell the truth: the good and the bad. I didn't hate him. I hated that he took me, but I wouldn't change it. I knew it sounded crazy, but I had Matty, and he was everything to me. Matty had stopped asking me about Daddy. I'm not sure if he'd lost parts of his memory because of his tetanus and resulting coma, or if time was making him forget. Dr. Brown said there is no way to tell. Either way, I see it as a blessing. He's happy, and that's all that matters.

Once Dr. Bates's next patient was settled in his office, I returned to reception to see Linda was already seated at the desk, placing things where she wanted them. She liked things a certain way, and so did I, but we were both learning to compromise. I reached behind her to grab my purse and jacket from the cubby behind the desk.

"Wow, you look beautiful today, Krissy. Have a great time."

"Thanks, Linda. And Dr. Bates promised to clean his office tonight. Make sure you hold him to it."

"Oh, honey. I wouldn't hold your breath for that one. He's got hockey practice at six and patients booked until five forty-five. He'll be running out of here with his hair on fire."

"Well, people are going to have to start wearing a mask in there. It's gross."

"Tell me about it. Bye, dear."

I headed out the door and down the steps. I pulled my phone from my purse as I walked, anxious to see if words appeared on the screen. There was a message: *Hey, Baby. Can't wait to see you. Miss you like crazy. Hurry up!*

I had to stop myself from running as a big grin broke out on my face. I was dating Jake, although, not officially. We were keeping it a secret until after the trial. Jake was worried about the fallout from his colleagues and even from the judge because he was so involved in my case. It made sense to keep it quiet. The press had finally stopped hounding me when they realized I wasn't going to say anything about my kidnapping. I didn't want to give them any reason to get interested in me all over again. Jake and I both agreed once the trial was over the interest in me would fade, and we could actually be a real couple.

I burst out the back door of the hospital into the quiet alley and chilly air. The first snowfall was imminent. I pulled my jacket up around my face and scanned the road. The black truck was parked where it always was. Jake leaned on the passenger door, his smoky expression turning into a smile when he saw me. "Don't run," I told myself as I tried to play it cool. As soon as I got within five feet of him it was impossible. I leapt into his outstretched arms and kissed his neck, his smell always made my knees weak. He held me in his tight embrace, kissing the top of my head.

"There you are. God, I missed my girl. That was a long morning."

I stepped back to look into his handsome face.

"I just saw you last night. How could you miss me that much?"

"Because I've been thinking about you every second since then. That can make time go pretty slowly."

"Oh, come on. You're ridiculous. So, where are you taking me for lunch? It's a special day you know."

"What do you mean a special day? What day is it? Is it your birthday?"

"Come on, Jake, you know when my birthday is. It's our one-month anniversary. Did you forget?"

"Is it? Wow, totally slipped past me."

As he spoke, he pulled a tiny box from his chest pocket. It was a beautiful robin's egg blue with a white ribbon.

"What's that? You got me a present? I didn't get you anything."

"It's just a little something. Besides, you've given me everything. I've never been so happy, Kris. I mean that."

He kissed me softly on the lips. His eyes told me he meant every word.

"I'm really happy too. I didn't think happiness was going to be a possibility for me after everything. You're like my knight in shining armour or something cheesy like that."

"Wow, that's a lot of pressure. I've always wanted to be a knight though. Just open your present."

I pulled the delicate white ribbon and opened the box. Inside was a beautiful silver necklace with a pale blue pendant. The color reminded me of the sky on a clear day at the cabin, but I didn't mention that to Jake. It had markings on it that I'd never seen before.

"Jake, I love it! It's stunning. What does it mean?"

"It's Sanskrit. The lady at the store said it means "protection for your heart." Just so you know, I'm making it my personal mission. I never want you to be hurt again, Krissy. You've had too much of it in your life. From now on, you deserve to be happy."

He took the necklace from me and put it on. The blue pendant sat right in the hollow of my throat. I couldn't stop touching it.

"It's looks amazing on you. Come on, let's go eat."

He opened the door and helped me inside the car.

33.

It was the first day of Jasper's trial. I was shaking. I sat in the courtroom, my mom on one side and Jill on the other. My lawyer wasn't sure if I would testify today or tomorrow. It depended on the length of opening statements and other details I didn't really understand. I bought a new black dress for the trial. It was structured and knee-length. It clung to my body and made me feel like a strong woman, not the little girl I was when all of this had started. Every time a door opened I jumped, thinking it was Jasper. I hadn't seen him since his arraignment six months ago. My stomach churned with anticipation.

Jake sat in the front row next to the lawyer. He had a huge part in the case and was set to testify as well. He wouldn't be satisfied unless Jasper got the maximum sentence. Although I didn't feel love for Jasper anymore, I did have a softness for him that I didn't think would ever fade. We had spent incredibly intimate moments together. I knew him better than anyone, where he'd come from and what a terrible childhood he suffered. He was sick, he needed help, but he wasn't evil. I didn't say any of this to Jake. We rarely spoke of Jasper.

Jake and I spent as much time together as possible, but we were taking it slowly, at least from a physical standpoint. He had never spent the night. I always sent him home, sometimes just before the sun came up, but I wasn't ready to cross that line yet. I'd never been to his place, which was strange. He always made excuses that his apartment was a disaster, which I found that hard to believe since his work desk was always immaculate, but I let it slide. I'm sure it was like a man cave in there. Maybe he had posters of half-naked women or something. It didn't matter. I loved him, and although neither of us had said the words yet, I knew he loved me too. The passion between us was explosive. I often fantasized about him tearing off my clothes and making love to me. I didn't know what I was waiting for. Maybe for the trial to be over, to truly be finished with Jasper and ready to give myself completely to Jake.

It was amazing to watch him with Matty. He had taken on a huge role in Matty's life and my son was never more than a few feet from Jake whenever he came over. After supper, the two of them would play on the floor, racing cars or doing Lego until Matty's eyes would start to close. Then Jake would bring him to me for a kiss and take him to bed. I would usually have to go in there and wake Jake up after half an hour, the two of them cuddled up, a book still open on Jake's chest. He was a natural father and more than I could ever dream for Matty.

The clunk of the big metal door at the front signalled Jasper's entrance. My breath caught in my throat. An officer came through, followed by Jasper and another officer close behind. He wore a dark grey suit, which looked completely strange on him. He was clean-shaven and thin, as thin as I had ever seen him. His cheekbones jutted from his face, his eyes appeared hollow, casting shadows on him. He looked handsome, as he always did, but like a ghost. The life had completely gone out of him. He walked toward the chairs at the front and raised his head just high enough that our eyes met. I wanted to go to him. Take him in my arms. Not like a lover but like a dying friend. The tears fell from my eyes, and he raised his eyebrows slightly before an officer pushed him roughly into the chair. He had been broken.

My mom passed me a tissue, and I wiped my face, trying to recover my composure. Jake's eyes burned into me but I couldn't look over at him. I didn't want to acknowledge the emotion Jasper could still evoke in me or see any hurt in Jake's expression.

Throughout the morning, we listened to the lawyers state their cases. The defense spoke of Jasper as a lonely boy who grew up without love, driven to this desperate act due to mental illness brought on by his years of isolation. He needed counselling, they argued, not prison. The prosecution fired back, pointing me out to the jury several times and reminding them that when I was taken, I was not the woman they saw before them now but a young, defenseless child. I was the victim of abuse of every kind imaginable: mental, physical, and sexual. My only hope for survival lay in playing along with the accused and his sick plan, becoming his sexual slave and eventually the mother of his child. If the child had not been on death's door and the accused had not shown an ounce of mercy, I would still be up in the mountains, possibly for the rest of my life. My face was scarlet as the lawyer spoke and people turned to look. Jasper continued to stare straight ahead.

The prosecution presented their case first. Dr. Bates took the stand. He looked very put together in his navy suit and crisp white shirt. His hair gave him away with its signature dampness, indicating he had probably been in the shower fifteen minutes before coming into the courtroom. I could just hear Linda now, complaining about how he had run out of the office late.

He spoke eloquently and used words I'd never heard from his lips before, showing why he was well respected in his field. He explained how when a victim is shown some small kindness by the abuser, even though it is to the abuser's benefit, the victim interprets that kindness as a positive trait of the captor or controller. When Jasper saved me from the river, I definitely felt a shift in my feelings for him. My isolation from other perspectives only further solidified my bond to Jasper. Dr. Bates spoke of more events that supplemented my situation, like sympathy for Jasper over his abusive childhood and something called "cognitive dissonance," which explains why people change their opinions and beliefs to support situations they find themselves in that do not appear to be healthy or positive.

I was proud of him and overwhelmed by his humility. He kept this level of professionalism so well hidden. When he mentioned other cases similar to mine, the girls in the book I had written to thank, I welled up. Knowing they too had to sit through trials, trying to explain the inexplicable to most people, gave me a twinge of comfort.

When it was the defense lawyers' turn to question Dr. Bates, they really drilled into him. What proof is there that Stockholm syndrome is in fact what I had? Was it not possible that Jasper and I were really in love? They quoted several lines from my statement: how I felt when Jasper saved me from the river, how I was the one who said I should stay until my legs were better. I noticed Jasper sit up a little straighter as these questions were asked. I remember rationalizing in my head how everyone would be fine without me. That I was better off with Jasper, who needed me. When I look back it seems completely crazy, but at the time it made sense to me. They were making very valid points, and I was filled with dread at having to explain myself. I didn't know how. At the time, those decisions felt right. Now, I see that choosing a life where I would never see my family or be a part of society again is not something I would want if I were in my right mind. But how would I explain that?

Dr. Bates handled the questions like the professional he was. He kept explaining to the lawyers that my actions actually fell perfectly in line with classic Stockholm tendencies. Throughout his testimony, the lawyers continued to interrupt him and demanded he only answer the questions with a "yes" or "no," but Dr. Bates used every opportunity he had to explain how common, and even expected, my feelings were given the situation I had been thrust into.

They let Dr. Bates go and recessed for lunch. I could think of only one thing, and after they led Jasper from the room and we were free to go, I rushed over to Jake.

"Can I talk to you in the hall for a second?"

"Hi, baby. How are you holding up?"

"Yeah, I guess. I just really need to talk to you."

Jake said something to the lawyer and then led me out of the courtroom. Every set of eyes watched us leave. He took me down the hall and into a room. It was empty except for a few chairs strewn about, like some kind of last-minute strategy room.

As soon as we stepped inside, he pulled me to him and held me tightly.

"This must be awful, Kris. It must be so hard to be in the same room with that guy again. I can barely control myself."

I gently pushed him away and looked into his face.

"Listen. I know you're not going to understand this, and I don't know how to explain it to you, but I want to see Jasper. I need to talk to him. Can you get me in to see him? Please?"

"You want to see him? What do you mean? What could you possibly have to say to him? He can only hurt you. You have a new life now. With me."

"I know, Jake. Believe me. I think that's why I need to see him. I need to have that closure to be able to move on with you. I tried to go see him in prison, months ago, but he won't put me on the list or something, so I couldn't. My relationship with you is so important to me, and seeing Jasper brought up all these feelings. I just need to talk to him. I don't even know what I'm going to say. 'Good-bye.' 'I don't hate you.' I don't know, something to release him. For him, but mostly for me. For us."

Jake looked hurt. I knew it was risky, and I despised asking him for this. I didn't want to do anything to jeopardize what we had. Jake had been so wonderful to me, and I knew he could be an amazing father to Matty. But I had a desperate need to talk to Jasper one last time, and this might be my last opportunity. Once he was back in prison, I couldn't reach him, and if Jake had his way, it could be at least ten years before he'd be out. I needed to do it now.

"Krissy, I really feel like it's a bad idea. And witnesses are not supposed to talk to the accused during a trial. I could lose my job. I don't know what you want to get out of this."

I reached up and touched his face and planted a soft kiss on his lips.

"A fresh start."

34.

Jake left me in the little room. He told me he would see if he could cash in some favours, but he wasn't making any promises. Seconds passed like hours. I really didn't know what I wanted to say to Jasper, but I knew I had to see him.

The door creaked open and Jasper walked in, followed closely by Jake. It was strange to see the two of them together: my past and my future. Jasper looked surprised, his eyes a little wider than normal. When he saw me his faced relaxed slightly, relieved but still unsure what was about to happen. What I might say. Jake looked angry.

"Sit down in that chair. Don't even think about moving."

Jake kicked a chair out and Jasper sat in it, laying his cuffed hands on his lap. Then Jake came over to me, taking my hands in his.

"Kris, you have five minutes. Even that's too long. If we get busted doing this…Just so you know, I'm doing it for you. For our future. I hope it's worth it."

Jake took a step toward the door and then turned and faced Jasper.

"If I hear that chair move I won't hesitate. Got it?"

As he said it, his hand glanced over the gun on his belt. Jasper remained silent, staring up at Jake with indifference.

"Krissy, if you need me, I'm three steps away."

He gave me a final look, like even he couldn't believe he was doing this, shook his head slightly and then stepped out of the room. I could see the back of his head through the small window in the door. I was amazed that he would actually do this. He was risking everything for me, and I loved him for it.

And then Jasper and I were alone. We looked at each other for a few seconds. He had so much pain in his eyes. I wondered what kind of hell he'd been through in the last six months. I stood before him, unable to sit.

"Jasper, I really need to talk to you. You didn't answer my letter, so you may not have anything else to say, but I do. How have you been?"

His eyes, so familiar, pooled with tears. I had no idea what he was thinking. All I knew was that he was incredibly unhappy. I had an urge to reach out to touch him but suppressed it. He cleared his throat.

"I've been fine, Kris. How about you? Is he taking good care of you?"

His question shocked me. Why did I feel guilty?

"I've been okay. I've been going to counselling and working through everything that happened. Dr. Bates, the doctor who was speaking this morning, he's my doctor. He's a really nice guy. I actually work for him part-time."

My palms were sweating. I was rambling. Jasper's eyes on me, being close to him again, was unnerving.

"That's great. You're doing really well. I'm proud of you. You look beautiful, as always. How's Matty?"

His voice cracked as he spoke his son's name. Once he'd gotten used to having Matty around, Jasper developed a fierce love for him, just as I had. It was a love that brought him to this horrible place. I knew it was the way things should be, that Matty was exactly where he belonged, but seeing Jasper's heart break at the thought of Matty was excruciating.

"He's so amazing, Jasper. He's fully recovered. Now he's growing like a weed. I swear he eats more than me. He goes to daycare in the morning and loves it. He's totally into Lego and trucks and, well, this was all in my letter. Did you like the picture?"

"Kris, I don't know what you're talking about. I never got a letter from you."

"What do you mean? I sent you a letter months ago, after I got your note. Which I thought was pretty shitty, by the way. I know you probably did it for my benefit, to let me go free, but it was harsh."

Jasper's eyebrows shot up in a look of complete shock.

"I really have no idea what you're talking about. I didn't get a letter from you, and I definitely didn't write you one. I've been in solitary confinement almost the entire time I've been in prison, which is the only reason I'm still alive. Your boyfriend's henchmen have had it out for me from the second I got there. Solitary is the only place they can't get to me, except for my food, that is. They like to put their own special touch on every meal I get, which is why I look like a skeleton."

He looked down at himself and lifted the baggy jacket away from his gaunt torso, showing how huge it was on him. I squeezed my eyes shut so I didn't have to see how he'd wasted away.

"I don't have friends in there, that's for sure. I don't know who sent you a letter, but it wasn't me. What did it say?"

I collapsed into a chair across from Jasper. Jake heard the noise and stuck his head in.

"You all right?"

All I could do was nod my head. I had no idea what was going on. Jake looked concerned.

"You have one more minute. That's all I can do."

He closed the door, and I looked back to Jasper.

"Are you serious? You didn't write me a letter?"

"I promise you. I didn't. What did it say?"

"It doesn't matter. Look, we're going to run out of time and I want to say a few things. I want you to know that I don't hate you. I'm still really confused about what happened and my actions up at the cabin. I thought we were in love, but Dr. Bates has helped me see the cracks in that. It wasn't love, Jasper."

My words burned him. He cringed like I touched him with fire.

"Krissy, I don't know what all these people around you have been telling you, or writing to you, and I don't care. When we were together, really together, it was like we were one person. Our bodies became one. Have you forgotten how great that was? Does he make you feel the way I did?"

Jasper nodded toward Jake. I wanted to slap him.

"That was sex. And how Jake makes me feel is none of your business. He didn't have to kidnap me and chain me up until I almost died in a river to get me to love him. That's the difference."

"So you love him? Wow. Then I hope you'll be happy, and I hope he's good to Matty. I wish I could have done things differently, made better choices, but it doesn't matter now. I have to tell you, the years we were together were everything to me. I live in that world every time I close my eyes, and it's so sweet. Making love to you, the way you looked at me after, was magical. No matter what you say, you can't take those memories away from me."

I felt guilty, like I was cheating on Jasper with Jake. He had this power over me. I thought it was gone, but being around him like this, talking about our relationship, was not good.

"Jasper, I know people don't hurt a person they love, and they don't keep that person from their family and everyone who loves them. So whether or not you thought you loved me, you hurt me. Deeply. But I hope you get help because I think you can be a good man and have a good life."

He looked shocked by my response. By my strength. The tears that were pooling in his eyes released down his cheeks. He was so alone. I hoped he could hang on.

"One more thing. I'm going to tell Matty about you when he's old enough to understand. I will tell him what I just told you, that his dad is a good man who did a bad thing. When you get out, you can call me. I'll make sure the prison always has my current contact information. We can arrange for you and Matty to meet and take it from there. I think that's fair to you and to Matty. I hope you can find some peace, Jasper. I believe you deserve it."

He wiped the tears from his face with the back of his hand, the handcuffs jingling as he did it. Jake spoke to someone in the hall. Only a few seconds remained.

"Thank you, Krissy. Whether or not you believe it, I loved you. I still love you. And I hope you find happiness. I'm so sorry I robbed you and your family of it for so long. Give Matty a kiss for me."

He looked up at the door, glaring at the back of Jake's head.

"And whoever wrote that note, make sure they have a good explanation. You've had enough hurt."

My hand went straight to my pendant, just as the door opened. Jake entered the room, looking from Jasper to me. Jasper's body language immediately changed, his defiance returning. I was still stunned by his final words. Was he implying Jake wrote the note? Could that be possible? And if he did write it, what would I do?

"Let's go."

Jake grabbed Jasper roughly by the arm and led him out of the room. I sat, unable to move. Jake came back a few minutes later, eyeing me warily.

"You look kind of sick. I knew that was a bad idea."

I was speechless. Blown away by everything that had been said. I hadn't anticipated Jasper talking about us, about sex, about Jake. His passion was like a drug I had given up, but the memory of the addiction still scared me.

"Yes. Sorry, that was just emotional. It's hard to explain."

"Did he say anything that upset you?"

He stood by the door, leery to come over to me. I made myself stand and go to him. Would Jake have gone out of his way to let me talk to Jasper if he'd written that note? And if it wasn't Jake, who was it? Was Jasper lying about it to sabotage the life I was trying to rebuild? That didn't make sense. Jasper did say those words to me in the holding cell that first night. He didn't want me to visit him in prison, he wanted me to get on with my life and be happy. So why deny writing it? I reached out and took Jake's hand, the concern in his face making me nervous. He pulled me to him and held me against his strong chest, kissing my forehead. His embrace felt like home.

35.

That afternoon the judge called me to the stand. After seeing Jasper, I was more anxious than ever about my testimony. Diving into the past and recalling my years with Jasper in front of strangers made me want to throw up. I wanted to move forward. But I owed it to myself, and to Jake, who put so much work into the case, to get up there and tell the truth. My lawyer and I had gone over the questions he planned to ask me, mostly about how scared I was when Jasper took me to the cabin, how I was chained and almost died when I tried to escape. I tried not to look at Jasper, his eyes never leaving me. We didn't get into a lot of the personal questions about our relationship but stuck mostly to the facts. The lawyer asked me about Jasper locking me in the cabin after Matty was born, and if I thought Matty might die. I said yes. I still didn't know why Jasper did that, but I remember the fear. A crack in the fantasy. I noticed Jasper cower slightly as I described it, like maybe he'd forgotten. Like in his mind, everything was complete perfection.

We took a short break after my lawyer had completed his questions, and then it was the defense's turn.

I sat stiffly at the front, anticipating an attack. His first questions were simple, as we went over the timeline, when Jasper began to let me off my chain, and when I attempted my escape. Then he dove head first into our relationship, and the courtroom became painfully awkward. Jake squirmed in his chair, concern on his face. Jasper looked up at me, never wavering. I could tell he relived everything as I spoke.

"Krissy, when was the first time you and Jasper consummated your relationship?"

"After I recovered from my infection, I guess. About two weeks after I got there?"

"You're stating that like a question to me, Krissy. You are the one with the answers. Is that when it was?"

"Yes."

Prick.

"And would you say your sex was consensual?"

"I guess so. Yes. I mean, at that point I knew I couldn't get away, and Jasper had saved my life, twice, so from what I've read I think I was already suffering from Stockholm—"

"Yes, will do. Thank you. Stick to the questions, please."

"I did."

I hated him.

"So within two weeks of arriving at the cabin you were having consensual sex with the accused. Is that correct?"

"Yes."

"And how many times did you have sex that first night?"

I peered at Jake. He looked like he might throw up.

"Four times."

"I'm sorry. Could you say that louder please? I don't think the jury could hear you."

"Four times."

I wanted to claw his eyes out. Jasper looked sympathetic, like he wished he could help me somehow. In the back of the courtroom there was a commotion. Everyone turned to see Jill pushing past people out of her row and slamming open the door. The judge called for order.

The defense lawyer continued to wade through my statement. Jasper hadn't added anything. They were all my words, but now I had to say them aloud for the world to hear. When I first told my story to Jake, he was only a detective. He wasn't my boyfriend. To have to talk about this again, with him and Jasper in the room, was excruciating. I wanted to crouch down behind the witness stand and magically disappear.

"So, Krissy, how many times would you say Jasper went for supplies in the four years you were at the cabin?"

"I don't know. Maybe eight times?"

"Eight times. So eight times you were alone for an entire day. You knew Jasper was in town, you weren't tied up, and you didn't try to escape?"

"Well, no. It wasn't that easy. I tried once and the river was almost impossible to cross unless you found the perfect spot, and even then I couldn't do it without Jasper's help."

"But wasn't it worth a shot? You knew your parents would be looking for you. Didn't you miss your family, Krissy?" He took a breath and lowered his voice slightly, as if he was going to share a secret. "Or had you been planning to run away, and now you had the perfect out?"

"What? What are you talking about? Of course I missed my family! But Jasper needed me. I was afraid if I left him he might—"

"He might what, Krissy? Kill himself? Was the life of your kidnapper more valuable to you than your family?"

"No! I just, I was confused. I thought I owed him for saving my life."

I broke down. Jasper stood up, pure rage on his face.

"That's enough. Do you hear me? Enough! You're treating her like a criminal. I'm the criminal! She did nothing wrong. Just end this, Your Honour. Give me the maximum sentence and end this."

The judge pounded his gavel on the desk.

"Sit down. Now."

The court erupted. I looked up through my tears to see Jasper and Jake both on their feet. Jake looked like he was about to come up to the stand, and both were going to tear that lawyer apart. The judge calmed everyone and decided to recess for the day. As I stepped down from the stand, Jasper mouthed the words *I'm sorry.* I gave him a small smile. It wasn't his fault his lawyer was an asshole. My eyes skipped from Jasper's to Jake's. He was watching our exchange with an unreadable expression. It had been a hard day for everyone. I walked past him and over to my mom. Her face was puffy and red, her hands shaking as she hugged me. I wanted to go home and see Matty.

That night Jake called to check on me. I told him I was holding up, which was a lie. It was like I'd been thrown into the sky by a tornado. He didn't ask if he could come over, and I didn't invite him. The day had confused me, and as much as I wanted to cuddle up with him and hear his sexy, comforting voice, I needed to process everything. I couldn't stop thinking about Jasper and the note. Had he really not written it? I had to find out.

I asked my mom to come over and stay with Matty, who was sound asleep. I told her I had to take a walk to clear my head. I bundled up and headed down the street. Twenty minutes later, I stood in front of Jake's apartment. His truck was parked out front and his motorbike was in his spot in the underground garage. I tried the truck door, but it was locked, so I pulled out the extra key he had given me so I could use his truck to get groceries. I got into the passenger seat, instantly feeling guilty for what I was about to do. But I had to do it. I had to know.

I rifled through the middle console and backseat pockets. Nothing. Then I popped the glove box. Inside were a couple of manuals, sunglasses, and a small black book Jake used to log phone calls he got when he was out of the office. I opened it up and then pulled the folded note from my pocket. I unfolded it slowly, but I didn't have to. I had looked at it enough times to know. The writing matched. Perfectly. I leaned back against the seat, the familiar feeling of confusion making me lightheaded. Why did he do it? Why the dishonesty? Jake was the last person I thought capable of lying to my face.

I sat up to put the book back. I needed to walk. As I set it under the manuals where it had been, I noticed an envelope stuck in one. I opened the manual and pulled it out. This time it was my writing staring back. The letter I had written to Jasper was torn open. The picture of Matty was missing. How did Jake get my letter? There was another envelope. It had no writing on the front. I looked inside. It was a stack of photographs. All of me. Most of them had been taken shortly before I'd disappeared: some with friends, at school dances, running track. I looked through my old life, wondering why Jake had these pictures in his glove box. At the bottom of the stack was an artist rendering of what they thought I'd look like now. It was close: same eyes, chubbier cheeks. There was a single word scrawled in pencil under the drawing: "Umbry."

36.

I didn't sleep much that night. I walked the streets for a while, furious at first. I knew why Jake wrote the note. I just wished he let me realize it on my own. And I would have. If he had feelings for me right from the start, it must have been torture to watch me declaring my love for Jasper and saying I was going to wait for him. I got that. But he lied to me. And how did he get my letter? I figured the pictures were just the ones he used when he was looking for me. Still, a seed of doubt had been planted. Could I trust him? With my life and with Matty's?

I was dreading going back to the courtroom today. The thought of sitting up there while that sleazy lawyer picked over intimate details of my life, like he was sorting through junk at a garage sale, made me sick.

I gave Matty a kiss and told the babysitter I'd probably be home later that afternoon. I walked through my apartment lobby and onto the street, and I saw Jake coming towards me. He walked with heavy steps and a dark expression on his face. Oh, God. He knew I went into his truck last night. He was coming to break up with me. My breath quickened and blood pounded in my temples.

"What are you doing here? Shouldn't you be in court already?"

"Krissy. I really need to talk to you. Can we sit in the lobby for a second?"

How could I screw up the best thing that had ever happened to me? I wanted to cry.

"Yeah, sure. What's wrong?" I squeaked out the question, full of trepidation.

He opened the door and held it for me as we walked inside. There was a shabby looking couch in the corner. We sat down on it. Jake looked so good in his black suit and dark wool coat. I swallowed the lump of regret in my throat.

"I have to talk to you about something."

I couldn't breathe, let alone speak.

"It's about Jasper. Something happened last night."

He exhaled and stared so deeply into my eyes I thought the world stopped spinning.

"Somehow Jasper hid his tie when he changed back into his jumpsuit yesterday. They're not sure how, but he did. Late last night he hung himself, Krissy. Jasper's dead. I'm sorry."

Everything swirled before my eyes. Jake moved in and out of focus.

"What?"

"He's dead, Kris."

I couldn't move. Jake pulled me to him, softly. I breathed in his scent, his coat rough against my face. It was over. Jasper was dead.

I cried. I didn't want to, especially not with Jake, but I couldn't help it. I wondered why now. Was it because of our exchange yesterday? Was Jasper trying to spare me another day of torture, or did he finally just see an opportunity and seize it? I didn't know the answer, and I would never know. Jasper being gone was like the ultimate end to everything that was my past.

After we sat for a bit, I told Jake I wanted to go back up to my apartment and see Matty. I told him he could come, but he said he had to take care of everything at the station. People were going crazy, and Jake was needed in about five different meetings. He said he'd call to check on me later and he left. I was sad as I watched him walk away. I really loved him. Thinking he was going to end our relationship had made that real. I wanted to be with him, regardless of whether or not he wrote the note.

Matty was glad to see Mommy again. I thanked the babysitter and sent her away. My mom called. She was already at the courthouse and had heard what happened. I said I needed some time alone with Matty. I spent the morning playing with him, watching this amazing little boy laugh and discover new things. Some of his facial expressions were Jasper's, especially when he was deep in concentration.

I went to the washroom and had another good cry. For everything we had been through, right or wrong, Jasper was an important person in my life. He always told me he wouldn't survive in jail, that he couldn't live in a cage. I hoped that wherever he was, he'd found peace. For a lot of his short life he was alone and very unhappy. No one deserved to live like that.

My buzzer sounded. It was late afternoon, and I was watching my phone, waiting for Jake to call. I didn't expect him to stop by. When I pushed the button and said hello, it was my sister's voice that answered.

"Hi, Krissy. It's me, Jill. Can I come up?"

"Oh, hey. Yes, come up."

It was the first time Jill had been to my apartment. I couldn't believe she was here. I opened the door and thanked her for coming. She was uncomfortable and went right over to talk to Matty. He was in the middle of building a playdough truck. Jill sat down with him, and we spent the next hour making an entire playdough city. Jill was like her old self, and I had to fight the tears from coming. I missed her desperately.

"Well, I better get going. I have to work in twenty minutes. Bye, Matty!"

"Bye, Aunty Jilly."

Her face beamed.

"Thanks for coming. It was so good to see you."

"You're welcome." She paused. "I'm really sorry about what happened with Jasper. It's awful. I know this is a little late, but I feel terrible about how I've treated you since you've been home, Krissy. This whole situation is completely fucked up, but I know you never asked for this to happen to you. It wasn't your fault. It's taken me months to be able to admit that. Dr. Bates has helped me a lot. He's made me understand where your feelings could come from." She swiped at a tear and looked past me as she spoke. "I couldn't stay in court and support you yesterday, and I want you to know it's not because I was judging you. I just couldn't look at him and think about what he made you do. It was too much." She took a deep breath and then looked directly at me. "I know our relationship will take time to repair. I have some issues of my own to deal with, and it was so hard when you disappeared. I missed you so much."

We hugged and cried. It felt amazing. I was going to get my sister back. We promised to get together the next day and talk more. And she left.

37.

Jake didn't call until eight, and I was panicking until then. He'd been on my mind all day. I didn't like that he had lied to me about the note, or that he had my letter, but I understood his motivation. I wasn't sure what I'd say to him about it, but I really wanted to see him. The tragic way Jasper's life ended would stick with me for a long time, but it was his decision. He'd made choices that got him to where he was, and living in that prison for ten years would have been impossible for him. Finally, the phone rang.

"It's me. Sorry it's so late. It's been a long day. How are you doing?"

"I'm processing everything, I guess. I was beginning to think you'd forgotten about me."

"Ha! Impossible. I've been in crisis meetings and protocol reviews all day. It's a mess down here. When something like this happens on our watch we get heat from every level. But it should not have happened. They're right. I'm sorry I had to be the one to tell you about it."

"To tell you the truth, I always expected to hear something like this about him. It was just a shock, that's all. Especially after seeing him yesterday."

"Yeah. Turns out we got busted for that. Looks like I might be stuck doing some traffic duty for a while, but I'll work my way back up to detective eventually."

"Jake! They demoted you over me! I'm so sorry! You warned me you were risking your job. I'm sorry. I'm so selfish."

"You didn't make me do anything, Krissy. I'm a big boy. Really, it was me being selfish. I just wanted you to be able to move past that guy. I think it backfired on me."

"No, it didn't. Can you come over here? I really want to have this conversation in person."

"Are you sure? I know you've had a hard day. I can give you some space and time to think."

"Get over here."

"I'll be there in ten minutes."

He hung up. I leapt into the shower and changed into a silky, cream-coloured slip dress I bought the week before, my blue pendant dangling from my neck. I pulled my wet hair into a bun on top of my head and was just dabbing on some lip-gloss when I heard the buzzer.

"Hi."

"Hey. It's me."

"Come up."

I buzzed him up, the anticipation fluttering in my stomach. I flipped the switch to turn on the tiny gas fireplace in the living room and waited for the knock on the door. When I heard it, I jumped.

"Hi. Thanks for coming."

"Hey. Wow, you are stunning. Seriously, Krissy."

My cheeks flushed as I ushered him inside. He'd showered too, his dark hair still wet. His jeans and T-shirt clung to his body beneath his leather coat. He looked incredibly sexy.

"I missed you. Come in. What's in the bag?"

"I picked up some sushi and wine. I didn't know if you'd eaten. I'm starving. At least, I was until I saw you in that dress. That thing is incredible."

"Thank you."

I took the bag from him and put it on the counter. Jake stripped off his coat and hung it on a chair, then opened the wine and poured us each a glass. We sat on the living room couch, and he held his glass up to mine.

"What should we toast to?"

I could tell he was feeling me out, unsure what state I was in.

"How about to fresh starts?"

Surprise crossed his face, and then a grin played at the corner of his lips.

"Sounds perfect."

We drank our wine, the tension between us palpable. I knew we should talk about Jasper, but I was so mentally exhausted from thinking about it all day. I just wanted to be with Jake.

"I'm really sorry you got into so much trouble at work. I never should have asked you to compromise your job for me. It was wrong."

"Don't worry about it. Like I said, I had personal reasons for doing what I did. Besides, those guys need me, and they know it. I'll have my desk back in a month. No one wants to take on that workload. Trust me."

As he spoke, his eyes wandered over my body.

"I'm sure that's true. And you're brilliant. Don't forget about that."

"Right." He rolled his eyes as he agreed. "So, you're really okay?"

"Yes. No one could control what happened to Jasper. He would have found a way eventually. I'm sorry it happened under your command. I just want to concentrate on getting better and being happy. With Matty, and you, I hope."

His smile said everything as the space between us disappeared. He put his glass down and pulled me over to him.

"I want to be with you and Matty more than anything in the world. I love you, Krissy. I knew you were special from the moment I saw that first picture of you. I was always so worried something I did, or didn't do, would keep you from being found. When I met you, you were so beautiful and brave and strong. I've never met a woman like you in my life. I want to be with you. I want to love you. For as long as you'll have me."

He kissed my forehead, my cheeks, my lips. Hearing Jake say he loved me was more powerful than anything I had with Jasper. I was a woman now, and I was making these decisions free of any influences.

"I love you too, Jake."

I whispered the words in his ear and looked into his eyes. We kissed. Jake pulled the dress over my head, and then took off his T-shirt as we tumbled to the floor. He was strong but gentle. His body rippled and strained as he moved, highlighting every muscle in his torso. I couldn't stop staring. His skin was darker than Jasper's, with just a few dark hairs lingering on his throat, his perfect chest, and making a trail that lead below his belt.

He laid me on my back, naked except for my ivory lace thong, and he kneeled between my legs to take off his pants. I watched him peel away his black boxer-briefs that clung to him. My body wanted him inside me. As Jake's mouth travelled all over me, I had to cover mine with my hand to keep from moaning and waking up Matty. I was lost in his hands and his intoxicating smell. He slowly slid my panties down my thighs. Jake's mouth came back to mine and, as he kissed me, he moved gently inside me. It had been so long since I'd made love, and I gasped slightly. He kissed me softly, until we couldn't control ourselves anymore.

We ate the sushi and drank wine, naked on the floor under a blanket. Sometime later that night, exhausted and giggling, we crawled into bed and Jake spent the night. I curled into him and slept contentedly, his strong body surrounding mine.

I awoke to a delicious smell. Jake wasn't in bed, but I could hear laughter coming from the kitchen. I glanced at the clock. It read nine-thirty. Nine-thirty! Matty had probably been up for two hours. I stumbled out of bed and into a robe. As I came out of the bedroom, I stopped in my tracks. Jake and Matty were in the kitchen. Matty was sitting on the counter, mixing batter in a huge bowl, and it smelled like pancakes frying in the pan. Jake was wearing my apron over his jeans, which were covered in flour. In fact, the entire kitchen was covered in flour. Matty was laughing hysterically as Jake put different pots and bowls on his head. My boys. Warmth radiated out of me. Before they noticed I was up, I went back into the bedroom. On the shelf was the black book that had become my diary over the past few months. I pulled it down, running my hand over the smooth cover, and then opened it up and pulled out the folded note. I didn't open it again. I just crumpled it up and threw it into the garbage. I didn't care. I didn't care if Jake wrote that note, or how he got my letter. He was trying to give me a life. It was the best gift I could've gotten.

"Hey, I thought I heard you get up. Are you hungry?"

He peeked his tousled head into the bedroom, flour smeared on his cheeks.

"Good morning. Yes, I'm starving. It smells amazing out there. So, let me get this straight: you're smart, funny, kind, incredibly sexy, great in bed, and you can cook?"

He chuckled and pulled me to him, planting a kiss on my lips.

"That's nothing. I haven't revealed any of my real talents yet. I'm saving them for later."

"I can't wait."

38.

After breakfast I stood at the sink washing the enormous pile of dishes Jake and Matty had managed to dirty. They were in the living room building some sort of Lego spaceship. The sound of their voices made me smile.

A loud pounding on the door shattered our blissful morning. I jumped, splashing soapy water all over my apron.

"Police! Open up!"

"What? Hang on a second," I yelled through the closed door.

"Jake! The police are here!"

"Fuck."

It was all he said, but the way he said it, the tone in his voice, scared me. I ran towards the living room, anxious to get to Matty. Jake was still on the floor. He was leaning against the couch, the couch we had leaned against last night, making love and talking long into the night. Matty was on his lap.

"Why are they here? What's going on?"

As I asked the questions, I reached down and scooped Matty off his lap, holding him tight against me. He didn't say anything. He just looked up at me with anguish.

"Open up, Ms. Mathews! We know Jake's in there."

There was some rustling, more voices outside the door. How many men were out there? I clutched Matty and looked frantically from the door to Jake.

"Come on, Umbry. Don't make us break your girlfriend's door down. Let's do this peacefully."

"Jake, answer me! What's going on?"

Slowly, he dropped his head to his chest and rose. I wanted to put my hands on him, but I didn't.

"Kris. I'll get off. Don't worry. They don't have any proof. This is such a fucking joke. I can't believe they're turning on me."

"Last chance, Umbry!"

Jake walked towards the door, and then came back to Matty and me. He brushed Matty's hair off his forehead. Matty reached out for Jake to take him, but I held him tightly.

"Kris, promise me you won't listen to them. They're going to try to pin stuff on me that I didn't do. You know me. You know how much I love you. We're going to be a family."

With that, he kissed my forehead and went to the door. When he opened it, men and testosterone filled the room and enveloped Jake. Matty started to cry.

"Jake Umbry, you're under arrest for the murder of Jasper Ryan."

The air was sucked out of the room. I gasped for breath, my knees threatening to give.

"Come on, guys. Not in front of the kid. Take me in the hall to cuff me."

The officers were on each side of him. Another grabbed Jake from behind and pinned him against the wall, frisking him up and down.

"Jake!"

"I'm fine, Kris. I'll call you later. I'll be out in an hour."

"I don't think so, Umbry. We've got a witness and some pretty solid evidence."

Jake murdered Jasper?

They grabbed Jake and led him out of my apartment. Two men who had been waiting in the hall stepped in. They were wearing regular clothes, their badges clipped to their belts. I recognized them both from my trial. They were usually sitting at the front with Jake.

"Hi, Ms. Mathews. I'm Detective Warren. This is Detective Samson. Can we have a word with you?"

"Can I get Matty calmed down first?" My voice was high-pitched and urgent. Matty looked at me with round, scared eyes, the tears streaming down his face. I didn't wait for an answer. I walked to Matty's room, whispering in his ear that everything would be all right. When he stopped crying, I set him up with some blocks on his bedroom floor and then stood to go back to the kitchen. Detective Warren was standing in Matty's doorway watching me.

"Oh! I didn't see you there! Can I have some privacy, please? I said I'd be out in a minute."

"Sorry, Ms. Mathews, but we need to make sure you're not hiding anything. Please come join us in the living room."

Hiding anything? What would I be hiding? My world had taken an abrupt turn.

I sat on the couch. The men moved two chairs from the kitchen into the living room and sat across from me. Detective Warren seemed to be the one in charge. He was chubby and balding slightly at the top of his head. The faint smell of cigarette smoke lingered in the air around them. The other one, Detective Samson, was younger and skinny, with a full head of red hair. His movements were jerky and his eyes darted around the room.

"Let's start with how you found out about Jasper Ryan's death."

I could see his mouth moving, but the words were coming more slowly than they should have. My thoughts swirled. Jasper's death. Could Jake really have anything to do with Jasper hanging himself? No. I knew Jake. He was a good man. This was impossible.

"Look, Detective. I know Jake had nothing to do with this. Jasper killed himself. He always told me he wouldn't be able to survive in a cell. I think he got his opportunity and he did it."

"Was Detective Umbry aware of the threats Jasper was making to harm himself?"

"Yeah, I guess. I think I mentioned them in my statement. But why does that matter? Jake didn't even see Jasper after the trial ended the day before yesterday."

"How do you know that, Ms. Mathews? Did he spend the night here?"

"Well, no. He called to check in from the office, and then he went home. He told me he was going home."

The detectives gave each other a knowing glance, and then Detective Samson couldn't contain himself any longer and jumped in. He leaned in as he spoke. It looked like he was trying not to smirk.

"So how long have you and Detective Umbry been a couple?"

"Not long at all! We really just, well, we were waiting until after the trial to really...not long."

I was a terrible liar. My voice still sounded shrill. I tried to soften it.

"Why does this matter? Jake and I have just been getting to know each other. He's a wonderful guy, and he only wants the best for me and my family."

"Yes. I'm sure that's true, Ms. Mathews. Did you ever ask Detective Umbry to harm Jasper Ryan in any way?"

"No! God, no. Why would I do that? Jasper was going to jail, probably for a long time. I never wanted him hurt. He's Matty's father."

"Right. And did Mr. Ryan know you and Detective Umbry were a couple?"

"Yes. He seemed to."

"What do you mean by 'he seemed to'"?

"I know you guys found out about Jake letting me talk to Jasper during the trial. That was all my idea. In fact, I begged Jake to let me speak to him. When I was talking to Jasper, he asked me about Jake. Jasper knew about us."

They looked at each other again. This time it was Detective Warren who spoke.

"How do you think he knew?"

I wasn't sure what to say. I didn't want to get Jake in any more trouble, but I wanted to tell the truth. I was positive there was an explanation for all of this.

"I don't know. Maybe just the way Jake acted with me? He was very protective."

"Yes. Have you ever been to Detective Umbry's apartment, Ms. Mathews?"

"Well, no. I haven't. He says it's really messy, and it worked better for us to be here, for Matty. His toys are here and, why? Why does that matter?"

"Is there someone you can call to come look after your son? We'd like to take you to Detective Umbry's apartment."

"I can call my mom. But why do you want me to see Jake's apartment? Isn't that invasion of privacy or something?"

"No. It's part of our investigation now. We'd like you to get an idea of what we're dealing with here. Please call your mom."

39.

I was in the back of an unmarked police car on my way to Jake's apartment. How could this be happening? The barrage of questions my mom peppered me with went unanswered. I didn't know what was going on. I didn't know how they could think Jake killed Jasper. I didn't know why they were taking me to his apartment. I didn't know.

She rushed over when I called, arriving out of breath and in tears. Speechless with shock, I hugged her and left. When we arrived at Jake's, we climbed the stairs to the second floor. I tried to control my uneven breath and the foreboding sickness in my stomach. I loved Jake. And after everything, I was finally happy. I didn't want to know what would put that in jeopardy.

A guard stood in front of Jake's door, which had yellow police tape marking an "X" behind him. He stepped aside as we ducked under the tape and walked in. It smelled like Jake, and a sob rose in my throat. I swallowed it down. We walked through a small hallway and into a large kitchen. As I expected, it was immaculate. Sparsely decorated, not a speck of dust, meticulously organized. It was Jake. A man in a white suit came from a hallway to the right. He had a camera around his neck. He looked surprised to see me, and then he lowered his eyes and walked past without a word.

"This way, Ms. Mathews. And let me warn you, what you're going to see is disturbing." Detective Warren led the way down the hall. Detective Samson lingered behind me.

Disturbing? We walked down the hallway. The door on the

right was a bathroom. There were two doors on the left. The first was open and housed a huge bed, perfectly made. His bed. We kept walking. The second door was open as well. I took one step into the second room and scanned the images before me. My brain was unable to accept what I was seeing.

Everywhere I looked, the walls were plastered with my face. Three of the walls were covered in images of me, severed from pictures with friends and family. Me laughing and running track, me on the ski hill. The only piece of furniture in the room was a desk in the middle. An officer sat at the desk, files piled before him. He looked up, saw it was me, and quietly excused himself. On the wall behind the desk, the only wall without my photograph, was a state map with pins and notes covering it. The detectives stood by the door, watching my reaction. I heard only white noise, as I stepped deeper into the room.

The pictures had writing, dates, and symbols that made no sense to me. As I came around the desk, I saw a framed picture of Matty, the one I'd sent to Jasper in my letter. The little motorcycle was held tightly in his hand.

"What is all of this?"

I looked over at them. Detective Samson opened his mouth to speak but got a look from Detective Warren and closed it. Detective Warren spoke instead.

"We're sorry you had to see this, Ms. Mathews. We need you to identify yourself, your son, and a timeline for when these photos were taken. I thought it was important for you to see these images here, instead of down at the station, so you can understand the full extent of what's been going on. It appears Detective Umbry has some serious mental issues we were unaware of. We knew he was more than vigilant about trying to find you, but he was young and, well, I apologize. We should have seen the signs earlier on." He held his hands up and motioned around the room as he spoke.

"Signs? Signs of what?"

It was rhetorical. I didn't want an answer. I collapsed into the chair. One of the files was open and again my photo stared back at me. I picked up a stack of images. Me walking to Dr. Bates's office,

Matty and me at the park, some of me through the window of my mom's condo. It was beyond creepy. Why was Jake watching me?

"Ms. Mathews, I know this must be incredibly uncomfortable for you. Detective Umbry is obviously very sick, and we want to put him where he belongs before he hurts anybody else. Specifically, you or your son. I have to ask you again: did you have any knowledge of Detective Umbry's intention to kill Mr. Ryan?"

I barely heard what he said. I was looking at the files: names of old friends, teachers, people I barely knew. In each file were pages and pages of notes. I noticed the name Blake Thompson scrawled in Jake's now-familiar printing on one of the file folders and pulled it out of the stack. Inside was a thick pile of paper with numerous dates on them, all leading up to the day when my dad and Blake fought. Jake must have spent a lot of time interviewing Blake, hoping to prove my dad's theory right. Hoping Blake would lead to me. There was a picture of Blake, which caught me off guard. I hadn't thought of his face or really mourned him since I found out he was dead—that my dad had killed him. He looked like a kid. I scanned the notes, reading an incredibly detailed description of what Blake and I had done together sexually. Where he'd put his hands, his mouth. It looked like a transcript of a tape recording:

JU: Did Krissy like what you were doing to her?

BT: I don't know. I guess.

JU: Did she tell you to stop?

BT: No. God, dude. I'm not some molester or something. She just seemed nervous.

JU: If she was nervous, why didn't you stop and ask her if she was okay?

BT: What does this have to do with Krissy going missing?

JU: Everything. I want to know every detail of every interaction you've had with her, or you'll be in a cell so fast you won't know what happened. And trust me, the other guys you'll be sharing it with don't show a lot of kindness to molesters, *dude*.

I slammed the file shut. Even then, Jake was protecting me.

"Ms. Mathews?" Detective Warren stepped slightly towards me from his spot by the door.

Why was this happening to me? I thought Jake was my saviour, the one man I could trust. Was there any man I could actually trust? Suddenly, I was furious, and I unleashed at the detective. I was screaming.

"Why is this happening? What the fuck is going on? Are all men psychos?"

He looked sympathetic and waited while I calmed down and wiped my tears.

"Sorry. What did you ask me?"

"If you knew anything about Detective Umbry murdering Mr. Ryan?"

"No. Of course not. All of this is completely shocking. How can you be sure Jake killed Jasper? He was found hanging in his cell, right?"

"Yes. He was. But it looks like Detective Umbry paid him a visit at about two in the morning. The guard he bribed is talking. Detective Umbry was unaware we moved another prisoner into a holding cell two down from Mr. Ryan's. The prisoner heard everything, and he's willing to testify.

"So what are you saying? Did Jake *hang* Jasper?"

I pushed back from the desk a bit, preparing to vomit on the floor if he said yes.

"Not exactly. But the two of them had quite a talk. Detective Umbry gave him some pretty good reasons to do it himself. We're unclear how Mr. Ryan got the tie. The surveillance cameras were shut off for the twenty minutes the men were together."

This still didn't make any sense to me. Why would Jake do this, risk everything, when Jasper was going to be in prison for so long anyway?

"I'm sorry, but I don't get it. What could Jake have said to Jasper to make him hang himself? If anything, I think Jasper would do the opposite of what Jake wanted. Jasper hated Jake. And, like I told you, Jasper always warned me he would do something like this if he ever got caught." He shot a look over to detective Samson again, as if to keep him quiet, and then spoke with a soft tone.

"I can't really get into all of the particulars, as this is an open investigation, but it looks like Detective Umbry suggested your son might have a terrible accident if Mr. Ryan didn't end his life."

I couldn't even imagine Jake uttering those words. He loved Matty. There's no way he would harm him.

"Are you sure? How do you know this prisoner is telling the truth, or that he heard correctly? That doesn't sound like something Jake would say."

"We're sure, Ms. Mathews. There's another piece of physical evidence we have as well."

"Oh yeah, what's that?"

"During Mr. Ryan's autopsy the coroner found a message inscribed on his leg."

"Something was written on Jasper's leg? With a pen?"

"Yes, something was written. But it wasn't with a pen. The deceased carved a message into his flesh with his own fingernail."

Oh, my God. The wave of nausea passed over me again. It took a few seconds before I could find my voice.

"What did it say?"

"It said, 'Jake did it.'"

40.

I wanted to talk to Jake. I needed to. If he was really capable of threatening to harm Matty and blackmailing Jasper, stalking me, and tricking me into loving him, then I wanted him to rot in jail. But something didn't feel right. We had spent hours talking. Never did I see any signs he wasn't a good, honest man. I knew he didn't like Jasper, and I couldn't really blame him. He dedicated years of his life to solve a crime Jasper committed. He only saw the pain Jasper caused me, and all the work it took with Dr. Bates to get to the place I was at now. He loved Matty. The whole thing didn't make sense.

After leaving Jake's apartment I walked home, promising to be available the next day to give a statement about what I knew, which wasn't much. I didn't mention anything to the detectives about the note Jake had given me, supposedly from Jasper, or the letter I'd written to Jasper that I found in Jake's truck. I was still turning those things over in my mind.

My mom was happy to see me come through the door. She wanted to know what they'd found at Jake's apartment. I knew she loved Jake and thought of him as a member of the family. It would tear her up to discover some of his intentions may not have been good when it came to being with me. I told her they found a ton of pictures of me and files on my case, and the detectives thought it was strange for him to have them all at home. And also that he may have spoken to Jasper the night he killed himself.

My mom was relieved and explained that Jake was under a huge amount of pressure to close my case and move on. Eventually, they had forbidden him from working on it anymore, so he had to do it from home. She thought it was ridiculous they would even attempt to pin Jasper's death on him.

My mom left and I put Matty down for his nap. I tried calling Jake, but it went straight to voicemail. Later my phone rang.

"Hello?"

"Krissy. It's me. How are you doing?"

"To tell you the truth, I'm not doing well. What the hell is going on?"

"I'm so sorry, but please trust me. I can explain all of this. These guys have had it out for me from the moment I got detective. I was smarter than them and worked harder. I made them look bad. They've been looking for a way to bring me down. Especially Samson. That little piece of shit is licking his chops over this whole thing because I've called him out about some stuff in the past. I just can't believe that they won't even give me the benefit of the doubt."

A twinge of hope ran through me. Was it possible this wasn't real?

"Please tell me you didn't go see Jasper in jail the night he killed himself. Did they make that up?"

It was quiet on the line for a second, and then he spoke.

"No, they didn't. I did go see Jasper, and I had to bribe the guy watching him to let me do it. But you have no idea what it's like around the station. I wanted to talk to Jasper about you and Matty, and I knew if I was overheard it would be gossip over coffee the next morning. I really wanted to keep our relationship private as long as I could. I turned off the surveillance video so the guard wouldn't get busted."

"What did you have to say to Jasper? Why was it so important you had to talk to him at two in the morning?"

"Kris, I know I screwed up. This is such a fucking disaster. Look, that day was really hard for me. When I saw how you were after talking to him, the effect he still had on you, and then the way he defended you in court, I guess I just wanted him to know that I understood he loved you, too. And Matty. I'm sure it was pretty hard for the guy to see his family with another man, you know? I just wanted him to know that I'd take really good care of you and Matty. Be the best dad I could until he got out. That kind of stuff. I'd been pretty harsh to the guy, especially when you weren't around. But I didn't try to kill him, or tell him to kill himself, or whatever they're accusing me of. You have to believe me."

Did I? Could I? Everything he said was making sense, and I wanted so desperately to believe him.

"Let's say everything you're telling me is the truth. What about the note from Jasper? Did you write it?"

I heard him sigh on the other end. Seconds passed. I waited.

"Yes. I wrote it. But I can explain that too. When I took you to his cell to see him the first day you were back, he said those exact words to you. It was so painful to sit by and watch you throw your life away, and your happiness, waiting for him. I thought if I could just remind you of what he said, what he wanted, you might reconsider. It was wrong, and I'm so sorry it hurt you deeply, but selfishly, I'm still glad I did it. It brought you to me, and even if it was just for a few months, they were the best months of my life, Kris. And last night was incredible. You're incredible."

"That's the thing. I would've come to you, with or without the note. I would have realized I loved you, in my own time."

I think he choked back a sob. I couldn't picture him crying.

"I'm so sorry about all of this. I hope you can stand by me. I promise you, I will be vindicated."

"I want to believe you. Desperately. How did you get out? What's going on?"

"They let me out on bail while they sort through the evidence, which shouldn't take long, since it's a pile of shit. They offered the other prisoner immunity if he testified against me. Of course he's going to say whatever they want him to. Not to mention, I was the one who put him in jail in the first place. This will never hold up in court. They have nothing."

"But Jake, there are other things. What about your office? I've been to your apartment. It's creepy. And then there's my letter. How did you get my letter?"

I was so overwhelmed. I wanted to curl up in a ball. It was all so complicated, and I had a son to think about.

"You have to trust me. I can explain it all. It's no secret I was consumed with you, with your case. I've told you that. I'm not proud of it, but I think I was working out some of my own demons: wondering if I was good enough to follow in my dad's footsteps, if I was too young, if these guys were right about me. I was so determined to prove myself that I took it a little far." He was speaking quickly and with a slight desperation that unnerved me.

"And then you showed up, and your story was so hard to believe. I kept following you to make sure you weren't hiding something. I didn't know what. Maybe that you'd run away, that you knew Jasper ahead of time. I didn't know. It just didn't make any sense to me. Your letter was returned to the station after it had been opened at the prison. Standard protocol. Jasper was in solitary, so they couldn't give it to him, and everyone knew I'd been working this case hard for the last four years, so anything with your name would get dropped to me. When I saw the picture of Matty holding the motorbike I gave him, I couldn't resist putting it on my desk. I was going to tell you, but I didn't want you to think I was reading your mail. I don't know. Like I said, I screwed up."

Could this all be a huge misunderstanding? What was I going to do?

"I want to believe you. I really do. But, there's one more thing: Jasper said you did it. Well, he didn't say it, but you know what I mean. His leg, Jake. Why would he do that if it wasn't true? I can't imagine the last thing he would want the world to know was a lie. How do you explain that?"

"I heard about that today and I felt sick. I really did. I didn't kill him. When I went to talk to him things got a little heated. We definitely had a knack for pushing each other's buttons. I guess that's not shocking. We both love the same woman."

My stomach flipped when he said this. I let him continue.

"I'm sure the thought of you and I together really hurt him.

When I talked about Matty he freaked. He said he'd never put up with me being around Matty, being his dad, that he'd find a way to break you and I up. That's when I realized going to talk to him was a bad idea. I left. I can only think that Jasper carved what he did into his leg to get me. To make sure neither one of us could be with you. I'd heard the time he'd spent in prison so far was rough, to say the least. I'm not surprised he didn't want to go back, but I'm really sorry it ended like this. I really am."

How would I ever figure this all out? Jasper was gone. It was only Jake that could put the pieces together. But did they fit? Would Jasper really make the last thing he did on this earth an act of vengeance? Did he hate Jake that much? Maybe he did.

"I need to think about all of this for a while. I have to think about what's best for Matty. I'm really confused and sad. I don't know what to do. I'll call you in a couple days."

"I'll be waiting. I just want you to know I love you and Matty. You guys are everything to me. But if you decide you can't trust me, that you want the courts to figure it out, then do that. I'm innocent. I'll prove it. But take all the time you need. I'll be here."

"Bye, Jake."

There was only one man I wanted to talk to, and I hoped he had some answers for me.

41.

Dr. Bates was waiting for me when I got to his office. There was a hot cup of tropical green tea, my favourite kind, sitting on the edge of his desk. I'd suggested he come to my house, but he thought it would be more like our usual routine if we met at the office. I needed all the routine I could get right now. When I walked in, I went to sit in the chair, but he came around the desk and held out his arms. I collapsed into him.

"Dr. Bates, what am I going to do?"

I cried on his shoulder until I ran out of tears. He eased me into the chair and brought over a box of tissue. I told him everything. He sat quietly, listening. The more I talked, the more confused I became.

"How will I ever know the real truth? It has to be a leap of faith, but what if Jake is lying? What if he really is crazy and he forced Jasper to kill himself? I might be putting Matty and me at risk. I just don't know what to do."

"I usually like to reserve my personal opinion and let my patient come up with their own solution. In your case, I think I have to interject. You know I think the world of you. You've really played a big role in getting me on track and organized."

As I looked around the disastrous office, the only change I could really detect was some sort of flowering plant that replaced the old grey one. Decaying petals littered the ground.

"Thanks. I would really love your advice."

"Remember when I warned you about jumping into any type of romantic relationship so early after what you'd been through?"

"Yes. Yes, maybe you were right."

"Of course I was right, but that's not the point. My point is that I think you're so vulnerable to making any kind of attachments that you may be too willing to overlook certain signs."

"Wait. What signs? I've had my eyes pretty open."

"Really, Krissy? You knew Jake forged a note from Jasper, which is a pretty big lie, before you slept with him. Didn't you think that was worth discussing before you jumped in with both feet?"

"Well, I didn't know what to do. I was confused, and I kind of understood why he did it. I don't know. I love him."

"Do you see what I mean though? You're willing to overlook a huge betrayal of trust to keep your relationship intact. This pattern of behaviour goes right back to your relationship with Jasper. Focus only on the perceived good, banish the bad. Sacrifice yourself and your morals to keep things status quo. Keep your partner happy. It isn't healthy and it isn't fair."

"Well that's a bit harsh. Jake isn't Jasper."

"No. He isn't. But there are comparisons that raise some flags. Both of these men are strong willed. Both fall under the hero archetype. There are studies showing unnaturally strong attachments can be formed with people who play a role as a hero or white knight in our lives."

"Please don't tell me I have another attachment syndrome! I love Jake. He is a strong, sexy, smart man and any woman would be lucky to have him."

"He may also be a stalker and a murderer."

We stared each other down. Where was I supposed to go from here?

"Krissy, I'm sorry. I don't mean to pick on you. I strongly advise you to take a break from men for a while. Keep your distance from Jake until a judge works this out. Concentrate on being a mother. Concentrate on getting to know yourself. Not who you were, but who you are now. You don't need a man for that. Let's see each other more frequently. Maybe three times a week, until you feel grounded again."

I took a deep breath. Dr. Bates was right. I needed to focus on me, and enough of this drama. Maybe I didn't know Jake as well as I thought I did. When I looked back, did I ever really have a choice about being with him? I felt like his property from the moment I walked into his office.

"Thanks. That sounds like a good plan. I can always count on you."

I stood and reached across his desk to hug him. He smelled fresh, like soap.

"No worries. I've got your back."

Epilogue

"He's getting bigger. He'll be starting college soon by the looks of him."

I spun on the bench to see Jake coming up behind me. I opened my mouth to say something, but when I looked at him I was stunned into silence. He was more handsome than ever in jeans that hung perfectly from his hips and a T-shirt clinging to his muscular body, his tanned face an attractive side effect of the six-month leave he had from work while his case was being investigated. My voice sounded a little breathless as I awkwardly patted the bench beside me.

"Jake. It's good to see you. Come sit down."

He walked around the bench cautiously but didn't sit. I looked up at him, his eyes had returned to Matty, who was completely engrossed with the sandbox he was digging in. Jake got slightly choked up.

"I've really missed that little guy. How was Christmas?"

Tears pooled in my eyes. I inhaled deeply, taking the fresh spring air into my lungs. I promised myself I would be strong. I had to be.

"It was great. Matty had so much fun. Of course my mom and Jill spoiled him rotten. I think we have enough Lego to build a life-sized house now. His favourite toy is still that motorcycle though. He doesn't leave home without it. He left it on the bus last month and I almost had to call you to find out where you got it, but luckily some nice person turned it into the school's lost-and-found."

As I rambled on, Jake stood and watched me. My cheeks were

on fire. Eventually he sat down a noticeable distance from me. Matty still hadn't looked up from burrowing his truck into the sand. I was hoping he wouldn't notice Jake, not at least until we'd said what we had come to say. Matty had been asking about Jake almost daily since he abruptly disappeared from our lives. I didn't want to have his little heart smashed into pieces for a second time.

"You know you can call me anytime. About a toy or anything else."

Even from the opposite side of the bench, I could pick up a hint of his cologne.

"I know. Luckily, we found it. And I called you today, didn't I?"

"Yes. You did. You look amazing, by the way. I'm having a hard time concentrating."

I blushed again and looked away. In the six months since I'd spoken to Jake, I'd been working hard at getting healthy. Jill and I had both gotten memberships at the gym, and we went together as often as we could. Jill was forty pounds lighter, off her meds, and getting back to her old self. We were planning to run now that spring was here. I forced myself to look back at him and acknowledge his compliment.

"Thanks. You look good too. Is that a tan I see? Have you been vacationing in Mexico or something?"

He laughed and relaxed into the bench a little.

"Yes, it is a tan. No, not Mexico. My mom came up to visit for a few weeks, and with the beautiful weather we've been having, we managed to get out for a hike every day. She actually said she liked it here, which was a first." He beamed as he talked about his mom. "It was just what I needed. A few weeks with my mom is like a year of intensive therapy. She really helped me work a few things out."

"That's great, Jake."

I struggled for what to say next. I knew I needed to dive into the heavy stuff, but I couldn't find the right words. Jake spoke before I had a chance.

"So, I saw you in court yesterday, but you disappeared afterwards. Thanks for coming."

"You're welcome. I think I owed it to you to be there. And congratulations, by the way. You were vindicated, just like you said you would be. You must feel great."

Jake looked over at me but didn't say anything. His expression was the same one he wore in court yesterday. After the not-guilty verdict had been read, he looked directly at me with a mixed expression of sadness and exhaustion, not the jubilation his lawyers exuded as they slapped Jake on the back and hugged each other. During the celebration, I'd slipped out the back door. The final decision wasn't a surprise to me or anyone else. During the course of the trial, Jake's lawyers had discovered faint audio on the surveillance tape from the night Jake visited Jasper in jail. After Jake left and turned the tape back on, Jasper and the other prisoner, a man Jake had arrested for drug trafficking, started whispering to each other. The prisoner was furious Jake had busted him, and wanted revenge. Some of Jasper's words were so quiet they were unintelligible, but enough could be made out to understand that he wanted to die, but he wanted Jake to take the blame. He believed Jake was hiding his true self from me, and he didn't want Matty or me around such a controlling guy. The other prisoner promised to tell the police Jake had threatened to kill Matty if Jasper didn't kill himself. The last words on the tape before Jasper died were from the prisoner whispering, "Are you sure you want to do this buddy?" and then the sound of the cot scraping against the floor as Jasper kicked it away. It was horrible. With the tape and Jake's testimony, the prisoner's story fell apart and the prosecution had no case. Things ended quickly.

Jake looked out to where Matty was playing again and then sat a little straighter on the bench and spoke.

"So, it's been a year since you've been back. That's quite a milestone. What have you been up to?"

The formality of the question struck me as funny, after everything we'd been through together. I wondered what that meant, how this was going to end.

"Well, I'm still working for Dr. Bates. Linda took some time off to travel with her husband, so lately it's been full-time.

I registered at the community college to finish my high-school education. I've been doing that online. I'm thinking about maybe going in to counselling. I'd love to try and help women who've been victims like me."

"That's awesome, Kris. I think you have a lot to offer in that field. I've been reading about that subject lately, too. Dr. Bates recommended some really interesting books on Stockholm syndrome for me. I have to say, I've learned so much. I wish I'd read them before you came back. It definitely would've made our first few meetings a little easier on you."

He looked away sheepishly while I stared at him. Jake had been reading about Stockholm syndrome?

"Really? When did you see Dr. Bates?"

"I called him."

"Why?"

"Because I wanted to learn more about what you were going through. The stuff he was saying during his testimony at your trial made so much sense when I thought about everything you went through up there. I wanted to understand more about how you were feeling."

"Thanks. I appreciate that."

"It's no big deal. I also wanted to tell you I talked to a buddy of mine on the parole board last week. He said things are looking good for your dad. His five-year mark is coming up, and with all the positive feedback from the guards he could be looking at getting out on parole soon. He's really made an impact on that place. He's a very special guy."

"Yeah. I know. I can't wait to have him back."

My dad and I had repaired the damage to our relationship. He had a new understanding of my experience. He told me he'd also been doing some reading. I brought Matty up to see him a few times. He fell in love with his grandson instantly. I think he asked me more about Matty than myself the last time I talked to him. Matty had become a shining light in the lives of my family, drawing us all together. Now that I was working full-time, my mom picked him up from daycare every day at three and had him to herself for a couple of hours before I came home. As I watched him playing in the sand, I knew there was only one thing missing from Matty's perfect world: a father.

For a moment, Jake and I sat in silence, watching Matty. I knew he would look up soon, want me for something, and then see Jake. Before that happened, he and I had to figure out what, if anything, we were to each other. With a deep sigh, I spoke first.

"I called you today to tell you I'm sorry. I didn't trust you. You told me you didn't do it, and I couldn't believe you. I couldn't stand by you. I'm so sorry. After everything you did for me, how understanding you were, how patient, how great you were with Matty, and I just threw it all away."

I put my face in my hands, trying to will the tears back into my eyes. I'd thought of him every day since the morning the police tore him from my apartment. From my life. I'd wanted to talk to him endlessly until he could explain it all away, but I didn't. The risk was too big to take. If I'd kept Jake in our lives for the six months before the trial, Matty and I falling more in love with him every day, and then he'd been convicted of killing Jasper, I would never have forgiven myself. How could I possibly let Matty spend time with the man who killed his father? I had to wait. I had to be sure. I was so afraid that by not trusting him, by pushing him away, I'd lost him.

"How could you ever think I would expect that of you? You and I were just finding our way, beginning to really know each other, when all of this came down. And the way the police stormed your place. I would have been terrified of me too. After enduring what you did the last four years of your life, trusting strange men wasn't exactly smart for you. I totally understand. You have Matty to think about. He has to be your first priority."

As Jake spoke Matty's name, he looked out to the sandbox again. We could hear him making beeping sounds as he backed up the big truck.

"I've kept my distance from you guys because I knew if I couldn't prove my innocence, I would be known as a murderer. Jasper's murderer. Definitely not someone you want your son to be around. Believe me. I get it."

I couldn't help but lean in closer to him as my regret got the better of me.

"I wish I'd listened to you when you explained everything. It all made sense, but I just got so caught up in what the police were telling me."

"I know. They were pretty convincing. It might sound stupid now, but I want you to know I was planning to take everything down the night that trial ended. I couldn't wait. I was so goddamn sick of looking at those pictures, but until they convicted him I didn't want to move one thing in case they screwed it up somehow and we ended up having to build the case again. Your case was my life, which I realize now was totally unhealthy. I think it had a lot to do with some issue I have with my dad. I was too focused on proving I was as good as him, and then I got your case and I couldn't solve it. I felt so bad for your family and the more I got to know you, through everything I was learning about you, the more I had this, I don't know, this *ownership* of you. You were my case: I needed to bring you home. I did some things I'm not proud of, Kris. I'm really sorry. I've never been that passionate about anyone before. Not being with you just wasn't an option for me. I realize now it has to be mutual."

"It was mutual! Maybe not at first, but after we started spending time together I saw that being with you gave me hope for the future. Hope that I could be happy again. Hope that the three of us could be a family."

I wiped at a tear as it slipped down my cheek.

"Jake, you make me so happy."

He broke into a big smile.

"God, that's good to hear. I've thought about everything so much over the last six months, I kind of forgot what parts were actually real."

In the distance I heard Matty say, "Momma…Jake!" His squeal of delight made us both laugh. Matty stood and ran in our direction.

Acknowledgments

Mountain Girl is the product of a promise. When I had my first daughter and found myself home, I quickly realized something: without the distraction of my on-hold career, I had hundreds of days to care for my baby, and—what else? The draw of daytime TV and Pinterest were magnetic, but I heard a faint whisper of opportunity. I promised myself that rather than maintain a stagnant identity, I would evolve. I would investigate the unexplored in myself.

Mountain Girl took many years (seven!) and many fails, before finally succeeding. I'd like to thank my first readers, my family, for being impressed merely with those giant piles of paper I handed them, regardless of the story's quality. You made it admirable to try. Ryan and Laura, Dallas and Rita, Al, Cece, and Mary. Jodi, your acceptance and friendship are incomparable. My parents, Don and Sally Cain, continue to support everything I attempt with commendable optimism and sacrificed so much to lay a foundation for me and my brothers that will support generations to come. I respect and love you infinitely.

I would also like to thank:

The ever-generous author Angie Abdou, who helped mold this book into what it is today. You are an unwavering cheerleader for Canadian literature.

Oolichan Press, thank you for stepping outside the norm and saying yes. Thank you. Thank you.

The very special community of Fernie, British Columbia. I continue to put my words, and my heart, into your open hands. You always make me feel at home.

The Bombers, who witness my many adventures, and disasters, and keep cheering for me. Special thanks to Brenda Maudie, my first editor, for giving me the confidence to keep writing, and Bob Maudie, my longest friend, who always makes me feel like he's proud to know me.

Tara Cunningham, my editor, literary therapist, fact checker, detail-demander, and supporter on the hard days. Thank you for believing and risking and seeing the good in Jasper, even though he's so flawed. You are awesome.

Wild Honey, for hopping on the dream train with me and riding it right off the cliff. Together, hand in hand—Jess and Laura. Barn—your presence in my life continues to astound, humble, and compel me to be better.

Riley and Sloan, two walking, talking, breathing "Aha!" moments. You make it all make sense. I do everything for you. I would stop everything for you. I am everything because of you.

Finally, thank you Steve. For letting me shine. For making me laugh out loud every day. For being my trusted partner in every adventure. Let's never stop. I love you forever.

"Life is about growth and change. When you are no longer doing that—that is your whisper; that is your whisper that you are supposed to do something else."

"Devote today to something so daring even you can't believe you're doing it."

~Oprah Winfrey

Shelby Cain was raised in Cranbrook, British Columbia, where she developed an obsession for nature and adrenaline. She now lives an hour away in Fernie with her husband and two young daughters. Writing is a new and exhilarating passion she has explored since having her children. She writes short stories, magazine articles, and a monthly column about her life for Fernie Fix magazine entitled "Family Stoke." *Mountain Girl* is her first novel.